Enthusiastic reviews for Lior Samson's novels –

Distant Sons

" [A] book that will stay with me, probably for the rest of my life, and that I know I'll read again. ... It enlarged my experience of being human."
— *M. Thornberg, author*

The Rosen Singularity

" The plotting is ingenious and the characters come through strongly."
— *Rebecca Goldstein, MacArthur Fellow, author*

The Millicent Factor

" A solid page turner. The author keeps the pace just right with action and chases ... and backroom dealings."
— *RJ Beam, author*

The Intaglio Imprint

" Super-realism and compelling rationale, ... an intricate and incisive creation."
— *George Church, geneticist*

The Drucker Proxy

" An edge-of-the-seat, emotionally gripping, intimate, arousing, techno-legal tour-de-force."
— *Phillip M. Samson, attorney*

Bashert (The Homeland Connection)

" Samson writes with a crisp elegance, like John Le Carré, and weaves his plot magically."
— *James A. Anderson, author*

The Dome (The Homeland Connection)

" An excellent read, and very highly recommended."
— *Midwest Book Review*

Web Games (The Homeland Connection)

" This extraordinary author has the ability to anticipate events. ... You will not put it down."
— *Alan Caruba, critic, BookViews*

Chipset (The Homeland Connection)

"[A] multi-dimensional thriller ... populated by flesh-and-blood characters."
— Avraham Azrieli, author

Gasline (The Homeland Connection)

"[A] great novel . . . high concept, flesh-and-blood protagonist, and realistic action. ... [It] will raise your blood pressure and make you think."
— Columbia Review of Books and Film

Flight Track (The Homeland Connection)

"Stunning, compelling, thought-provoking. To the book's broad scope and expert pacing, add three-dimensional, engaging characters."
— M. Thornburg, author

The Four-Color Puzzle

"[A]n authentic thinking person's ideal mystery; an eloquent feast of words and an excellent story."
— Jeanie B. Clemmons, author

Exit Plans

Exit Plans

by Lior Samson

GESHER PRESS

Gesher Press
Rowley, Massachusetts

Gesher Press and the bridge logo are trademarks of Gesher Press.

5 4 3 2 1

ISBN 978-1-7326091-3-6

Cover and book design: Larry Constantine
Cover background photo: "Jerusalem Street," public domain
Set in Alegreya, titles in Aila Black

To Ed Howe: friend, confident, consultant, critic, and world-traveling adventurer

Often when you think you're at the end of something, you're at the beginning of something else. – Fred Rogers

Chapter 1

WITH ITS TIRED CHUG-AND-WHINE persistence, the window air conditioner struggled against the muggy early evening that stubbornly refused to cool. In the years since Gaspar Pembroke arrived in southern Brazil to realize his retirement dream of making wine, this had been the warmest autumn, one that followed an entire summer of untrustworthy weather. Inside the annex that had once been a stable but was now the offices of *Vinhos de Curitiba*, he and his manager were using the quiet hours to catch up on paperwork.

Gaspar finished outlining the pruning plans on the new vineyards, closed his notebook, and slid it into the center desk drawer. The slim ruggedized computer, with its brushed titanium finish, was a holdover from an earlier, more peripatetic life. It no more seemed to belong atop the exotic hardwood inlays of his handcrafted desk than Pembroke belonged in the state of Paraná. His lined Slavic face wore the leathery evidence of years in the field even before he had moved to Brazil, and his Brazilian Portuguese was by now polished to near native-speaker perfection, but Pembroke did not belong. Pembroke belonged nowhere. Self-imposed exile would never be a substitute for a lost and distant homeland, but he would admit to himself, in quiet moments like these, that the lush and sometimes luxurious setting of his own winery and vineyards was compensation—much of the time. He particularly reveled in the ever changing challenges of growing grapes to create wine, something alive with beauty and so in contrast to the sometimes ugly work of his pre-retirement years.

He had been sitting too long, and his bad leg was beginning to bother him. He straightened it and leaned back, staring up at the bare boards and open beams of the stable annex, their wood oxidized into a heavy red-brown patina. The old bullet wound in his leg throbbed. Time to knock off for the evening and stroll the grounds, he told himself. As he reached to turn off the desk lamp, the lights flickered, dimmed, and went out. The air conditioner sighed into silence.

"Not again, dammit." Under his breath, his cursing continued with a more extreme invective in yet another of his many languages. Electricity in the region had become progressively less reliable in recent years, with interlocked but inferior power grids that could spread massive blackouts like spilled India ink across Argentina, Paraguay, and portions of Brazil. Pembroke's office went black for several seconds. He held his breath until the winery's emergency power kicked in.

The viognier had been a gamble at these latitudes, but this year's crush looked promising. From here on out, the quality of the fruit-forward wine he planned hinged on the newly upgraded temperature-controlled stainless fermentation tanks. Between the solar arrays, wall-sized Tesla batteries, and diesel generators, the winery could hold out for days, more if the sun cooperated, as it usually did. If need be, the winery would prioritize fuel and stored power to keep the tanks cooled for even longer.

He listened as the air-conditioner resumed its struggle against the warm humid air. "'Fredo," he called out, "have you heard anything? Do we have any idea what caused it this time or what to expect?"

Alfredo Cippolini had been manager of *Vinhos de Curitiba* since before Pembroke had arrived to take charge of the winery in which he had been quietly investing for decades. The solemnly efficient and always deferent Fredo called from the adjacent office. "*Não, senhor Gaspar, nada.* No, nothing yet, but I'm checking."

The lights flickered and went out again, which should not have happened. In the quiet dark, Pembroke held his breath and listened. Cautious footsteps. At least three men straining to advance without sound through a building that accompanied every movement with its own creaking descant. He shifted into semi-automatic mode. Acting from instinct and long disused but never forgotten training, he silently reopened the desk drawer. By the cold haze from the emergency lighting in the hallway, he located the loaded Beretta stashed behind the notebook computer. At the creak of floorboards in the hall, he grabbed two extra magazines and picked up a banded stack of passports, only one of which was genuine.

By this time, the little red intrusion signal at the base of the desk lamp should have been winking. Someone must have disabled the alarm system along with the backup power. Pembroke mouthed silent curse words. Muted pops from the next room sent him into overdrive. To his well-trained ear, the sounds were both sharp and subtle, like 5.56mm NATO rounds from a rifle with a suppressor. Professionals. He dropped to the floor and slithered as fast as he could toward the doorway opening onto the deck. As he pushed his way out, the sliver of moonlight beneath the door became a blue-white wedge across the carpet.

Automatic weapons fire erupted in the office behind him just as Pembroke plunged off the deck into a tuck-and-roll on the manicured grass. Despite his leg, he was nearly to the tree line when the yard was flooded with light from halogen head-lights, and bullets churned the ground all around him.

Chapter 2

THE SUN WAS HOURS from rising and the bedroom shades were drawn against the perpetual lights of the city. Arkady fumbled in the dark for the phone that kept playing a Bach invention. Had he been fully awake, he would have deciphered that the ringtone meant the phone didn't recognize the caller. There was nobody on the line when he answered. He put the cellphone back in the drawer of the nightstand and rolled over.

"Who was that?" Barbara asked, pushing the duvet aside.

"Nobody." Despite their shared past in law enforcement, they were an unlikely couple. In all their years with the FBI, even teamed up as partners, they had never progressed beyond a functional friendship in which Arkady mostly deferred to Barbara as his superior. Barbara Delacroix had been a married, by-the-book player on her way to a senior position at the Bureau when a shootout in Pennsylvania helped her into early retirement. Arkady Pohl had been a perennial single, a loose cannon who bent rules and made side bets with unofficial players of uncertain loyalties. Only after Barbara lost her husband and Arkady had materialized to offer his support, did something real and personal begin to grow between them.

The cellphone started playing Bach again. "Well, sounds like nobody seems to be calling. Again," she said.

Arkady picked up the phone, intending to reject the call.

He didn't recognize the calling number. He let it play for a few more bars just to see if the caller might give up. It kept looping the same eight-bar phrase. He swiped the little green handset icon and put the phone to his ear. "Yes?"

"Wolf cub?" The voice was distorted by distance and digital enhancement, but the words were penetrating.

"What in hell?"

"Right again, little brother. I'm the what. And seven tomorrow night, I'll be at the same old place."

"Wait, where are you? What's up?"

"No time. Tomorrow." The click was followed by a tone Arkady recognized as indicating a satellite connection by a specialty carrier. He put down the phone.

"Who was that?" Barbara sat up in bed.

"Dima."

"Who did you say?"

"Dima, Dmitry, my brother."

"I thought he was . . ."

"He is. Was. The dead walk again. At least it looks that way."

"My god, what does this mean?"

"It can't be good. Maybe *HaVered* has been reactivated."

"*HaVered*? Reactivated?"

"You were already retired by that time. *HaVered* is Hebrew for the rose.

"I know. I picked up a lot from my years married to Abe."

"Good. Yeah, well, it was a rogue group of Israelis and scattered others who took on self-assigned wet missions. They were behind some rather spectacularly messy takedowns with a whole lot of collateral damage." He took a deep breath and let it out slowly. "But, of course, I never said that to you. Okay?"

She shook her head in a chill-out way. "Honey, we're both ex-agents. And we're married now, in case you forgot. I think we can trust each other with old stories."

"Maybe, but this old story may not be over. It's like those Hollywood superhero franchises that seem to keep generating sequels. Forever. And each one worse than the one before."

"What are you going to do?"

"Meet my brother for dinner tomorrow night."

"I'll join you."

"No way. If Dima sees you—or anyone else but me—he'll spook and we'll never hear from him again. No, this I gotta do on my own. Besides, it could be dangerous."

"All the more reason for me to be with you."

"No. That's final."

"An order? Hey, remember, I always outranked you, so don't pull any of that male 'that's-final' bullshit on me."

"Never would, o captain, my captain."

"That's better. So, where are you going now?"

"To make coffee and . . . well, to wipe the dust off some of my old, uh, tools."

"Shit you are, mister. I'm going with you, like it or not." She swung out of bed and slipped on her robe. "You make the coffee, and I'll get to polishing the damn tools, as you call them."

≈ ≈ ≈

Luigi's Little Napoli was a modest eatery that had survived war and peace, economic downturns, shuffled administrations, and aggressive gentrification to become an almost immortal institution among DC foodies savvy enough not to walk past its understated entrance below street level. In its latest incarnation, the logo on the door had been modernized, red leatherette benches had been replaced with varnished hardwood, and the chandeliers had been swapped out for multi-hued LED mood lighting. The tables were no longer covered with white tablecloths, but they were still set with red napkins and can-

7

dles in ruby glass, only the candles were now battery powered and controlled via infrared remotes.

Arkady sat on one of the benches along the side wall, facing the door, watching, alert to his surroundings even as he scanned the menu. He recognized nothing on it. A new chef, direct from Firenze, had taken over, bringing post-modern molecular culinary technique to bear on traditional Italian fare. Some of the names of dishes were the same, but the descriptions might as well have been drafted on another planet. Topping the menu was a sous vide cutlet, flame-finished, served over rosemary and green tea infused pasta topped with artichoke and radish foam swirls. What next, Arkady thought.

While Arkady was distracted for the third time by the waiter asking if he wanted a drink, Dima slipped in on the far side of the table.

"He'll have a vodka tonic with a twist," Dima said. "Make that two."

"Certainly. I'll be back with another menu." The waiter took a step back before turning with a stylized toe-pivot flourish.

"Well, Dima, I was beginning to wonder whether you were going to make it."

"Taking my time, wolf cub, making sure I was clean. I led your lovely lady on a merry chase through the subway mall. I assume she'll catch on soon that she was made and I'm long gone. Knowing how the Bureau boys and girls of your vintage were trained, I figure she'll send you a one-word text message any moment now to let you know I gave her the slip."

Arkady's phone buzzed once in his pocket.

Dima put on a self-satisfied grin. "Right on time, just like I called it."

"You do realize how old we are, Dima. Don't you think it's time we stopped playing schoolyard games with each other?

It's not a competition. I think you even once said something like that to me."

Dima looked his brother in the eyes for several seconds. As schoolboys they had looked so much alike that they could be mistaken for twins. With the passing years and their diverging lifestyles, they now were barely recognizable as siblings. Arkady's was the padded, pasty face of an easy American early retirement, with none of the scars and few of the lines that his older sibling carried. "Yeah, I suppose you're right. I probably did say that to you, but old habits die slowly. And I already know how good you are or I wouldn't be here now. So, do text former agent Delacroix and tell her to join us."

Arkady pulled out his phone and thumb-typed a quick message. Before he could slip it back in his pocket, it buzzed again. "She's already nearly back to the apartment, says I can catch her up later. By the way, she wants me to ask whether you spotted your other tail, the bald guy with the moustache."

Dima picked up his water glass and pretended to be interested in it as he surreptitiously checked the room. "I don't see him. I must've ditched him in that round of the old men's-room shuffle. But I guess I am a little out of practice. The slower lifestyle of the other hemisphere takes its toll." He smiled to cover his embarrassment.

Arkady put away his phone. "So, what happened?"

"They came after me. Whoever 'they' is. I'm guessing it's an old contract still floating around. I have no illusions that the most recent collapse of the regional power grid was orchestrated for my sake. The wet team that invaded my estate were simply opportunists."

"Well, you got away again."

"I always get away, even when it's my own brother who comes after me. You wrote me a rather strongly worded message to get lost and packaged it in a bullet from a cheap handgun. I still limp. But, I'll always get away, at least until I don't."

"Always the philosopher."

"Always."

"So, I take it you've been living in South America all this time."

"Brazil, in the state of Paraná, not far outside Curitiba. You know where that is? Truly lovely city, a cultural center with world-famous museums, concert halls, and a growing elite with an appreciation for local wines with character and for fine Brazilian estate-grown coffees. Well, I have . . . had a winery there, with a wine bar in the city. It was a good life being Gaspar Pembroke for a few years. Now . . ."

"I'm sorry. I was hoping you had finally found someplace to call home."

"I never called it home. As they say, you can never go home again. In any case, I have only one homeland, *Eretz Yisrael*. You know that."

"I guess I do." It was an old strain between them. After growing up in the Ukraine, Dima had made *aliyah* to Israel, where he had joined Mossad; Arkady had emigrated to the United States and eventually found his way into the FBI. To Dima, that had been a broken boyhood promise by his weaker younger brother who habitually took what seemed to be the easier road.

Arkady made a show of closing his menu, signaling the waiter he was ready to order. "So, what do you think about all the power outages down your way?"

"I think a lot about them, especially this last blackout."

"Because it provided cover for an attack on you?"

"No, the timing was significant, but not for the attack on the winery."

"Timing?"

"Yes. Twenty-four hours nearly to the second after the tweet. I checked."

"The tweet? Are you talking about a tweet from . . ."

"Yes, from the man in residence in a big white house just a few miles from here. It's hard to believe. Who discloses state secrets about offensive cyber capability and then brags about it by personally threatening a man like Vaslav Petrov? And why? A dare? In my mind, it does not compute."

"I missed that tweet. I admit I don't follow POTUS as closely as I once did."

"Well, your dear President Donaldson doubled down on his earlier admission that the NSA's Tailored Access Operations had planted malware throughout the Russian electric grid. He told Petrov that he was ready to give the go ahead to 'shut down your entire damn country' if Petrov didn't stop helping the Iranians with their attacks in the Gulf of Oman and the Straits of Hormuz and missiles targeting American bases in Iraq. You can bet the head of the TAO team went apoplectic. I knew Joyce Roberts at the NSA when she was just the smartest, cutest hacker in the lot, but already she was not somebody to be crossed or messed with. I don't know how she and others in the American intelligence services put up with a president who vilifies her and her colleagues, denigrates their work, and then breaks both protocol and the law."

Arkady shrugged. "The few real pros left in town must all be going nuts. It's bad enough that Donaldson keeps taking us to the brink of war in the Middle East. Now he has to threaten an egomaniac kleptocrat like Petrov in a game of cyberspace chicken. Is that why you're here?"

"I'm here because I thought you might know something."

"About the hit team or about the grid?"

"Either. Both. Maybe even something I don't know. That would be fun. And a first."

"Dima, I'm retired. I'm on the outside. I moonlight as a consultant for antivirus software makers. If it's not on CNBC or in the *Post*, I know nothing about it."

"Okay, good enough. Let's eat before I disappear again. I have to cover my tracks and fill in a few holes in my new identity. I'm a little out of practice, but I've always been a quick study."

"The attack, was it . . . ?"

"No, this wasn't *HaVered*, at least not the network I knew. Too sloppy. We . . . *HaVered* was always professional and polished."

"Except when they weren't, when they had to improvise. Then it became monumentally messy. I could mention a few instances."

Dima raised his hands in surrender. "Like I said, I figure these were bounty hunters."

"How did they find you? Before I retired, I did a little digging, just as an exercise, to see if I could locate you. I was able to trace you to Alaska, but the trail went cold there. No pun intended."

Dima laughed. "I was never in Alaska. That was just a false way-pointer. So, it seems you can trust me to disappear again where at least your American colleagues of comparable skills won't be able to track me. As for my old mates at Mossad, they probably could find me, but I don't think they have enough reason."

"Who are you this time."

"Dmitry Pohl to you, as always. I don't want you to know my new identity. Safer for you that way. And me."

"What about the mercenaries?"

"They're off my trail, whether or not they've already been neutralized."

"How did you manage that?"

"I returned fire to keep them shooting while I ducked into the battery shed. When I pushed the button, the fireball would have lit up the whole estate. Once the fireworks started, they weren't going to stick around trying to confirm a kill by trying to recover a charred corpse from a chemical-fed fire. Of course, I didn't see it. I was already down my rabbit hole and on my way off the property. Every entrepreneur knows you have to have exit plans. You need to know when and how to go out of business, how to manage the exit interview, and where to sock away the severance bonus. There will likely be something on the wire services about an explosion at a winery in Brazil triggered by raiding banditos. 'Tragic loss of life, including the owner, one Gaspar Pembroke, and the manager, Alfredo Cippolini.' Sad. I don't know if they took out anybody else. I'll have to wait until I see the news."

"How like you to be so broken up at the loss of life. What about this Cippolini? A friend?"

"A manager, pretty good. Nothing much I can do about it now. He's dead. And so, little brother, am I. Once again I'm dead. Maybe I can stay dead this time. Never too late to learn from one's failures." The waiter arrived with their drinks and another menu. Dima opened it and closed it after a speed-read of the first pages. "Two of the Chef's Special and side salads," he said, scooping up Arkady's menu and thrusting both at the waiter.

"Which salad will that be, sir?"

"Your call."

"With the house dressing?"

"Of course."

"Excellent choice." The waiter did his step-turn routine again and disappeared into the kitchen.

Arkady leaned across the table. "So what are we eating?"

"I have no idea, and maybe it's better that way, what with all the postmodern mumbo-jumbo on the menu. I always figure whatever the chef is proud enough of to call his specialty is probably going to be good. But tomorrow, if I'm not already ten-thousand miles from here, I'll take you to an authentic Brazilian *churrascaria* I know of over in Adams Morgan. A Brazilian barbecue—now that's real food. Meat, meat, and more meat. And none of this"—he gestured with his pinky—"sous vide and propane torch silliness. No, just open fire, wood, flame, and smoke: that's the proper way to cook meat. At the winery, we would host this harvest barbecue with a hundred-plus guests. People loved it." His look turned wistful and far away. "Maybe the kid, Paolo, who apprenticed himself to the cellar master, will try to get it going again. He was always ambitious. I should have thought more about the succession options in my exit plans. Somehow I didn't think both Cippolini and I would leave at the same time. Alfredo was a good manager: a bit on the uninspired side, but solid. Good Man.

"Well, we'll see, I guess. We'll have to keep a watch on developments down in Curitiba."

≈ ≈ ≈

From a bench in the tree-dotted pocket park down the street, Ted Baumer watched, waited, and pretended to read *The Washington Post*. He had years of practice in all of these things, especially the waiting and pretending. Still, he had almost lost track of Dmitry Pohl when Pohl had backtracked in an attempt to lose the woman who was also on his tail. You Ukrainians, he thought, you always underestimate us Russians. And you are out of practice. Like a rabbit, torn between running and freezing, when you do move, you move too fast and stumble over the trip wire. We knew within hours that you were back. As soon as you used that passport to fly out of São Paulo, we knew. But, of course, we already had an eye half open on your brother, so you were both doomed either way.

Fyodor Sokolov, who had been American travel agent Ted Baumer for nearly nineteen years, was a debt collector. He tracked down deadbeats who had failed to pay what they owed to the Russia they had abandoned—or screwed over. Then he offered them a payment plan. Some were expected to make regular payments: bits of information, casual observations, occasionally a cellphone shot of a location or a document. Others were told they could rest easy until they were called on. Of course, many did not rest easy, and some even tried to slip away. Tried. Sokolov was a very good debt collector, and he had ways of dealing with the deadbeats who didn't pay up. He had always found that word resonant: deadbeat.

The Pohl brothers debt had been compounding interest since they had defected. Dmitry, whose sins were the greater, was the deeper in debt. It mattered little that it had then been the Soviet Union they had turned against. Sokolov smiled to himself. Russians could be sloppy in some areas, but they kept meticulous account books in indelible ink over such matters. Our lives may be short, but our memory is long, he thought.

With the twilight fading, the streetlamp by the bench automatically came on, allowing Sokolov to continue his subterfuge. Over the top of his newspaper, he watched as the brothers came up the concrete steps from the restaurant and turned at the top in opposite directions without any farewell ritual. Sokolov pulled a flat-billed cap from his waistband and slapped it on his bald head. The vest had already been swapped for a pullover sweater. It was more colorful than the drab wear he preferred, but highland patterns were a flash fashion this spring, so it was actually a way of blending in. He waited until Dmitry was past and already well around the corner before lowering his *Post*, folding it, and chucking it into a recycling bin. He studied the cars for several seconds before jaywalking at a trot through traffic, dodging like a basketball forward and reaching the curb without having triggered a single horn tap.

He was grinning as he rounded the corner.

Chapter 3

FOR DIMA, IT WAS a judgment call, made on-the-fly as always, in a sport he had played most of his adult life. If you're the rabbit and you spot the hound tracking you, what do you do? If you lose the tail too quickly and easily, they might realize they've been made. Once shed, the hound might get on your trail again, whether now or later, without being spotted. You might even turn and confront the tail, if you have reason to believe that might buy something worthwhile, but it can also be useful just to know who is following you without letting on that you know.

In the end, Dima was persuaded by his brother's earlier remarks. They were getting too old to be playing young men's games. Information was a valuable end in itself. Better sometimes just to know who was on your tail than try to outrun or elude them. At the streetlight, left-handed Dima pretended to get a phone call and put the phone to his ear. As he waited at the corner, he turned his head to the side and back as if trying to decide whether to cross to the left with the light or to wait for it to change straight ahead. In that partial turn, he snapped a picture of the scene behind him. He finished the pretend call and, with the phone lowered in front of him, checked the shot, zooming in on faces. He immediately recognized Fyodor Sokolov. Are you still at it? he was thinking. You may be a master of tradecraft, but you never did catch on to how distinctive your lopsided face is. Every spook has his blind spot; that's yours, what's mine?

Dima kept his pace steady all the way to the hotel. The early evening crowds made it easy for Sokolov to blend in but hard for him to make any move. The well-lit lobby of the venerable Hotel Meredith, with its soaring ceilings and grand-canyon spaces, would make it impossible. The chase is over, Dima thought, score one for the rabbit who now knows what breed of hound is after him. The hound is Russian, a wolf hound, a sleeper, a sleeping dog to let lie. He crossed over to the lobby bar where President Donaldson's fat face filled the television screen as the chyron below declared: Donaldson doubles down on demands. Russia denies role in Brazilian outage.

Dima took a seat at one of the tiny tables dotting the lobby bar area and raised a finger to get the attention of the waitress delivering drinks to a couple of over-the-hill tourist types with a city map spread out in front of them.

"What'll it be?" she said, putting a small dish of bar snacks on the table. He pushed them away.

"A glass of port, tawny."

"We have a selection of ports and cognacs. Would you like to see a list?"

"Bartender's choice."

The woman's smile broadened in a round face that made Dima think Pacific islanders. "Right away," she said, knowing that the bartender would pick toward the expensive end of the list and her tip would be all the better.

She was just short of the bar when the TV screen went black and the lights winked out. Almost instantly, the blue-white light and shadow of emergency lighting replaced the warmth of the lobby's huge central chandelier and multitude of downlights. Out of the corner of his eyes, Dima, spotted a face in the lobby, its irregular contours heightened by the harsh light and deep shadows. Sokolov was getting overly confident. Let him close in, he thought, while I pretend to be oblivious.

Before the management could begin herding guests out, the lights came back on, and the TV resumed its drone of disaster and pending disaster.

The waitress arrived with his drink and a tab. "I hope you like this," she said, doubling down on her bid for a good tip. "Armando at the bar said the older Taylor Fladgates are his favorite."

"Thanks. You can charge it to my room." He scribbled a number and signed the tab with a flourish. Before she could pick it up, he reached for his wallet. "And this is for you." He folded a twenty and slipped it under the tab.

"Well, thank you."

"You're welcome. This happen often? The lights on and off? I'm from overseas."

"Not really," she said. "But I have a friend who works over at . . . at Fort Meade. Well, he says we can expect more of this."

"What, because of climate change? I mean, it is a warm spring and all, but I thought demand for electricity would be down, if anything."

"Well not that kind of climate change. Like the political climate, you know, international, the guy in the Whitehouse and the guy in the Kremlin."

"Your friend in—where did you say, Fort Something—he knows about this stuff."

"Well, yeah, except he can't really talk about it with me. You know what I'm saying?"

"I think I do." What he didn't say was that he thought her

boyfriend already talked too much, considering his probable employer.

"Yeah, well this is DC. Everybody works for the government, you know. Except for those of us like me who wait tables or change sheets or clean up their crap. Sorry. It's been a long day."

"No apology necessary. I'm not American, but I understand. We have much the same where I come from."

"Where are you from?"

She was playing into his script perfectly, giving Dima plenty of time to keep the bead on Sokolov while appearing to be busy chatting up the waitress. "Greece," he said, improvising. "Athens."

"Now that's funny. I had another Greek in here, like on the weekend. But you don't sound like him."

"I'm on the road most of the time. I've pretty much lost my accent. And you? Where are you from? Are you a local gal?"

"No, I'm from Hawaii. You can't tell? People pick up that I sound like I'm from somewhere else, but they usually guess the wrong place. I followed my boyfriend when he got a job out here."

"The guy at Fort Whatever?"

She laughed. "No, no, the guy I came out with was two boyfriends ago. Look, I gotta get back to work, even if the lights go out again." She retrieved the tray with the tab and his twenty.

With nothing to be gained by moving, Dima took time to savor his port. Let Sokolov grow impatient, see what his move would be. The news on the screen had been replaced by some talking-heads commentary when the lights went out again. This time they stayed out.

Dima savored the last sip of port in the semi-dark and rose slowly. Time to go for a stroll, he thought. Let's see whether

Sokolov, having tracked his rabbit to its lair, will give up or renew the chase.

He was nearly at the main doors when there was a commotion behind him. He turned to see a knot of people around a woman kneeling next to a man who was stretched out on the floor. "I think it's a heart attack," she said. "Somebody, call 9-1-1."

As the small crowd shifted, Dima got a glimpse of the man's face. He did not wait to learn more. Time to move on, he thought. Way too much action here in DC. Emerging from the hotel, the reflection in the glass door gave him a glimpse of someone behind him. The man pushed ahead and nodded for Dima to follow. It was Arkady.

Chapter 4

WHETHER FOR EXPEDIENCE or to make a point, Arkady set a pace that was difficult for Dima to sustain. Half way across one of the new pedestrian bridges, with the pain in his leg mounting, Dima finally spoke up. "Slow down, wolf cub, I can't move this fast."

"I want to put some distance between us and the hotel." He stopped at a point on the bridge that was in shadow with a good view back. "But we can take a break."

"Thanks. I meant to ask: did you have anything to do with what happened back there in the lobby?"

"I had something to do with it, but I didn't do it, if that's what you're asking. After you left the restaurant, I rounded the block and spotted your tail. While he was focused on you, I followed him and contacted an old buddy at the Bureau to suggest they might be interested in this guy. I didn't expect they would be quite so fast or openly aggressive in confronting him. I think everybody is on edge, what with the power out and this business with the Russians escalating. And, from their reaction to my description, I think they may have had some notion of who he was"

"So, what did happen back there? I was already on my way out, so I didn't see it."

"I didn't either, just that a pair from the Bureau entered

shortly before the lights went out. They pretended to ignore me and not to be interested in the mark, but when the lights went out they began moving in. Finally, with one on either side crowding him, it looked like they were asking him for some ID. Next thing I know, he was on the floor."

Dima looked skeptical. "I didn't think the open-and-above-board FBI was into that sort of thing. I thought taking out targets on American soil was a job for foreigners."

"It still is—yet another reason not to close our borders completely—but I don't think that's what happened. Maybe it was a heart attack, maybe the guy ended it himself. I don't know who he was."

"Fyodor Sokolov, Russian, ex-FSB. I knew him from an operation in Berlin. He should have opted for plastic surgery long ago. In his line of work, you want to have a forgettable face." Dima leaned on the hand rail and looked out over the city, a patchwork of blackness with sporadic pools and spots of light where there were emergency generators. Overhead, a police helicopter patrolled with its searchlight. "A blackout can bring a certain stark beauty to an ugly city."

"I've heard you say that all cities are ugly."

"All but Jerusalem." He started quietly humming *Yerushalayim shel Zahav*, an Israeli pop classic by Naomi Shemer. *Jerusalem of Gold* had become for Israel what *America* was in the US: almost an unofficial national anthem. He stopped humming in mid phrase. "I'm beginning to wonder whether I'll ever see the City of David again."

"You will, if you want it badly enough."

"You're talking to an old *katsa*, a field agent, like an alley cat who long ago had used up his allotted lives. I don't know, wolf cub. Do you think your FBI friends are doing some checking at the hotel. It would help if I knew whether my cover is also blown with the Americans."

"I didn't say anything to them about who it was that, uh, Sokolov was tailing, and I don't think you did anything that would have drawn their attention. They might check the hotel register, or the police might if there was anything suspicious about Sokolov's swan dive. You might have to switch identities again before moving on."

"I'll have to switch again anyway, I suppose, since the Russians already had me made. The rest of my 'spares' might also be compromised. I should assume that. Sokolov is an object lesson, too. Maybe time to change my appearance, but if I have to construct an entire new identity from scratch, it'll take time. And I don't know enough about the local resources these days to even know where to start."

"I can probably help, but you'll need to take some time off the map." He tipped his head back in thought. "I think you should stay with me and Barbara. The three of us can take a little vacation at this summer place in Virginia we share with another couple. This time of year they won't be using it, and there will be nobody around. We even have an excuse, since the cabin is off the grid with its own power. I can put the wheels in motion to get a passport for you before we leave the DC area."

"So, the old wolf relies on the cub for help. Okay, we'll do that, but I need to return to the hotel to recover a few things. Now, while the power is still out, is a good time. I'll make it quick and clean."

"You can't make it quick with that leg of yours, and you're already too dirty to make it clean. If the Russians were watching you, they may be keeping an eye on me as well, but we have another option. We can get Barbara to do the snatch-and-go."

"Good, but we also need a temporary place that we can be sure isn't being staked out. Just until we are ready to leave for your cabin. You already put yourself on the radar with the Bureau, so your place is out."

Arkady chewed on his thumb as he thought, a very old habit. "Let me see if I can set up something with a guy I know from the NTSB. He lost his lady a few years back."

"You mean the *schwarzer?*"

"I doubt he would like your label, but yes, his father was African-American. You know Sam Parsons?"

"I . . . I don't really, but . . . well, it is a rather small world we travel in. I know his work, shall we say. Something about pipeline explosions? And again, that lost airliner."

Arkady had noticed Dima's uncharacteristic hesitance but said nothing of it. "Yeah. He was the semi-pro fall-guy. Ended up being forced to put his name on a government cover up because nobody wanted to admit that our natural gas transmission network was so vulnerable to hacking. Then, after he switched over to the air-safety side of the NTSB, his aircraft cybersecurity program was killed. Nobody wants to admit how insecure the electronics on commercial aircraft are."

"Let me count the ways."

Arkady pulled out his phone, looked at the screen, and shook his head. "No bars. With everyone in the DC area panicking and everything on backup power, cell service is going to be crap. I'm going to start with trying to get a text through to Barbara and get that plan in motion. Next I'll switch over to connecting with Parsons. It's going to be a nightmare getting around, and we don't know how widespread the outage is yet." He started thumb typing on his phone.

"I know how widespread it is. The hotel Wi-Fi worked long enough for me to call up a map on my phone while I finished sipping my drink in the dark. It's DC plus pretty much all of the Mid-Atlantic States and some toward the west. I'm guessing it's all part of the same subnet or whatever it's called. Not my specialty."

"So, it's not local, but it's also not the whole goddamn grid."

"Apparently it was possible to keep it from spreading up into New England and farther west by isolating parts of the grid, but it is a big mess. I would still also say it looks like a surgical strike compared to what it could be. Last information I got said Virginia still had power, I guess because they are part of a different section of the grid. The real question is how it was accomplished. Some ways can be countered faster than others, I would assume. Again, not my field."

"You're making this sound like you think this is a cyber-attack from the Russians."

"I don't think it, I know. Twenty-four hours after your president's second twitter salvo against Petrov, your nation's capital goes dark. This time Petrov didn't fire a warning shot across the bow using a swat at South America. This time he punched America in the belly button, with a shot below the waterline, to mix my metaphors. Donaldson can't just shoot off his mouth again with another Twitter storm. He's a weak man, but completely invested in not appearing weak. He has to do something. It's getting scary how far this could go. Just how long could we hold out in your wilderness cabin?"

"Not long enough to wait for the return of civilization after Armageddon. You may be a survivor, but you're no survivalist—unless you joined some new clubs and picked up some new skills while you were hiding out in Brazil."

"I'm always picking up new skills, but I didn't join any of the post-apocalypse brigades. The American ones are too focused on stockpiling weapons and food and not enough on what they would really need if the whole system collapsed."

Arkady shook his head slowly. "Some of them even seem to

be hoping the whole system collapses. Since this grid-wars posturing started, FLAG2 has been marching and demonstrating, launching social media storms, egging the president on with protests and chants of 'Turn the lights off. Turn the lights off.' Weird."

"FLAG2?"

"Freedom Lovers of America Group. First, Last, and Always Great. Take your pick—both/and. It's a relatively new coalition, an umbrella organization for every ultra-right, nativist, and neo-anarcho apocalyptic conspiracy wing-nut group with their AR-15s, red caps, and camo."

"All that? That's quite an ideological stew. My take is that the collective IQ goes down proportionate to the number of competing orthodoxies you cram under one umbrella."

"Could be. Look, we better start walking if we're going to intersect Barbara with your stuff. You can keep up the lecture as we walk."

"Wait, I didn't give you my room number or where to look or what to grab."

"Don't worry, she'll figure it out. She may be retired, but she's still pretty good doing the limbo. You'll have to trust her, because my second text message still won't go through."

"How do you know she's on her way, then, and where she'll meet us, and . . ."

"You've never been married, Dima. You wouldn't understand."

"It's not like there have never been women in my life. I've had relationships."

"Women in your life is hardly the same, although it took me a long time to learn all the differences." Spotting a knot of strobing red and blue lights ahead, he turned and headed back down the pedestrian bridge.

27

"Why are we turning around."

"To take a different route. I don't like the color of the lighting in that direction."

At the bottom of the pedestrian overpass, Arkady spotted something in the bushes. "Squirrels."

"What?"

"That's what some of the locals now call them around here: the battery-powered rent-a-scooters. You know, like squirrels: they hide out in the bushes; they suddenly skitter in and out of traffic. With the power out, I doubt if we can unlock them with our phones, but I know how to jimmy them."

He pulled the two cinnamon-brown GoFarr scooters from where they had been abandoned. "These'll be a lot faster way to get around—and easier on your leg. You know, I am sorry about that, but I could tell at the time that you weren't going to be persuaded by verbal arguments alone that you really, really needed to retire."

It took him a couple minutes to work his magic with a pocket knife on the scooters. "Looks like both have a fair amount of juice left. See, now this is real survival skill," he said, closing his pocket knife. "You think you can handle one of these things?"

"I can if you can." Dima mounted the scooter, studied the control handle, then made a wobbly start along the sidewalk.

Arkady caught up and pulled smoothly alongside. "Now, you were saying, big brother, about survivalists."

"Well, I'm no expert, but—"

"You say that a lot, even as you keep showing off your supposed expertise."

"Whatever. Anyway, I would not be gathering guns and stockpiling ammo. Ammunition might be good for a decade or so, but if you are talking about the end of civilization, it'll go bad, eventually, and if you run out, your handguns are nothing more than weird-shaped doorstops and your long guns are useless except as awkward clubs." Finally getting the hang of the scooter, he accelerated.

"So, what would you stockpile?" Arkady said, keeping pace.

"Tools, seed, and a couple of good crossbows. You can always make new crossbow bolts. Bullets and smokeless powder, not so easy."

"So, did you stockpile those things in Brazil?"

"Hardly. I'm no survivalist. I'm a survivor."

≈ ≈ ≈

The text from Sam Parsons came in just as they were meeting up with Barbara.

overseas. u r free 2 use apt. keypad code 102923.

"Well, we have temporary quarters. Parsons is out of the country. Interesting."

"Where is he?" Barbara asked.

"Didn't say. After taking the sword-fall for the gas pipeline explosions and the failure of his airline security group, he has become more reclusive, especially since his partner was killed, and . . . I don't really know what he's been up to these last years."

Barbara handed the gym bag she was carrying to Dima. "Heavy."

"Tools," Dima said, knowing she would catch his meaning.

"Already? You just arrived."

"I've learned to move fast. I met with a dealer right after I landed. How'd you know which bag to snatch?"

"The others still had baggage tags. They went through airport security. This one was brand new and no tag."

"I'm impressed. I assume you two are carrying. Clean out

your closet?"

Barbara laughed. "Emptied the shoeboxes. Once an agent, always an agent. But that bag has more in it than a concealed-carry permit would cover."

"A craftsman always uses the right tool for the job. Sometimes you need a long bladed screwdriver, sometimes just a stubby. You know what I mean?"

She nodded. "I'm glad I didn't know how serious the contents were. The streets are crawling with police. I'd hate to get caught with whatever is in there."

"So," Arkady said, "let's get ourselves off the streets. We're bivouacking in Sam Parson's apartment. You remember him?"

"Fond memories of West Virginia and Pennsylvania and being shot at," she said. "Oh, yeah, I remember Parsons."

Chapter 5

DOUGLASS "DB" BOTTENEAU looked over the group assembled in conference room A of the Scenaria Security Systems headquarters. Half of his core management team was missing. He took a last sip of his black coffee and, in an act of reluctant discipline, pushed the untouched donut away. Under the stress of a business downturn, it was becoming harder of late to keep from regaining the pounds he had shed on his way to the executive suite. "Okay, people," he said. "We're going to have to assume that the others are doing their best to get here. They know the drill."

Dune Huang, polite to a fault, raised a finger and waited for Botteneau to recognize him. "Doug, shouldn't we wait for Girard? She is CTO."

"The roads are parking lots between here and Columbia, Maryland, where Maude moved. I'm sure she's trying her best. You can act as her alter ego until she gets here." Dune Huang, who had been Chief Technical Officer before Maude Girard, had taken a lateral "promotion" to Chief Scientist in order to get out of management so he and his husband could more easily share the parenting of their adopted son. Like Maude, he was a veteran of the company's crack code-deconstruction team that worked in the company's high-security underground isolation facilities known as The Vault. Seated next to him was Rufus Baumgarten, current head of that team, now

31

officially designated as Special Cybersecurity Analysis Operations but informally referred to as Cybops or the Bumpus crew, after the nickname that still trailed Baumgarten from his days as a coding cowboy.

Suze Kerchoff, Chief Security Officer, nodded to Botteneau, a private signal for him to pick up the pace. Tall and athletic, she was a decorated veteran who had served in the military police in Iraq and Afghanistan before going into private security with the elite team at Saltmarsh Services and from there into Scenaria management. That she and DB were living together was hardly a secret, but they both strove to keep things all business at work. "Okay," he said, "status reports. Operations?"

Ed Idris, raided from Kaspersky, one of Scenaria's biggest and most successful competitors, was still more or less an outsider. "We're good. The blackout has been isolated to RFC, the grid security region that includes DC. Most of Virginia is controlled by SERC, a different part of the North American Electric Reliability Corporation. And, of course, here we have our own beaucoup backup power. Cellphone service is poor owing to overload, but landlines, for those who still have them, like we do, are still good. The internet is wobbly. Again, owing to demand, but the internet infrastructure does not appear to have been the target, at least not yet. Our server network is good, with load shifting automatically to the Northwest and Northeast."

"Cybops?"

Baumgarten responded without looking up from his notes on his tablet. "It looks like the grid takedown may have resulted from Trojans planted long ago and undetected until now. Our people are onto it, and we're also working with several of our industrial customers who are helping us get on top of it.

From our intel, the attack not only took out parts of the grid but did actual physical damage. One of the two generators at Comanaugh in Pennsylvania was shut off and allowed to spin down. It's toast. The public doesn't know yet, and there probably will be some BS cover story when it gets out."

"And they can't just order a new one?" Idris asked.

DB answered, "They can, but they'll be at half capacity for many months. It's not like they keep spare turbine-generator units in a warehouse somewhere."

Baumgarten continued as if never interrupted. "If this was Russia, which is what the Whitehouse is tweeting, it's tantamount to an act of war. Things could get a lot worse. A lot worse. The current administration is not known for its diplomatic subtlety."

DB shot him a look. "I was asking for a technical analysis, Bumpus, not a CNN political report."

"Right. As I said, we're working on it. We'll let you know the moment we find something."

"I want signatures for the malware and then removal tools, and I want Scenaria to be first to the goal square. Let's show Eugene Kaspersky and the others that we are the undisputed leaders in industrial cybersecurity, okay? Security?"

Suze Kerchoff looked up from her laptop. "We're good, went to orange alert. I've been in touch with my old pals at Saltmarsh and they are sending a couple extra people over. We don't have any reason to believe our campus is under any threat, but an abundance of caution makes sense with the lights out and public safety resources strained." She glanced at Dune. "Dune and I agreed that we should trigger deep scans of all our own systems, but nothing turned up. Our people have always been good at digital hygiene. As soon as Cybops knows exactly what we're looking for, we'll launch a fresh round of deep scans throughout the company—all sites."

"Okay, good work everybody. And remember, the rest of the world is not in the dark, so it's also a regular workday. We can't let customers think we've been wounded or are under attack. Ed, do we have contingency plans for customer service?"

"Already in place. Calls and web queries are being rerouted from the West Virginia operation to a backup call center in Utah. Wait times in the queues are a little high for this time of night, but they're not worrisome."

DB tapped the table. "All right, everybody, back to work."

The group started to disperse. "And Rufus, as soon as your team has a signature, I want you to do a push-and-ping to our entire installed software base—industrial, commercial, personal, and government. We need to get a handle on how widespread this thing is and exactly who and what the malware has infected. It's a good bet it got into industrial control systems through openings in business, administrative, and supervisory systems."

"You want us to force polling the installations even before we have a removal tool?"

"Even before. I just want to know how big the invasion is. Okay, people, back to the barricades."

Suze kept typing on her laptop until everyone else had left. "What aren't you saying, Doug? I could read it on your face."

"Am I that transparent?"

"Only to me."

"Okay, I got an encrypted email from my former boss."

"Wait a minute. Richard Talpa?"

"The one and only. He wants to know if the backdoor in our antivirus software is still open in case there is need."

"And what did you tell him?"

"I didn't. I wanted to talk with you first. And Maude."

"I'm guessing, then, that we left the backdoor in place, a gaping security hole in our own security software."

"Not only that, we've ported it to as part of the operating core of every new version and product. Maude is the only other person who knows this. Now there's three of us."

"Well, four with Talpa." She covered her eyes and hung her head. "Why? We're a security outfit. Why build in a security flaw just waiting to be found by somebody. That would be the end of the company."

"No one is going to find it. It's old and obscure and buried too deep. Besides, if anyone was going to find it, they would have long ago. And the why is easy: insurance, just in case we ever needed it again. Look, I doubt we're the only ones. That's the thing about antimalware software. It has to burrow deep down into the hidden bowels of the computer operating systems, and it has to be nearly invisible even as it gets privileged access to system resources."

She stared at her screen and sighed. "I can't say that I agree with your assessment of potential need, and I'm not comfortable with your decision to keep Talpa's trick coding in place. What are you going to tell him?"

"Maybe nothing. I would imagine it would not be hard for him to confirm on his own whether his code was still intact."

"Then he's setting you up by asking."

"How so?"

"If the backdoor is used and things go sour, you're the one on the line."

"Him too."

"Are we talking about the same Richard Talpa, the invisible inside-outsider ensconced in some Holy of Holies over at the NSA, who gets by with murder and never gets caught or charged? He lives up to his Italian name: mole. Talpa is the ultimate survivor, always the last standing, the watcher who shrugs as those around him are going down in flames."

"It's not the way I've come to see him. I'm not saying I trust the man, but events suggest he isn't all bad."

"Events? Suggest?" She stood, looked around, and then walked over to kiss him on the top of his now balding head. "You, love, have a real gift for words."

≈ ≈ ≈

The sky was turning into swirls of charcoal and muddy orange in the east when DB finally started the hike along the winding walkway to the condo that he and Suze shared in Reston. He was tired from the all-nighter but jazzed by the brisk early morning walk. Suze had promised to finish up and head home within the hour. He almost didn't notice the vibrating in his jacket pocket. He fumbled for the phone and put it to his ear as he stepped off the footpath to let a jogger pass.

"This is DB."

"Arkady Pohl here."

"Well, this has been a night for unexpected calls. What can I do for you? I'm assuming it has something to do with the power plug being pulled."

"Indirectly. I just wanted to make sure you weren't thinking of using your cabin right away."

"Are you kidding? With the fallout from this latest grid attack, I'll be lucky to get away from the office for more than a couple hours a day. In fact, I'm walking to the condo right now in hopes of grabbing a bite and a few Zs before sprinting back to the frontlines. So, the mountain place is yours."

"Thanks. We'll be there for a week or so."

"Must be nice to be retired and without responsibilities."

"Well, the retired part applies. Responsibilities never stop. You got any inside poop on the blackout?"

"Some. It was surgical. Bumpus and the kids in the Vault are getting signatures on the delivery vehicle and are trying to deconstruct the payload. Payloads, plural. This is a race we want to win, big-time. It's a very big feather in our caps if we can be first with a full diagnosis and cure. You know how that works."

"I do. Er, just curious, are you and Suze Kerchoff still . . . ?"

"Still. You and, uh . . . ?"

"Barbara. Delacroix. Yeah, we tied the knot. We already knew too much about each other. We had to do it. National security, you know, for the good of the country."

DB laughed. "I'll have to try that one on Suze. Not sure she'll buy it, but it's worth a try. She's rather, uh, independent."

"Barbara is more the marrying kind. I'm her second edition, after Abe died. Not complaining, just being realistic. Look, if there's any way you can keep me in the loop . . . I mean without breaking any rules. You know you can trust me and Barb."

"Sure. If something comes up I think you might want to know, I'll send a secure text—our usual protocol. Okay?"

"Sounds good. I guess it's never completely over for us old guys, at least not until . . ."

The line went silent. "You all right, Arkady?"

There was several more seconds of silence. "Yeah. I'm all right. You know where to find me. And if you and Suze also need, you know, to get out of town, the place is big enough. I just didn't want you to be surprised to find it occupied or for us to suddenly drop in on you guys."

"No problem. Enjoy your stay."

"Yeah. Enjoy. Not likely, but cheers."

Chapter 6

A WAXING GIBBOUS MOON, now high in the sky, stained the stone walls of Jerusalem's Old City with cold light. Above the narrow streets and alleys, the persistent haze of urban light pollution had been replaced by slices of blue-black sky dusted by bright stars. With long-legged grace, Roni Zimro hurried through a darkened city lit only by the moon and the occasional candle or lantern in an open window. Her visit to Jerusalem friends had been interrupted by the call on her cellphone that arrived several hours after the electricity had cut off, leaving the group laughing and drinking by candlelight.

Roni reached the avenue where she had left her scooter, unlocked the chain, and checked her phone again for texts from isGrid ProFence, the startup where she worked as a software engineer. She was her family's rising star, a star who, in high school, had outshone her three lay-about brothers to be recruited by Israel's elite intelligence group, *Yehidah Shmoneh Matayim*, Unit 8200. On leaving her military service in the IDF, she had worked her way up the engineering ladder at Israel Electric Corporation before joining with several other Unit 8200 grads to form isGrid, another of Israel's many technology startups but one of the few founded by members of the country's Ethiopian immigrant community.

Her oval face, as dark as the night around her, tensed in

concentration as she thumb-typed a response to a fresh text.

on my way. what's up?

The one-word response was almost instantaneous.

greeks?

It was an insider joke referring to malicious software: "Trojans." A rush of adrenalin pulsed through her. Her boss was already speculating on the cause of the power outage that was blanketing much of Israel from the Golan Heights in the north to the Negev desert in the south. This was the chance she had been waiting for, that the whole company had at once dreaded and dreamed of. Their contract with Israel Electric to provide emergency forensic services had never before been invoked, but now the power establishment, a bureaucratic empire that predated the founding of the modern state of Israel, was turning to the often marginalized newcomers for help.

Roni shivered in the middle-of-the-night chill as she buzzed along mostly deserted roads toward the Har Hotzvim Technology Park where her company was headquartered. In her mind, she was channeling Gal Gadot as Wonder Woman, becoming the grownup reification of her own childhood fantasies, dreams of heroic rescues and of revenge—revenge for the isolation of being a black face in a white community and for the taunts of "kushi" she had endured whenever she scored a goal against an all-white soccer team or aced an exam on which others had struggled.

As she turned into the parking lot at the Technology Park, Shimon Molla, the CEO of isGrid, playfully raced her in his Mercedes. He was lanky, bright, and handsome—and he was single. He was also too old and too out of reach. Rumor had it that his girlfriend was a Yemeni Jew, with straight black hair and skin as pale as the straw-tinged moon that lit the street ahead. Even among her own, Roni had always been the dark one, complemented for her beautiful skin as a backhanded way of telling her she was too dark to be beautiful.

She parked her scooter next to the bicycle racks and caught up with Shimon at the entrance. He waved his keycard at the security pad, and the door lock, on its own backup battery, clunked in response. He smiled as he held the door for her. "So, are you eager to kick some ass?"

"With both feet at once, if necessary. Fill me in."

"Oh, that's what you're supposed to do for me." He reflexively flicked the light switches inside but nothing happened. He scanned the gloomy, ill lit hallway ahead. "I expect you to get the lights back on within the hour. All the computer equipment is on our UPS, but you'll have to work by the emergency lighting for now. When Asaf and Kfir arrive, remind them that you're in charge, but have them check in with me. Okay?"

"Okay." She was again Gal Gadot as she trotted down the hall to begin her all-night marathon. Asaf and Kfir were both good, but she could code circles around them. Unlike the two young men she supervised, she had a secret weapon, an almost preternatural gift for seeing patterns, her own mental Lasso of Truth that made her a demon at deconstructing malicious code to discover its true objective or at analyzing the root causes of misbehaving software and equipment to get them to do her bidding.

She pushed open the door to the open-office bullpen where the company's software matadors outsmarted their counterparts on the other side of an invisible but very real digital divide. It was a tournament without timeout. They probed their clients' systems for vulnerabilities needing to be patched over and studied recent malicious attack attempts even as their adversaries, the dark armies of cyberspace, scouted out new openings and devised fresh exploits in endless rounds of digital thrust and parry with never any clear winners. At its heart, cybersecurity was high-stakes cerebral jousting, a contest of hackers against hackers in which noble knights at keyboards fought against unseen hordes of freelancers, thieves, and armies of well-funded state actors bent on chaos, extortion, or destruction.

The two-meter folding table where Roni's computer was set up was shared with Dara, a newly recruited software engineer in-training who had not been called in for the emergency. The company, still in ramp-up mode since its launch a year earlier, did not consider furniture to be a top investment priority. Roni decided to take advantage of the circumstance by commandeering Dara's computer. She woke it up, logged in, and paired her Bluetooth headset, then established a secure link to her counterpart at Israel Electric. Bruce Latham was an Australian who had made *aliyah* sometime after finishing university with a degree in electrical engineering. Since then, he had settled into a corkscrew career path that wound up with him leading a grid security team at Israel Electric.

Roni pinged his chat app. "Bruce, you there?"

"I am, mate. Juggling backup systems."

"Do you know where it started?"

"Pretty much all over the map, but it looks like central Haifa and the port went black a bit ahead of the rest of the corridor. We're having trouble bringing sections back on line. The SCADA network seems to be dropping commands. We're sending guys out to reset regional systems and substations manually."

"All right. Let's tunnel me in from here and start looking together at signs and symptoms. Which version of Scenaria

PowerShield are you running?"

"We're a release behind but our subscriptions are all current. Let me bring up the logs on a shared screen."

They quickly settled into an easy collaboration, made all the easier by their disembodied voices. His Hebrew carried a vaguely Anglo accent; hers was the guttural, high-volume firehose of a *sabra*, an Israeli born and raised in the country. The domain of their discourse was technical, peppered by arcana and terms of art, the specialized, highly condensed lingo of insiders to an obscure specialty, but there was also a friendly, almost flirtatious undertone.

"You're not wrong there, Roni. If we can trick the software into thinking it's operating in a different environment, then it should act on the new instructions."

Roni grinned with satisfaction. Then, as if being watched or filmed, she put on a serious-minded expression that she hoped projected into her voice. "Let's launch your code with my modules and see if it works." She knew better. It would work— despite the modifications on which Bruce had insisted. This was her life: convincing males, especially older, light-skinned males, that they were the ones working the magic, doing the stuff needing to be done. As Gal Gadot, she was simultaneously smug and resentful. It was a thought she shared with soul sisters: inside, we know we are superior. We know who is really in charge.

On the outside, her hands shook as she typed the command to insert the new counter-malware code into the power plants at the epicenter of the blackout. Then she corralled them all in a giant Lasso of Truth as she tapped out the rest of the command sequence.

Silence. Darkness. Seconds stretched into long minutes. Then the schematic display on her computer turned one dot from red to green. The lights started to turn on in waves that swept slowly outward from Jerusalem, exactly as she had configured the code to do. "Never miss a chance to make a statement about who's in charge," she said into the night air.

"What?" Bruce said.

She had been so absorbed that she had forgotten that they was still connected. "That'll show them, whoever 'them' is."

"Yeah, and I bet military intelligence is also wondering just that."

"Were you in Aman when you served in the IDF?"

"Never served. Took too long to get my degree from the University of Technology, Sydney, then spent a couple of lost years going walkabout before landing in Tel Aviv." There was a pause filled by the rattle of typing on a keyboard. "There. I just sent a note and a code sample to the people at Scenaria."

"You beat me to the punch," she said, but she was thinking that it was so like men to do that without first asking. What would Shimon do when she brought him up to date on her work? She'd find out soon enough. "Gotta go, Brucie. My boss is waiting to hear the story." She blinked. "And here come the lights. Isn't electricity amazing?"

"Yeah, and us. We made quick work of that attack. It was almost as if the black-hats made it easy to spot the code and defeat it."

"Almost as if," she said, thinking ahead about her and Shimon's ties to Unit 8200. Maybe this was the moment to renew some old contacts.

Chapter 7

BINYAMIN MARKHAM PACED in front of the class, compensating for what he lacked in stature with an athlete's energy as he wrapped up his remarks in a rushed delivery. Israeli-born but with U.S. dual citizenship, intensity and intelligence were the currency in his lifelong competition to convince others—and himself—that he belonged. He was carrying on family tradition, the legacy of ancestors who came from elsewhere and were perpetual inside-outsiders.

"So, any questions?" It was an academic ritual replayed on a regular basis by reluctant pedagogues around the world. Wait until five minutes before the class ends, speed through the last slides or a quick derivation on the whiteboard, and then, when time was running out, take questions with the unspoken hope there would be none. Markham loved his subject but loathed teaching it. His happy space was a quiet office where he could spend his days building and testing mathematical models. He had onetime had that, when he was working at the Center for Advanced Adaptive Systems Studies, a now-defunct defense-funded think tank adjacent to the Massachusetts Institute of Technology in Cambridge. Once it was no longer needed, the Center had faded from view as quickly as it had sprouted. Now he was adjunct faculty lecturing at the Technion in Haifa. His wife, Marwa, had been recruited; he was the plus one.

Bearded Tal Magen in the front row raised a pudgy hand. "Is this going to be on the quiz?" In a room full of young geeks, he was not the youngest but he was definitely one of the geekiest.

"This?" Markham waved a hand toward the densely covered whiteboard. "Which 'this' are you asking about?"

"Well, like, all of it?"

"Oh, that this. Yes, that 'this' will be on the quiz."

Groans accompanied the clicks of closing computers. Tal persisted. "Wait, like, you mean also the model-fit metrics?"

Markham turned toward the whiteboard. "Hmm, model goodness-of-fit measures. Ah, yes, there they are, pretty much most of what we talked about for the last hour. How can you know if your model is any good without them? Yes, I would say that will be on the quiz." He closed his laptop and slipped it into his backpack just after the second hand reached the apex on the clock. "See you all next class."

He was meeting Marwa for lunch at the other side of the three-hundred-acre Technion campus, and he needed to hustle. Binyamin hated being late, Marwa hated being early. If she arrived ahead of him, lunch would start like a badly spun dreidel, a top wobbling for a time before landing on the Hebrew letter *nun*, signifying that the whole thing had come to nothing. They both hated that: time wasted, time lost.

Marwa Khalidi was the misfit social scientist already well on her way to tenure at Israel's fabled tech-centered university. A Canadian-educated Arab Israeli, fluent in Hebrew, Arabic, French, and English, with advanced degrees in anthropology, linguistics, and social psychology, she was suitably overqualified, ticked all the right diversity boxes, and, since being recruited, had made all the right career moves. She brought the mindset of modern social sciences to bear on security and

45

threat analysis. With her dark-eyed beauty and crisp, quotable responses to questions, she had become the Israel media's go-to talking head after every fresh cybersecurity crisis. Of late, there had been no shortage of such media moments.

≈ ≈ ≈

Binyamin, always in pursuit of the precise, lengthened his stride without breaking into a run as he approached the little café at the edge of campus. He grabbed a sidewalk table, slouched purposefully into the wrought-iron chair, and slowed his breathing just as the dark and slender Marwa rounded the corner with a wiry energy like a wound spring. The residue of resentment for having to rush left him as she greeted him with a growing smile that transformed her face into a beam, a personal superpower that could melt him in mere seconds. How did I get so lucky, he was thinking.

"Sorry I'm late," she said, a trope between them that had marked the opening bars of meetings for most of their years together. "My grad student is floundering. I hope you haven't been waiting long."

"Not long. Don't worry. Is this the student who wants to do semantic analysis of social media feeds or something like that?" It was conversational, but tinted by a certain disdain.

"He did. Now he's thinking that's been done and redone. I'm trying to steer him into doing something with multilingual real-time voice processing driven by adversarial deep-learning algorithms." They were both geeks, though of different species, and even their most casual conversations could be peppered with geek-speak. "Maybe bring in Professor Rachamon to co-supervise, we'll see. Anyway, it's the same-old story. First year PhD students always go through this wash-and-rinse cycle. I sure did. Both times."

Binyamin was on the verge of saying that he wouldn't

know, but held back. He had bailed on his own graduate education and had never gotten over a certain sense of inferiority for his lack of an advanced degree, a lack that life often reminded him of. "You want to order?" he said.

"In a minute. There was something I wanted to . . . oh yes, this arrived for you just after you left the apartment this morning." She handed him a courier packet.

Biniyamin's heart started jogging when he saw the imprint on the outside. He zipped open the outer envelope, tore the inner one, and quickly read the message on official stationery.

"What is it?"

"I'm being called up, the reserves, on a Decree 8, an emergency. I report next week to *Shmoneh Matayim*."

"Really, Unit 8200, military intelligence? Are you sure?"

"Here, read it yourself."

She read it with a single sweep of her eyes. "Why Aman? This says OSINT. Open-source intelligence is my area."

"It's not like you have a monopoly. Everybody is on this bandwagon. Social media and public channels are supplanting spies on the ground. As to why they didn't call on you, could it be that you never served in the IDF? Is it also possible that military intelligence is not all that keen to call up Arab Israelis? All charges of discrimination to be denied, mind you." It was a sore point between them and between their communities-of-origin. Israeli Arabs could serve in the military but were exempted from mandatory service. Those who did serve, a small minority, gained a shared experience that led to lifelong connections but often at the price of criticism and isolation from their own communities.

She gave him a spare-me look. "So, what's really going on?"

"How should I know, at least not yet? And I certainly wouldn't be able to tell you if and when I do find out."

"Wait a minute. I seem to recall us working together at the Center in Cambridge. We both had the same top-level security clearance. And I'm your wife."

"That was then, this is now. That was Stateside, this is Israel. And, we went rogue. Once you go off the reservation, the tribe is understandably hesitant to take you back."

"Well," she said, gesturing at the letter, "they seem to want you back, despite your rogue ops. That must mean it's pretty big."

"Maybe. Maybe the IDF is just short-handed or Unit 8200 needs my more mature hand to help the herd all those kids they have there hacking away at the world's computer systems. That was me, once."

"Well, at least Herzliya's not that far."

"No, but I'm not reporting to headquarters at Camp Glilot. I'm headed for the desert, the Negev, Be'er Sheva."

She sank down in her chair. "You realize, we've never been really separated, not since we got married."

"We've hardly been separated since we were office mates in Cambridge. And here we are, married." He looked down, studying the pattern of the table for a moment. "I could never have imagined."

"Is it really that much of a stretch?"

"Well, you were married before, and he wasn't Muslim, so maybe it's less of a stretch for you."

"Oh, now I get it. And you never dated any gentile girls?"

"You know I did. We've talked about this before, but . . . well, anyway, I guess we're going to be apart for a while. Maybe a break from . . . well, from routine will be good for us. Commuting between here and Be'er Sheva is probably not an option. It's, what, nearly three hours by train? Until I report, I'm not going to know when I'll be able to get away on leave."

"This sucks. And you were doing so well at the university."

"You want to know what sucks? For real? Adjunct Professor Markham sucks. I really was not cut out for teaching. Give me a copy of R Studio and a really hairy stats problem to solve, and I am content. Make that C++ with the right toolkit, and I'll gleefully write malicious code to target any system or network of your choice. Ask me to stand in front of a bunch of students every day trying to pound statistical models into their brilliant but distractible and argumentative brains, and you have one unhappy mathematician."

"I didn't realize you were so unhappy."

"Of course you didn't. How could you? When I'm with you, I'm happy. Period. I'm happy now. Happy and hungry."

"I'm not. Neither hungry nor happy. I can't believe they're separating us. It's one of those things about . . . well, about here. At least when we were in the States, our lives were more or less our own."

"More or less. Look, it won't be all that long, just until this crisis, whatever it is, passes. It's like the power outage this week. It'll be over, and I'll be back before you can miss me."

"If it's like the blackout, then I am worried. I thought Israel had the world's only hardened, hack-proof power infrastructure, and then we learn that we, too, can be hacked."

"If it was a cyberattack. We don't know for certain."

"Trust me, we know for certain; we just aren't admitting it yet. Politics, spin, managing the narrative—that's what it's always about these days. And now this. The timing is suspicious. No, not suspicious, conclusive. With Donaldson in the States and Petrov in Russia playing chicken over who has the faster, fatter cyber missile, I don't know. My student doing the media-tracking project says things are heating up way faster than official storylines are portraying."

"You put more faith in those soft analyses than I do. Always have."

"Hey, I use the same statistical techniques as you do in your work."

"Sure you do, but the difference is I do it with real data." It was a perennial debate between them that had decayed into a certain mock seriousness without ever completely losing its edge. Their unspoken rules required one of them to change the subject before it escalated out of the mock and into the real. Bini was trying to think of a suitable non sequitur to avoid conflict, when Marwa jumped in.

"You know what we should do?" she said. "Let's head up to Mount Hermon for the weekend."

"It's going to be too warm to ski by now."

"These days, pretty much everywhere on the planet has become too warm to ski, but we don't have to ski. We don't even have to get out of bed." She winked at him.

"This is beginning to sound like a good plan." He winked back. "You've been so busy with your teaching and research lately that we hardly see each other except over lunch. But we can't go right away. We're with my folks Wednesday night for a Passover seder. Lev and Anat are coming up from Tel Aviv."

"I forgot. Passover. Of course. I've been so heads-down into research and teaching. Growing up, we just ignored the Jewish holidays. Or pretended to ignore them. I'm still not used to paying real attention to the Jewish calendar. It doesn't make sense to me."

"Hey, what about me, what I have to deal with? Ramadan always seems to come out of nowhere."

"It does: eleven days earlier every year. Islam does it for real, a pure lunar calendar, none of this half-hearted lunisolar stuff with fudged interpolations."

He picked up on her teasing. "You just don't want to admit that the Jews and the Christians did a better job reconciling the calendars."

"Maybe, but the Arabs gave you your numbers—and algebra, which is an Arabic word, remember—for which you, of all people, ought to be most grateful."

He lowered his head. "I bow in gratitude. Anyway, as you know, even in our barely observant family, Passover is a big deal."

"Will Shoshi be there? I really like your kid sister."

"No, she'll be celebrating Pesach on the base. I still don't know exactly what she does in the IDF, but they seem to need her. Anyway, we can do both. We'll have to drive up to Mount Hermon the next day, but we can still spend the rest of the time in bed once we get there."

"See, so maybe this crisis is not such a bad thing."

"Maybe. I should know better when I report in the Negev next week. Right now, I'm ready for falafel and a cucumber salad. If you're really not hungry, you can watch me eat if you wish."

She stuck her tongue out at him and he mirrored her.

≈ ≈ ≈

By the time Bini and Marwa arrived, the apartment was a beehive of last-minute prep. The décor in the two-bedroom apartment on a hill looking down toward the bowl of Haifa's harbor bore the marks melding Bini's parents: Shira's artistry coupled with Karl's compulsive need for order. Shira welcomed them both with hugs and cheek kisses, then leaned back to give Marwa a more thorough up-and-down, with a pointed pause at her midsection.

"Ima," Bini said, "you have all the subtlety of a she-goat. Hint, hint, wink wink. Something about grandchildren?"

"I'm not getting any younger, you know, and neither are you two."

"You had me and Shoshi rather later in life, and look how we turned out."

"That's what I was thinking. A son who now lives not fifteen minutes away and we only see you once or twice a year. What mother would not want to have grandchildren, so she has somebody to see while she can still make it up and down the stairs? Someday you'll understand, Marwa, if you are, uh, so lucky enough as to have children who are so . . . so attentive."

"Ima, please. You can't run that Jewish guilt thing on Marwa. It won't work."

Marwa smiled at Shira before turning back to Bini. "Oh, maybe it works better than you think. She's right. We should come over more often. And none of us is getting any younger."

Shira grinned triumphantly at both of them. "And I have to get back to the kitchen to oversee the two old guys who were finishing up with their annual ritual of messing up my kitchen by making something new that no one ever heard of. This year it's some spicy Moroccan dish they insist is authentic."

"Hey, Marwa," Karl called out from the kitchen. "Come and give this old guy a hug. And bring my prodigal son with you." He aligned his spoon on the spoon rest and quickly but carefully washed and dried his hands, untied his apron, and hung it on a peg before reaching out to Marwa to repeat the hugs-and-kisses ritual with her. With Bini it was a one-armed hug and handshake, both held long. He and Bini kept nodding as they held each other's gaze. "It's been too long, Bini."

"It's always too long, Abba, always too long." He finally dropped his hand. "So, how's the book coming."

"There you go, having to spoil a perfectly good father-son moment."

Lev Novikov, who had been grinding away with a mortar-and-pestle, peered around from behind Karl. "I'd shake hands too, but my hands are all sticky, and I don't have your father's obsessive-compulsive personality, so I'm not going to pause to wash my hands for a second time. We can save that ritual for the seder."

"Sure thing. But you know, we usually don't do that whole hand-washing ritual, so you might end up on your own at the sink. And how is your book coming?"

"Done. It's off to my new publisher in New York. The whole series is doing quite well. It was the right move to start writing in English. You wanna know the ironic thing? Another of my thrillers for the American market is now being translated into Hebrew for the Israeli market. All my years with Mossad are finally paying off with the fictional exploits of the intrepid but invented Avi Barak. I keep telling your dad that he should develop an action character and turn it into a franchise. No, he wants to write, quote, literature." He shook his fruit-stained hands heavenward to emphasize the last word.

Karl shifted to the side to block Lev. "He's just jealous because I can really write. What he does is called typing."

"Who's jealous? What you do is called retyping and retyping—l'olam va'ed, to the horizon and again, endless."

Marwa took Bini's arm and gently tugged him away. "Let's go check out the seder table."

Karl followed them into the living room, where the small dining table had been moved and extended with an extra leaf to accommodate all the guests. "So, you two, what's new in your lives?" he asked.

"I've been called up," Bini said. "I'm headed for the Negev next week, Defense Intelligence."

"I'm not surprised, what with Petrov and Donaldson squaring off for a cyber duel. Lightsabers at dawn. Rolling blackouts across the Americas, and then we get hit. You two wouldn't know anything about that, would you? I mean, what with your contacts and all."

"Ask Marwa. Her students researching social media seem to know more than all the intelligence services combined. If you think Unit 8200 shines in open-source intel, they have nothing on the grad-student analysts she has working on their dissertations at the Technion."

"He's just jealous," she said. "But, yeah, it's pretty clear from text analysis that the Russians were the ones turning the lights out here as well as in the States. The feud with the U.S. is pretty obvious, but the strike at Israel is perplexing. I'm not ready to go on record about any of this, but our data is pretty compelling. It's especially clear when you separate and highlight all the fake accounts the Russians set up, which is not always easy. Spotting the American fakes is not as hard. I think they're still playing catch-up ball in the online deception game. And then we have some new stuff we're still trying to track down. We're thinking there might be another player in the game."

From the kitchen, Lev spoke up. "I still don't understand how you can reach conclusions like that based on just tweets and blog posts." Lev was ex-Mossad and second generation in the intelligence services. Despite his technical background, he was deeply skeptical about social media and open-source intel.

Shira positioned her small frame in the doorway, arms outstretched to the jambs as if blocking the way. "Stop, everybody. Enough politics. It's all I ever hear, even in the shop. A lovely young couple came in not two days ago, looking for me to make them wedding bands, and within two minutes they were arguing over party politics. They finally left with a promise to come back later, but I still haven't seen them."

Marwa nodded emphatically. "I'm with you. Let's set it all aside for a while." She reached to realign the candlesticks on the table: delicate glass towers, flaring at the top, each wrapped with a filigree of silver wire forming a stylized tree. "Are these yours, Shira? Did you make them?"

"Yes. I wanted to do something that somehow melded a contemporary look with classic details. I'm working on a series I call *migdalim katanim*, small towers. What do you think?"

"I think they're beautiful. The combination of, well, the transparency of the glass and the weighty delicacy of the silver really works."

"I like that: 'weighty delicacy of the silver'. You should write ad copy for me."

"It's supposed to be *etz chaim*, right? The tree of life."

"Yes. And it's also expedient art. Silver is so expensive. Besides, I've always wanted to learn glassblowing, and this lovely Chinese woman in the next building has been teaching me. These are my first big project: not quite good enough to sell, but good enough here."

"So, where are the rest of the family?"

"Anat is running a last-minute errand, but Shoshi is supposed to be spending the whole of Pesach on base."

Bini plunked down on the sofa pushed against the wall. "It's hard to believe my little sister is not only in the IDF but in a combat unit. I remember when she wanted to be the Israeli Shirley Temple."

"It still could happen," Shira said, "although she now talks more about winning the Eurovision. That is, when she is not talking about becoming a cantor."

"Now that I can see, she always was the most observant in the family."

55

Karl sat down beside his son. "Hey, what about me? I've always been observant. We writers are always observing."

Shira groaned and turned to give him a raised-eyebrows look, just as Anat Dorfman, Lev's wife, entered carrying a small paper-wrapped package. Karl reached for it, but Anat shifted it behind her. "Oh, no. You'll have to wait. A little surprise for later." She playfully tapped him on the head with the package as she brushed past to give her husband a hug in the kitchen. "That, dear, looks interesting," she said as she bent over the bowl he was giving a stir."

"Moroccan *charoseth*. An old family recipe."

"Old family my foot. Novikov is as Ashkenazi as they come."

"Ah, but my mother, of blessed memory, was from Morocco, and my taste buds might as well be. I've always been partial to Sephardi and Mizrachi food. The Ashkenazim tend to overcook and over-salt everything. Anyway, there, it's done. Want a taste." He held out a spoonful toward her.

She gave it a suspicious onceover and shook her head. "I'll wait. Everything in order. It's called a *seder* for a reason."

"And I love it," Lev said, lifting the bowl from the counter and carrying it toward the dining table, "how everybody here becomes suddenly so orthodox, so strict and observant this time of year. Even Karl." Lev set the bowl down near the center of the table.

Karl feigned being offended. "Hey, I've never aspired to be orthodox. I am a proudly unorthodox Jew, always have been. Here, my unobservant Israeli brother"—he expertly frisbeed a blue-and-black skullcap across the room—"put on a kippah and come to the table."

≈ ≈ ≈

They were partway through the seder, building their Hillel sandwiches, spooning spicy date-apricot-and-pistachio charoseth atop the horseradish on their matzohs, when there was a knock at the apartment door. "It's too early for Elijah," Bini said.

"You're closest," his mother said. "You get it." Bini folded his napkin, rose, and opened the door.

The young woman in uniform was his height, with curly brown hair cut military short. They stood, unmoving, for seconds before embracing in silence. Both wiped their eyes as everyone around the table stood.

"Well, aren't you going to invite Elijah in?" his mother said.

"You knew. And you didn't tell me Shoshi was coming."

"No, we didn't know. Not until a couple hours ago,"

"I only have a few hours," Shoshi said, "and I have to catch the bus back, so this better not be one of those interminable seders singing every song and discussing and debating every page of the Haggadah. Okay? And I refuse to do every bloody verse of 'Chad Gadya'. Okay?"

"As you wish, princess." Bini took a slight bow.

"And you, smart guy, I can take on if you give me any crap. I'm trained in krav maga, you know." She made a mock judo gesture.

"Likewise. So let's just eat and catch up. They let you go?"

"Yeah, after I made a stink and said it would be my third Pesach away from family."

"But it's not been that long, and the year before you were . . . where? On some study cruise or something."

"Yeah, but they don't know that, unless they connect the dots, and by that time, I'll be back. Besides, they don't really need me." She brushed a hand through her hair. "Not yet, anyway."

"You do know, little sister, this may not be a military base, but we do have rules. And just so you know, the protocol for tonight is strictly no politics, no talk of international crises, global warming, or sea-level rise. Moses parted the sea once, but we will not be discussing any contemporary need for his services tonight."

"I'm fine with rules, bro, but remember, we are Israelis. Well, all except Abba, and he's honorary, even if not necessarily always honorable."

"I see what serving our country does to you, young lady," Karl said.

"Makes us realists, is what it does. I give us ten minutes—twenty tops—before someone makes a political crack and the voices get loud and the gestures dramatic."

"A shekel says we make it to dessert." Karl pointed toward her.

"You're on, Abba. Now, can we all sit down and get on with this thing before our putz of a prime minister pisses off the Arab world again."

Bini playfully rabbit-punched her, Shira looked heavenward, and Karl ceremoniously took off his glasses and did a face-palm. "Not even five minutes," he said.

≈ ≈ ≈

The somewhat streamlined Passover Seder concluded with dessert: a platter arrayed with an assortment of fruits and chocolates along with Shira's matzoh kugel, an elegant recipe from her growing up in England that borrowed the berries and the sherry of an English trifle. Anat excused herself and returned from the kitchen with a small plate arrayed with green, orange, yellow, and red jellies shaped like fruit slices.

"Is that what I think it is?" Karl asked.

"The real thing: Boston Kosher-for-Passover Fruit Slices. A friend brought them back with her from a business trip to your home town."

"Adopted home town. Erstwhile. I grew up in a small city on Michigan's Upper Penninsula—the far-north middle-of-nowhere, for those of you ignorant of North American geography—and now my home is Haifa. Home is where my hat is." He patted the yarmulke on his head. "But, wow, that is so sweet. I have such fond memories of those fruit slices."

Shoshi slipped her cellphone from a pocket and glanced at the screen. "I ordered a taxi with the Gett app. It's waiting at the bottom of the street." She grabbed an ersatz orange slice as the plate passed her. "I've gotta go."

Bini pushed his chair back and stood. "Marwa and I will walk down with you. I could use the exercise. You all right with that, Marwa?"

She hesitated before nodding. "We'll be back, everybody. You haven't gotten rid of us yet."

The leave-taking dragged on to the point that Shoshi had to start down the stairs on her own. In the street, Bini and Marwa trotted to catch up. "I'm sorry," Marwa said as she pulled alongside. "Military punctuality was never in my repertoire."

"I can testify to that," Bini said. "In fact, she turns being late into an art form."

Marwa rolled her eyes. "He's his father's son. Despite growing up in Israel, he never caught on to Middle East Standard Time. Israeli Arabs may not always be on time, but we are always *in* time. Anyway, look, can I ask you something, something about what's going on?"

"You can ask. That doesn't mean I can answer."

"What's happening? Are we going to be without power as Israel fights for its survival?"

Shoshi stopped to give her a look with layers of confusion and concern. "You and I haven't really had much chance to get to know each other, but . . ."

"If I understand what you are saying, don't forget, I'm Israeli, too. My older brother not only volunteered for the IDF, but he died for his country—your country, my country. I won't pretend not to have pulls that tug at my sympathies, but I could never have married your brother if I weren't clear about where my commitment lies."

"I'm sorry. I just never had many Arab friends . . . Muslim friends, you know."

"Yeah, that's one of the problems. We grow up in these separate worlds that are only a few miles or a few streets apart but with walls between that are at once invisible and opaque. Despite me being born in Israel, Bini was the first Jew I really knew, really, as a person rather than as an object or as a role or a symbol of something else. And I also went to school in liberal, multicultural Canada, where the unacknowledged boundaries are just as real."

"I said I'm sorry."

"I know. Me too. But it will take time. I assume we'll get there, you and I, because I can see how much you and your brother love each other, and he is the man I love."

Shoshi started walking again. "Okay, okay. But you know I can't really say much of anything about what I know."

"That says something. It means you know something."

"And I assume you can add that to Bini's orders and come up with a sum."

"What unit are you in?"

Bini, who had stayed out of the conversation, caught up. "Didn't you notice her uniform? She's in Aman, military intelligence. It's a family tradition to be in intelligence work, although I don't know what she does."

Shoshi, shifting from a stroll into high gear, spoke in word bursts. "I'm doing. What I'm good at. What I. Always was. And there's my taxi. *Shalom. L'hitraot.*" She sprinted ahead and got in the waiting car.

Marwa slowed to catch her breath. "What was she always good at?"

"Besides singing and acting, she's got an ear for languages and has always been a people person, far more than me." He stared off at the retreating car. "I just hope she's not getting involved in forward reconnaissance."

≈ ≈ ≈

After Bini and Marwa returned to the apartment, Karl caught up with his son during an odd lull amidst the ordered chaos of clearing and cleaning up. "I'm heading out onto the balcony with my espresso. Join me?"

"Sure. It looks like things are under control." Bini glanced toward the kitchen. "Marwa seems to fit right in with Ima and Anat."

"We don't pick people at random, Bini."

"Do you ever have, like, doubts? You've been married a long time, but, I mean, how can we know?" He was thinking of recent tensions. "Things change so much, so quickly, so easily these days."

Karl turned from the view to look Bini in the eye. "You know about me and your mother, right? How we got together?"

"Well, you guys did tell us the story of the mysterious way you met, about the *mezuzah* with the message and about being *bashert*, you know, that you were meant for each other, fated."

"But do you know that fate had a name? Your father was Mitchell Rossing. He took the name Migdal Rozen after he converted and became an Israeli citizen. He was fate, the Fates. He orchestrated this elaborate thing of a meeting with me and then the whole sequence of events afterwards, all just to bring Shira and me together."

"Why? I never understood why he would do that."

"Because he loved her so much. When he realized that his life was likely to end soon, he made sure that she would be all right, in good hands." Karl tried not to choke up. "Now that's real love. That's being faithful above and beyond."

"I don't remember him. I was so young. I mean, I can picture him because I've seen his pictures, but I don't remember anything that actually happened. You have always been Abba to me."

"Not always, but we did hit it off pretty quickly. You liked my goofy stories."

"What was he like?"

"Your father? You know, I didn't really know him in those days, only much earlier, back when we were in college."

"So?"

"He was, truth to tell, a bit of a poseur, a kind of con man of sorts, bluffing his way through life with outrageous bravado. I understand that served him well in a distinguished career in the Mossad. And he was brilliant, as are you and your sister."

"Technically, she's my half-sister."

"Right, so that means all the good stuff you have in common came from your mother's side. My own father advised me to marry one of the smart ones—as he did—and now it seems you're carrying on a family tradition with Marwa."

"But you and Ima, you're both Jewish. Marwa and I are . . . well, what could be more of a mismatch than a Muslim and a Jew?"

"A beautiful and talented Jewish artist and a nominally unspecified doubter and writer wannabe, maybe? Like your mother and me?"

"But, I mean, you're Jewish."

"So you say. So I say. So your mother says. And it is true, in a sense. But you know, I didn't know that I was born Jewish until you were about to enter the IDF, when I discovered that bunch of letters between my mother, the woman who raised me, and my mother, the woman who gave birth to me."

Bini turned to the railing and stood beside his father. "I don't know what's going to happen. What would our kids be? Marwa and me, I mean. I keep wondering about that, how we should raise them. Would they be Jews, Muslims, something else?"

"They'll be who they are, just like you and Soshi, just like ... hell, any of us." he downed the last sip of his espresso. "Now, let's go back in and act all surprised and apologetic that the women have finished the cleanup without us."

"What about uncle Lev?"

"He doesn't count. My guess is he's been kibitzing while making notes in that damn red journal he carries with him everywhere. He's such a wonk, a real writer, and you know I love him and hate him for it—for every big royalty check and translation deal of it."

Chapter 8

THE SMALL, UNASSUMING HOTEL Marwa had booked was some miles from the ski resort, but it had a reputable restaurant with a good wine list. "You've corrupted me," she told Bini over dinner, as she lifted her glass of a Vortman malbec. "I once was a good Muslim."

"You still are a good Muslim, as I am still a good Jew." He took a sip from his second glass of the cabernet. "And this is a good wine. We have just both become more—what shall we say?—more flexible. Admit it: even to the extent that we were observant, which in my case was hardly at all, neither one of us were rabid believers."

"I still have doubts about . . . well about pretty much everything. Do you really think we can make it? I mean, you and me, in the long run?"

"What brings this up now? We're coming up on four years. That bodes pretty well, I'd say."

"I was married to Seth for four years. We know how that ended."

"Except with me, there is no one else and never will be."

"You say that, but men say that all the time and then screw around on the side."

"I'm not 'men', Marwa. I'm me, Adam Binyamin Markham. I may not be much in the faith department, as you well know—

hell, here I am a Jew married to a Muslim—but I am faithful. That means a lot to me."

"And me." She reached across the table and took his hand. "But you know, the world, this country, has no room for us."

"What do you mean? No one is giving us any grief."

"Yes, because mostly nobody knows or sees. But what if I took up the hijab and you started wearing a kippah everywhere? How do you think our countrymen would react as we walked down the street holding hands? And what about our kids?"

"Kids? I . . ." Bini was still trying to understand the question when the first explosion shook the windows. "Iron Dome! At least I hope so." As the sirens sounded, the waitstaff were already herding patrons toward the shelter in the cellar. Bini and Marwa joined the orderly rush. "Syria," he said. "It's gotta be. Gaza doesn't have anything that can reach this far north."

The man ahead of Marwa snorted. "Those Palestinian swine. They get so-called humanitarian aid and use it to buy missiles. We should wipe the whole Gaza Strip clean, sterilize it and start over. Nothing good ever came out of Gaza."

Before Marwa could launch into a counterattack in Arabic, Bini put himself between them. "*Lashon hara*," he said to the man. "It is a Commandment. The 'evil tongue' is forbidden, even during an air raid. My wife came out of Gaza. Nothing good? What are you saying? Huh?"

"Well, at least your wife is not Palestinian."

"And if she were?"

Before the man could reply, a woman with an emergency radio app on her cellphone snapped at them. "*Sheket! Sheket, bevakasha.*" Shut up, please. The room went silent for the tinny voice announcing that three surface-to-surface missiles out of Syria had been intercepted over the Golan Heights by Israel's

Iron Dome missile defense system. Simultaneous rockets out of Gaza were also intercepted before they could reach Tel Aviv.

The rest of the report was uninformative, and the room erupted into Israel's number-one sport: heated debate. When the all-clear sounded, Marwa took Bini's hand and held him back until the shelter had emptied. "Something is going on. I'm scared. For you, for us. If there's war . . ."

"There's always war someplace. If it's here, one thing you can count on is that Israel will come out on top."

"Not if the whole . . . well, the Arab world is . . ."

"Yes, even if the whole Arab world is on the other side," he said.

"And what about me, my family. We're Arabs, Arab-Israelis."

"Not the same. Besides, we've been there before and here we are. Still. The Gaza thing I can understand. It's not so much Gazans as Hamas. That they keep lobbing rockets at us is self-defeating but predictable—and almost understandable. But Syria?"

"As I've been trying to tell you, Bini, my research shows it may be Hezbollah, but Russian fingerprints are on everything. They're supplying arms, intelligence, training, and cyber weapons, directly or indirectly through other proxies. Plus there may be other players in the mix; we're working on that one. And now Iran is flexing its muscles, seizing freighters, downing civilian aircraft, and once more rushing toward nuclear capability after the U.S. backed out of the nuclear agreement."

"The U.S. didn't back out, the Tweeter in Chief reneged on the deal."

"A distinction without a difference. The consequences are the same."

"Well, we don't know just what the consequences are."

"Yes we do. You're being called up, and I'm afraid of losing you."

"Unit 8200 is SIGINT. Look, I'll be in a bunker, staring at a computer screen and analyzing code. Or nodding off in some briefing. I'm not going to be a foot soldier."

"How do you know? 8200 now has its own tactical combat team, you know."

"How do I know? All I have to do is look at my driver's license and I know. Do the numbers from my date-of-birth, and you know I'm too old to be wearing olive-drabs and toting an assault rifle."

Chapter 9

IN THE BACK SEAT of the Mercedes limo, Maksim raised his glass of Dom Pérignon and toasted. "*Na Zdorovie*! Better than working ransomware for a few hundred a shot, wouldn't you say, Yuri?" He took a sip, then kissed the woman in his lap, a tall blonde whose name he couldn't remember and who pretended to enjoy his boozy attention.

"All the same. Money is money," Yuri said, staring with stoned indifference out the tinted glass windows as the garish colored lights of the Moscow night streamed by.

"But this money does not send us to jail. This money comes from high places."

"Does it? We have no idea how it appears in our accounts or where it really comes from. At least when we were playing the ransomware game, we knew who the suckers were and who our partners were. Antonov supplied the lists, and Stradchik cleared the Bitcoin ransom. Now we don't even know who the targets are, much less who pays."

"Well, we do have IP addresses for the targets, but it's not smart to look too closely, especially with such easy money." Maksim tapped the palm of his hand. "All we do is mod the code they send us and inject it through the DeusEx network. Afterwards, the numbers with strings of zeroes show up in our accounts."

Yuri shook his head and tried to ignore the woman in his lap, figuring that she was an informant or prostitute in the employ of Russian intelligence, the FSB—or both. It was not that she was not pretty, but she was sophisticated and aggressive—not his type. His type were frail and insecure, naïve but ready to surrender, not already practiced at giving a well-rehearsed performance. With the money he and Maksim now had banked, he would find his, the innocent girl who would willingly and sincerely do the things he wanted. Perhaps it was time, time to exit the game, while the exit was still open.

"You are arrogant, Maksim. Giving yourself that screen name after Russia's most storied hacker. BOGACHEV2, indeed. You're always drawing attention to your exploits. And you are too easily seduced. Zeroes are cheap, like these two. The strings of zeroes can contract as easily as they expand. The girls can disappear with the dawn. When they are through with us, pffft!" He flicked his fingers like a magician vanishing a playing card.

Maksim ignored him and leaned forward to tap on the jury-rigged Perspex screen bolted in place between them and the driver. "Hey, we're going to be late. Let's move it. We don't want to miss the first act. This is a premier, you know."

The driver nodded and touched his hat. He accelerated smoothly as he started switching lanes on the broad avenue. As the traffic light ahead turned yellow, he stepped on it and sailed through on the red. "See," he said, knowing his passengers were not listening. "You will make it to your fucking premier."

≈ ≈ ≈

On a side street a few blocks short of the theater, two men sat talking in a lorry, one with a cellphone to his ear. He held up his finger to silence his partner. "*Da, da, mnye pora,*" he said into

69

the phone in heavily accented Russian. It was time. He could do this. He slid the phone into his shirt pocket and pulled out from the kerb.

As he approached the intersection, he slowed. Timing was everything. Wait until the petrol tanker was in position, rolling to a stop just beyond the intersection, in the left lane of the broad avenue. Watch for the limo. There it was, but it was coming too fast, speeding through lights. The lorry driver revved the engine and popped the clutch, relying on his experience running supplies and dodging incoming in Afghanistan to time the impact. At the last second, he spun the wheel as if trying to avoid a collision and slid sideways into the limo, ricocheting , but sending the limo directly into the back of the tanker. The driver of the tanker was already hopping out of the cab when the limo struck with enough momentum to raise the rear of the tanker into the air. Seconds later, a fireball erupted as the lorry sped away.

≈ ≈ ≈

Within hours, Russian media were rife with stories about an attack on Russian soil staged by foreign agents and resulting in multiple civilian deaths. President Petrov announced a massive manhunt to locate the perpetrators, believed to be Americans or operatives in their employ. Eyewitnesses reported seeing the driver of a gasoline truck fleeing the scene on foot just before an explosion killed several pedestrians as well as the occupants of the limousine that collided with the tanker. A search was launched for two men in a damaged delivery van that was also seen speeding away.

The Whitehouse responded with official denials of any knowledge of or connection with the incident, while President Donaldson tweeted that Petrov was merely trying to create an excuse for dangerous "esculation[sic] of the situation." Fox

News lauded the president for his determination in standing up to and calling out the Russians. CNN took the President to task for sabre rattling and ridiculed his spelling.

Chapter 10

SPRING HAD COME EARLY, wet, and warm to Virginia, and trees that should have been skeletal or sprinkled with pale green or pink buds were already fully leafed-out. With the south-bound side of the two-lane road heading in the direction of Spring Falls moving like the slow drip of sap from the sugar maples, there was plenty of time to take in the verdant hills.

Barbara sighed and inched the car forward. While Dima rode shotgun and texted on his burner phone, Arkady dozed in the back. The two days in Sam Parson's small apartment had been a chorus of discordant agendas, as the three of them struggled to lay low and get ready for departure. Barbara leaned out the window to try and see how far ahead the bumper-to-bumper traffic stretched. Unlike others in line, she never used her horn. To her, it was not only pointless but went against her low-profile personality. "Looks like everybody has pretty much the same idea of heading for the hills. I wonder if it's as bad heading north from DC. Maybe we should have gone to the Poconos."

Dima shrugged. "Probably not." He swiped and tapped on his phone. "Pennsylvania and Maryland are still mostly without power."

The space ahead opened up a bit as the line of cars started rolling for a few seconds before the guy in the red Hyundai in front of her hit his brakes. Barbara slammed on hers and was startled by a sharp crack as a small round hole with a spider-web halo appeared in the lower right corner of the windshield.

"Everybody down!" Dima was already sliding out the passenger door as a second bullet took out the rearview mirror. "Pop the trunk, stay down." Before Barbara could say anything, Dima was behind the car grabbing his backpack. He moved in an awkward crouch alongside the stalled cars ahead as he readied his newly acquired Rucksack Rifle, the compact and collapsible Remington 5.56/.223 CSR becoming popular with right-wing nationalists and sniper fantasists who could afford it. To get his, Dima had paid more than double the retail price.

He jerked open the passenger door of a blue Dodge Ram and waved the carbine at the startled driver. "Police. Set your parking brake and don't move." He locked the scope in place and jammed in a magazine as he positioned himself behind the bed of the pickup.

He peeked over the edge and scanned the hills opposite. "Now, you bastard," he said to himself, "take another shot." There it was, the bright muzzle flash followed quickly by the bang. "No suppressor. You need the range. So do I." Through the scope, he panned left to pick out the spot in the thicket of trees atop the hills. "Come on, fucker, take that shot." Another flash. "Okay, got you." With no time for adjustments, he estimated the distance to the tree line at over three hundred yards. The rifle had been zeroed at a hundred, and he guessed the added bullet drop at about a foot. As he steadied the rifle on the edge of the pickup bed and began to squeeze the trigger, the driver of the truck panicked and suddenly lurched forward, spoiling the shot and leaving Dima exposed. He dropped to the ground in front of the BMW that was now rolling steadily toward him. With absolute focus, he worked the bolt and raised the rifle slowly to get a fix on his target. A round ricocheted off the pavement inches from his left elbow. He squeezed off his shot and rolled right, working the bolt. The pavement erupted where he had been a split second before. The driver in the BMW slammed on his brakes, and Dima calmly squeezed off another shot before shimmying backward and dropping into the ditch.

The space in front of Barbara's car had opened up by a couple of car lengths, and drivers behind were starting to lean on their horns. Dima scrambled in. "Let's get out of here before everybody in line is calling 9-1-1 or uploading to social media. Make a U-turn and head back. We'll need to switch cars, too." He raised the butt of his rifle. "Cover your face," he snapped, as he knocked out the rest of the shattered windshield. "Now you can see where you're going."

"Did you get him?"

"I think so. If not, we'll know in a minute. Whoever it is, he's not the best shot on the firing range, but he sure is persistent."

With horns behind her now blaring, Barbara pulled out of the line, swung the car around, and floored it.

≈ ≈ ≈

It was afternoon with Dima driving when they finally arrived from the wrong side of the mountain and turned with their newly acquired rental car onto the grown-over track leading to the cabin near Spring Falls. The modest vacation home was newly renovated but designed to blend in, with rustic cedar-shake siding, a full-length front porch, and fieldstone chimneys on either end. "So this is the place," Dima said, "the fabled Talpa retreat."

Barbara looked up from her phone, which no longer had a signal. "Fabled, maybe, but not his anymore. It was deeded over to Scenaria after he left in disgrace over using his antivirus software to spy on customers." She and Arkady had let Dima drive while they spent the time on their cellphones, using their FBI connections, creating a clumsy but plausible cover story for the mysterious shootout on the highway, and arranging for discreet disposal of the car and a replacement. For that, they had drawn on connections of Barbara's late husband, Abe Feingold, who had been one of the *sayanim*, the loyal, silent, and secretive network of helpers always standing ready to assist Israel's Mossad. They had been instructed to abandon Barbara's car at a drop spot where it would be picked up later. "You know, I loved that car," she said. "I should have known we were in for trouble the moment you insisted on swapping out the plates."

"Routine to switch plates," Dima said. "And that's also why the *sayan* disabled the tracking on this thing." He swung the rental car around to the side of the cabin where it could not be seen from the road. "If you want to disappear, you don't leave a trail of breadcrumbs behind you."

"Well, we left something behind us—or you did—because it certainly seems like your freelancers from Brazil were still on your trail."

"Maybe. But I don't think so any more. After the switch to the rental, I swapped SIM cards, took the corkscrew route Arkady suggested, and kept my eyes glued to the rearview mirrors. I think we're clean. Now, let's get settled in."

As Arkady mounted the front steps, he looked down. "Clean?" he said. "Really?" He pointed to a drab UPS packet barely noticeable against the weathered wood on the porch. "It's for you, Dima. Too small to be a bomb."

Dima caught up and stopped him from reaching for it. "Not really, and not too small for other equally fatal contents."

He twisted his head to read the label. "Holy shit." He got out his phone and scanned the barcode. "I can't double check with the UPS website—no signal out here, and that might not be a good idea anyway, considering we don't know who we might alert—but the barcode appears to be genuine. I think we can open it." He picked it up as Arkady tapped an entry code on the keypad by the door.

Barbara arrived from the car with her bag. "What's up?"

"We have a package waiting for us. Somebody knew we were coming."

"The guy from Scenaria who shares the place did."

"Yeah, but . . . no, DB would have told no one. At least I think."

Arkady sneered. "So much for our secret hideaway and not leaving breadcrumbs, brother. We are going to have to be on high alert the entire time we're here."

Barbara pushed past and entered the cabin. "Who's it from?"

"Some company I never heard of," Dima said, "but it was posted last week at the UPS office at 66 Hebron Road. In Be'er Sheva, Israel."

Chapter 11

BINI EXITED THE ROUND YELLOW HATBOX that was the main hall of the Central Train Station in Be'er Sheva and stepped into the shade of the overhanging roof. A hot, arid breeze swirled around the supporting columns—welded girders of steel sculpted to resemble abstract trees, as if the architect had tried to make up for a lack in the landscape. An IDF recruit in olive drab trotted over to Bini and shook his hand. "I'm Eitan," he said, taking Bini's bag, then striding ahead toward a car without another word until they were underway. "I can't believe you're coming to work with us," he said. "Wow. Binyamin Markham. You're iconic, a hacking legend. I mean, you were just a teenager when you started doing anti-terrorist shit."

"I know, I was there. And mostly I was lucky. And too cocky to know I was way out of my depth."

"But I heard you stopped an attack on the US power infrastructure."

"I helped. It was a team effort. These things always are. How old are you?"

"Eighteen, sir." Binyamin was nominally a warrant officer in the reserves. He would have to get used to the occasional sirs and salutes from the young recruits on their mandatory service. The youngsters were the mental muscle that powered Unit 8200, one of the world's foremost intelligence gathering groups, on a par with the American NSA in everything but size and budget. Like the NSA, they not only hoovered up terabytes of data for the military and the rest of the intelligence community, but their crack computer programmers also devised sophisticated cyber weaponry, software that could worm its way into systems and sweep them for information or lie in wait for the green light to blow up natural gas pipelines, take out a power grid, or wipe bank records clean. Or, as they had done on one famous occasion, trick the Iranian uranium enrichment centrifuges into self-destructing.

"Are you on the acquisition or the offensive side, Eitan?"

"You know we're not allowed to say."

"So, cyber weapons and tactics."

"I . . . I really can't talk about my work. I'm sure you'll be briefed as needed."

"How long will it take to get to the new signal base? It's near Urim, right?"

"Uh, we're not headed for the base. I was told to take you to Gav-Yam Advanced Technologies Park. That's the new commercial cyber-tech center here in Be'er Sheva, opposite the university."

"What? My orders are to report to Unit 8200. Why am I going to some glorified office park?"

"Maybe it's because of . . ." He stopped himself. "I wouldn't know sir. I have my orders."

"It's okay. I won't let on about what you told me about your work." The driver's face paled. "Just kidding. Relax."

≈ ≈ ≈

For Bini, it was a disappointment not to be headed for a homecoming, a return to familiar, all-but-forgotten territory: long rows of recruits, their nimble fingers tapping away at keyboards, their agile minds intent on the screens arrayed in front of them. The equipment would be different—the monitors were now all high-resolution touch screens, the computers faster and more compact, and the channels to the world all that much broader—but the essence was unchanged. The bright young recruits were still the soul of the unit, chosen for their technical skills, their creative minds, and their problem-solving prowess.

As they approached the cluster of buildings, a group of soldiers lounged in the central plaza. It was their faces, their impossibly young faces, that struck him. "Was I ever that young?" he mused quietly.

"Sir?" his escort asked.

"Nothing. Just remembering when I was one of those tapping at the keyboards, keeping Israel safe from the raging nations."

"Yes, well, here we are. I'll show you where."

≈ ≈ ≈

The briefing room was a temporary setup in a secured wing of a commercial building marked only by a sign with initials in Hebrew above and Latin letters below that didn't match. The room was equipped with a projector, a portable whiteboard, and two rows of folding chairs. At the front, a man in a blazer and civilian khakis stood with his back turned, twirling a blue dry-erase marker in his hand as he pondered an elaborate multi-color network of lines and shapes on the board. To the side, a recruit with a tablet computer was busy updating a digitized copy of the whiteboard diagram.

Bini saluted the officer who rose and turned from the front row. "General, Sir, Warrant Officer Adam Binyamin Markham reporting."

The general returned the salute without his hand quite reaching his forehead. "We don't stand on protocol around here, Markham," he said, switching to English, "except with the recruits when they first show up. Besides, we're not on the base." He held out his hand. "I'm Daniel Shapiro—General Shapiro when we are with distinguished visitors or newbies, Dan the rest of the time. I'm heading this op."

"Which is?"

"In due time. Say hello to our team." He gestured toward the group lined up in the folding chairs. Bini recognized none of them as they turned toward him, but their faces—earnest, young, intelligent—were familiar. They might as well have been his students at the Technion. Two among them stood out: a short recruit at the end of the second row, whose freckled face was topped by military-cut hair the color of candle flames, and the tall woman in the next chair who towered over him and whose confident smile in a polished ebony face drew Bini in like a lasso. She looked at him as if she recognized him and nodded almost imperceptibly.

"Introductions at mess," the General continued. "For now, let's let the professor continue with his lecture." He pointed toward the man at the whiteboard, who turned slowly and smiled. "Richard, this is Binyamin Markham, mathematician and hacker extraordinaire."

The man's smile broadened. "Yes, we've met. More than once."

Bini tried without success to hide his confusion. "I'll have to take your word for it, professor, but . . . Was it at the Technion?"

The man laughed as he walked slowly toward Bini, each step measured. "You probably don't recognize me with the beard and without my wheelchair. I spent so much of my life in one sort of wheelchair or another that it was almost a part of me, especially in the eyes of other people."

Open-mouthed, Bini shook his head. "No, that can't be. I thought you lost your legs in . . ."

"Well, it can be. There's only one Richard Talpa. I had the resources and the connections, so I worked with the neuro-prosthetics team at Worcester Polytechnic's Bioengineering Institute to take their work to the limit—neuro-myoelectric control with adaptive balance-assist technology, fully functional powered knees, articulated ankle joint, energy storing artificial tendons, a power pack with all new battery chemistry, regenerative supersonic motors that feed power back into the batteries with every move I make with my own muscles—the works. So, now I have legs," Talpa concluded with a double thumbs up.

"Forgive me for the geek dump, but this is so amazing to me. Best of all, dear old DoD paid most of the tab under their defense research programs for combat-injured vets. Which was me, although Nam was a very long time ago."

"How do you . . . ?"

"You mean how does it work? Advanced sensors, a lot of computer power in a very compact package, and six freakin' months of practice and rehab while the controller software and I learned to talk with each other. But, I can sit, stand, and walk, although that's still a work in progress and stairs are a bitch, especially going down. It's not like my old iBot wheelchair that always kept its balance on its own. Balancing on two legs again took practice and still takes some concentration." He closed the distance to Bini and shook hands. "Richard Talpa, at your service."

Bini took a step back to look the man up and down. "I can't believe it. You gotta be the Energizer Bunny of cyber intelligence. And now you're a professor in Israel."

"Well, I am in Israel, but I'm no professor. That's just what they call me around here, maybe because I'm always lecturing." He did a slightly jerky pirouette. "Not bad for a legless seventy-something Viet Nam vet, eh?"

"Definitely not bad. Although, last time I saw you, you were still a bit of a bad boy in the intelligence community."

"I've never been a bad boy, just a survivor. Survivors have certain things in common, foremost being luck, followed closely by a finely tuned sense of self-interest. The truth is that, ever since my somewhat ignominious exit from Scenaria, I have been paying penance, working on the side of the angels."

"As you define them."

"Fair enough. But I try. And I'm here. That has to atone for something, fighting for the Holy Land."

"Spoken like a true outsider. We don't usually call it that, except in brochures for tourists."

"Outsider I am. Always. Hey, would you believe that I actually considered applying for the IDF Lone Soldier program?"

"No, I don't think I'd believe that."

"Well, they wouldn't take me anyway. Too old. So I'm here as a civilian consultant. No charge. Building up bonus points with the angels, which is a good idea at my age." He walked back to the whiteboard.

"I still can't believe it. I mean, you were amazing with that high-tech wheelchair that could rise up on two wheels, but this is off the charts."

"Yeah, I am the bionic man incarnate. Wanna see?" He pulled up his pant leg to reveal the elaborate titanium and carbon fiber mechanism. He lifted his foot off the ground. "I can even point my toes. And stand on one foot." The very faint whine of actuators was just at the edge of hearing. "Not for long, though. I can already feel the battery pack in the small of my back getting warm." He lowered his foot. "Again, forgive me. I'm like a kid with his first pogo stick; I can't stop showing off."

"Understandable. But now, tell me, why am I here? Why are you here?"

"You're here because I told them to call you up."

"Gee, thanks."

"You're welcome. I'm assembling my dream team, trying to pull together the best I've worked with, although I can't seem to locate that guy who led that NTSB flight-tracking group. Anyway, we're here"—he pointed toward the ground—"because they wouldn't let me into the real heart of Unit 8200 and, well, there's you and . . ." He cleared his throat. "Well, we are all here because of this." He faced the whiteboard and spread his hands.

"Which is?"

"A dependency diagram. And what, do you ask, are the dependencies being modeled? They are the relationships and contingencies among diverse parties and players driven by the egos of a small group of men with too much power and too little perspective. I speak, of course, with particular reference to two presidents and an ayatollah."

"Don't forget our man," the general said. "Prime minister Natan Yehud is part of the picture, even if we are not sure exactly how, which is why there are so many question marks and tildes and plus-minus signs on that part of the board. You'd think we would know one of our own, but maybe we're too close to see clearly. At least that is what the professor here has been teaching us."

Bini was shaking his head in slow motion. "Why are you . . . why are we doing this? I assume it's more than just some academic exercise. Frankly, I've never been terribly impressed by these sorts of socio-tech models—and I use the term in its loosest sense. They often seem like little more than attempts to reduce something of insurmountable complexity and near to-tal uncertainty to some"—he waved at the whiteboard—"some polychromatic illusion of understanding."

Talpa laughed. "Wow, so many syllables. I see you haven't lost your gift for words, Bini. You always had a special knack for delivering sarcasm wrapped in excess verbiage."

"I keep in practice on the faculty at the Technion. And you're the one they call Professor. But please, what in hell are we doing this for?"

The general put his hand on Bini's back. "We are trying to map out how close we are to *Megiddo*."

"There you go again, Dan,"—the voice came from the back of the room—"always such a Hebrew purist. He meant to say Armageddon, as the rest of the world calls it. Or Doomsday. He's an immigrant; only made *aliyah* ten years ago. Forgive him."

Bini turned around, confused again. It was another general. Bini started to salute, then hesitated, then completed the salute. "Sir!"

"At ease. I'm Yishai Barg. We never met, but it was on my orders that you and your family were exfiltrated from Miami when you were just a teenager. I'd be heading this op, too, except it really needs younger heads at the keyboard."

"Then why do we have that decrepit old cripple standing at the whiteboard?"

"Ata boy, Bini." Talpa slapped his titanium knee. "Now you're delivering the digs without the verbal baggage. 'Decrepit old cripple.' Nice resonance to the consonants."

Bini ignored him. "Wait a minute, General Barg, uh, Yishai. You wouldn't be related to Dafna Barg with Mossad, would you?"

"She's my niece."

"She took over Technical Services when my aunt, Anat Dorfman, retired. Dafna must be something, because she was my aunt's handpicked successor."

"I know Anat well and worked with her on more than one occasion."

Talpa tapped the back of his marker on the whiteboard. "Schmooze on your own time, people. You only have me for another week, so let's get this sketched out so these kids can program the model under Bini's supervision. He's a whiz with these network models, graph theory, cut sets. Right, Bini? Then I have to get back to my fortified bunker."

"And where would that be?" Bini said.

"Not Saying Anything." NSA. It was a variant on an old joke in the intelligence community, and the assembled group joined in a chorus of quiet groans and coughs.

≈ ≈ ≈

Talpa had finally retreated to his temporary quarters in the new hotel at the edge of the complex when his phone burped in his pocket. He looked at the caller ID and smiled. "Hello, Dima. I see you got the satellite phone I sent."

"It's Arkady here, not Dima."

"Just as good. I assume your big brother must be with you."

"Who is this? Barg?"

"Good guess, but no, it's Richard Talpa. I want you to set up the sat phone as a hotspot and check out this website—gotta pen?" He rattled off a string of alphabet soup in the .INFO top level internet domain, which Arkady scribbled on the outside of the UPS package and read back for confirmation. "That's right. Check it out and you'll understand. I gotta go."

"Wait. How did you know where . . . ?"

"You forget, I have my sources. As soon as the Russians

knew, we knew."

"So then you must know that somebody tried to take out Dima, and your Russians were on his tail here in the States."

"We knew. Plus, your brother is far more predictable than he thinks. We only had to narrow the options some. My whiz kids calculated what destination would bring the odds of missing your brother close to zero—at least close enough for government work. And speaking of which, you all have your work cut out for you, so you better get busy. Cheers." Talpa hung up. He was thinking that, late as it was, his workday was only just beginning.

Chapter 12

ARKADY OPENED HIS LAPTOP on the kitchen table, configured the satellite phone to serve as a hotspot, and launched a web browser. The URL copied from the back of the package led to a site that prompted him to download new software: a custom-encrypted browser. "No way, Talpa. I trust you but not that far." He exited Firefox and launched a sandboxed browser that would keep anything they acquired from the internet in an isolated virtual machine, a software room walled off from the rest of the computer and prevented from making any changes to the computer or operating system itself. He went again to the designated website and dutifully downloaded the new custom browser. When he launched it, he watched the swirling wait-state cursor for a long time before finally getting a browser home page and a message. "PIPE-IT has detected it is being run inside a virtual machine. Please note this is not recommended and will seriously degrade performance."

"No shit, but I guess that's the price we pay for internet hygiene. Now what?"

Barbara was looking over his shoulder. "Well, try typing in the same address again. There, see, a new page. This browser is using a different protocol, something nonstandard." The page was black except for a menu across the top: HOME | FILES | MESSAGES | LOGIN

"Let's try them all." HOME just refreshed the black page; FILES gave them an ACCESS DENIED message; MESSAGES took them to an empty inbox; and LOGIN gave them a completely blank screen without even a flashing cursor in the upper left corner. "Now what? We have no idea how to log in."

"Talpa would assume we knew, or maybe Dima would know."

Dima came over to the table. "Dima would know what?" he said.

"How to log in from this screen."

Dima took a step back. "I hope to hell not." He closed his eyes for several seconds..

"What's wrong?"

"HaVered used a blank screen like that for its login. No prompt, not even a hint that anything is listening. Shit. Are they back? Is Talpa now tied up with them? Was he all along?"

"Too many questions at once," Barbara said. "There's probably only one way to find out anyway."

"Even if you're right, what is the price of finding out? If it is HaVered, the moment I log in, I'm dead. I left. I betrayed them."

"You don't have to do this," she said. "You certainly owe nothing to Talpa, and you already know how far I trust him, which is only about as far as I can reach, and Israel is way the hell out of reach for me."

Dima sat down next to Arkady and pulled the laptop toward himself. "This is a real puzzle. If it is actually looking for my login credentials for HaVered, how could Talpa have acquired that?"

"From Operation Hedgerow," Arkady said, "the attempt to take down HaVered which he took part in. We should have assumed that whatever we did would just be sucked up, sorted, and stored by him and the NSA."

Barbara paced behind the two men. "I've always wondered about his role with the NSA. Is he really an insider or does he just have connections? You know, my contacts there always denied even knowing who he is. That's not surprising in itself, but along with everything else about him we know—and don't know—it's part of a pattern. It was always hard to be sure which side Talpa was on."

"No it wasn't," Arkady said. "It was always crystal clear. From the outset, he was on the side of Richard Talpa and no one else. If he is a Fort Meade insider, I would assume they would be smart enough to keep him on a short leash."

"Well it certainly looks like he is not at Fort Meade at the moment," Dima said, "considering the package was posted in Israel. I wonder if he's living up to his Italian name. And if he's a mole, whose mole is he?"

"As you said: Richard Talpa's," Barbara said. "Wherever he is, he's looking out for number one, which made me wonder why he ever helped Arkady and why his crew attacked HaVered?"

Dima shook his head. "Isn't it obvious? Think about it, Barbara. What was HaVered's stock in trade? Talpa must have been on someone's target list. And he figured that the only way he could survive over the long haul was to eliminate the threat."

"Speculation."

"Perhaps, but it makes sense. The question is: what does he want with me now? And what is his connection with the attempts on my life?"

"There's the login screen, brother," Arkady said. "As Barbara said, only one way to find out."

"Perhaps not. I think I know another way." As Dima typed a

long string, the screen remained blank. He tapped the tab key, then typed an even longer string followed by the enter key. Nothing changed. The screen was still blank.

"It didn't work," Arkady said. "Are you sure you got it right?"

Dima looked at his brother and smiled. "Oh, I got it right; it worked. And now I'm pretty sure this is not HaVered reanimated." He quickly typed another pair of strings and let his finger hover over the enter key as Arkady and Barbara leaned forward in anticipation. This time, when he tapped the key, the screen refreshed with a desert panorama in the banner at the top above the original menu options and a bold message below: "Welcome Dmitry Pohl. Click here for further instructions."

Barbara looked confused. "What did you do? Did you have to type your login twice?"

"No. The first login was legitimate . . . but only for Ha-Vered, and only their system would know it. It was generic, a duress login. You know, a code to be used by any of us if we were being coerced to login or forced to reveal our credentials. This system didn't recognize that, so it wasn't HaVered reincarnated. The second time I logged in using my actual credentials, the ones associated with me, meaning the ones Talpa or the NSA would know if they had looked over my shoulder or tracked me with a keystroke logger or something similar. We don't know for sure this is Talpa, but it's not likely to be Ha-Vered."

"Well, let's find out. We're still safe inside the sandbox. Let's click for our 'further instructions', okay?" Barbara pulled over another chair and crowded in next to Arkady.

Dima moved the mouse pointer over the link but didn't click on it.

"What's wrong?"

"I thought I was through with this crap. I thought I was running a winery."

Arkady put his hand on his older brother's shoulder. "We're never through with being who we are, who we were. It's always there, somewhere."

Dmitry Pohl nodded, took a breath, and clicked for further instructions.

Chapter 13

THE LIGHTS IN DC had been on for a few hours, and now they were off again. Either Potomac Electric was having trouble with restoring power or it was a fresh attack. The encrypted email with its terse message from Richard Talpa had thrown DB off balance, and the call from Arkady Pohl had finished the job. He had been on edge now for days. After the automated text message received from the entry lock at the retreat, he knew that Arkady and the others had arrived at Spring Falls— or at least someone had.

DB was making a desultory review of a cybersecurity industry news feed on his tablet when his assistant, Ross Matranga, entered the inner office. Ross was the rare find in an era of ambition squared: trained as a butler in Switzerland, his forte was organization and coordination, and his goal in life was to use his ability to solve problems to serve others. DB did not know his sexual preferences, only that the man's understated good looks and firm but gentle manner made him the object of fantasies from both sides of the gender aisle— and in between. "There's someone at Reception to see you who is not on your calendar," Ross said in his baritone voice. "He refuses to say his reasons nor to speak with anyone else."

"Who did he say he was?"

"Pohl. That's all he would say. No card, no full name. 'Just tell him it's Pohl.' Word for word."

"Show him in."

"He has a couple of other people with him. Should I alert security?"

"No, I don't think so. Have them given visitor badges and escorted in."

DB paged out of the feed and brought up a password-protected file, which he started to skim. He looked up in time to see them enter. "Arkady. A personal visit. I thought you all were getting some fresh mountain air."

Arkady, trailed by Barbara and Dima, crossed the room with his hand extended. "We were. But then we got our orders. Can we . . . ?" He glanced toward Ross.

"Right. Ah, Ross, please get us all some coffee, will you? And have the librarian find me the hardcopy original of the file I just opened on my desktop."

"Right away." Ross nodded to the visitors and left the office, closing the door behind him.

"Well, Arkady. And Barbara. And I presume this is the long elusive Dmitry Pohl." DB arched his eyebrows.

Dima did not smile but nodded without saying anything. DB stood and stepped from behind the table-size desk to shake hands all around. "Please, have a seat. Can anyone bring me up-to-date? What's this visit about?"

"We should know ourselves in a few minutes," Arkady said. "We believe your mailroom is holding a package addressed to A. Pohl, Director of External Services. Could you check?"

There was a rap on the door and Ross entered carrying a coffee service on a tray, which he placed on the round conference table opposite DB's desk.

"Ross, can you check with the mailroom for a package addressed to A. Pohl? What was that, Director of External Ser-

vices, right? Please check in person, not by phone." DB rounded the table and started setting out the coffee cups with their
blue-and-green company logos. "Oh, and on your way, drop
this off for Kerchoff." He handed Ross a blank business envelope.

DB insisted everyone join him around the conference table
where he played host and fixed coffee for all. "And there it is for
you, Dmitry: black and strong. Not the Israeli coffee I imagine
you prefer, but a pretty good Swiss pretender. I hope your vacation, short as it was, was pleasantly uneventful."

"I wouldn't say that, but, well, we'll see." His face was unreadable.

"And Arkady, when was the last time we were in the same
room? I think we were working on problems in—what shall we
say, 'graph theory'?—trying to find a way to slice up a rose gar-
den gone feral."

"Yes. And, of course, Dima already knows that chapter of
HaVered. Rather intimately, I would say. And Barbara can be
trusted."

"Yes, of course. And here's Ross again. Success?"

"Yes." He held out a US Postal Service flat-rate mailer plas-
tered with stamps. "This arrived this morning, posted overnight from DC, probably from a mailbox, judging from the
stamps. The mailroom wasn't sure what to do with it and were
debating calling Kerchoff."

Dima reached across the table. "I'll take that."

Ross hesitated a moment and looked to DB, who shrugged
and nodded toward Dima, who took the packet and set it on
the table in front of himself. Both Arkady and Barbara edged
their chairs around a little closer. "Oh," Ross said, "Suze Kerchoff is here to see you, Dr. Botteneau."

"Tell her I'm with some people and will be with her in"—he

glanced at his watch—"in short order." It was a private pass-phrase that DB knew Suze would understand. She was being asked to stand by on alert.

"I'll do that," Ross said, as he exited.

"So, it's Doctor Botteneau now?" Arkady said.

"Yeah, I went back to school part-time to finally get some real credentials. Georgetown. Computer science, of course. Graduated in January." DB looked expectantly at his three visitors. "Well? Or do you want to be left alone?"

Dima turned the mailer over. "No, we're good. Do you have a pocket knife, Arkady?"

"Of course. Always. Since we were scouts together in Kyiv." He handed Dima a black Victorinox.

Dima opened the small blade and carefully worked the tip into the bottom corner of the mailer as DB watched with curiosity.

Arkady laughed. "I see that you remember, Dima."

"Yes, little brother. You never kept your knife sharpened, and you never used the small blade." He slit the pasteboard packet for the full length and carefully slid the contents out onto the table: two smaller envelopes, one addressed to D. Pohl and one to A. Pohl, plus a new 128 gigabyte SD card still in its blister pack. He tipped the envelope up and three Canadian passports fell out. He opened one to the picture page and handed it to Barbara. "Not a very flattering photo." He opened the next, closed it, and passed it to Arkady. "Same for you. Also not flattering." The third passport he pocketed without looking at it. He flipped the pocket knife in his hand and gave it and the marked envelope to Arkady. "Your turn first, little brother."

Arkady repeated the ritual with the knife blade, not opening the envelope flap but carefully slitting the bottom open.

"Well, I must say, the drama has my attention," DB said.

"What's with opening from the bottom?"

"Instructions, just following instructions." Arkady tipped up the envelope and a transparent vacuum-sealed sous vide cooking pouch slid out with a folded gray paper note inside. Rather than pull the red "open-here" tape across the top, Arkady slit the bottom as before. The note that slid out was thick, like blotter paper. He unfolded it as Barbara and Dima leaned in to read the message. Uneven letters, in all caps from an old manual typewriter with a faded blue cloth ribbon, marched across the page.

```
READ QUICKLY AND CAREFULLY.
RETRIEVE FILES AND HAND DELIVER TO ME.
DIMA KNOWS FROM WHOM.
ARKADY KNOWS FROM WHERE.
NO TRACKING NUMBERS!!!
NO ELECTRONICS!!!
PICS FOR DB. JUST PICS.
RT
```

As Arkady handed the note to Dima, who was on the other side of Barbara, it started to feel warm, and the corner crumbled in his fingers. It quickly fell apart into a small pile of fine speckled powder on the table top.

"Wow," DB said, "shades of Mission Impossible. I didn't know any of that kind of stuff was real."

"Real enough," Dima said, "just very rarely used. The paper is coated to react with the air and fall apart. That's why the vacuum seal."

"Why the melodrama and special effects?"

"Probably because electronic communications can never be trusted to be fully secure, especially if certain parties are involved. And digital trails are forever."

96

DB scanned the grim faces of his visitors. "Well, people, what did it say?"

"I think that's on a need to know basis. But the SD card is for you. Pictures, I think. Maybe that will explain." Arkady handed the SD card in its blister pack to DB, who turned it over and started to open it from the cardboard back. "Wait. I think we should stick to procedure here." Arkady took the pack back and carefully opened the bottom with his knife. He slid out the SD card and passed it to DB. "If there are already pictures on it, they're for you. Maybe they'll answer your questions."

DB hesitated, then retrieved a tablet computer from his desk. "We're not supposed to do this, but I'm going to disconnect from our Wi-Fi and take a peek." He tapped and finger-swiped around for a bit, then slipped the card into the SD slot. After a short delay a sour chord sounded. "It's contaminated. Our anti-virus software says it has malware on it. I'm going to have to turn it over to my team down in the Vault."

Arkady shrugged. "Do as you wish. We have our marching orders."

"I don't," Dima said, as he reached for the pocket knife and slit open the bottom of his envelope. Through the plastic of the vacuum-sealed packet inside could be seen the typed words: EYES ONLY. "I guess this is just for me." He slit open the plastic, unfolded the note, and read it. His face stiffened. He placed the note face down on the table to wait until the small gray tent powdered and collapsed.

Arkady looked at him. "Well? Also from Talpa?"

"Not exactly."

"Who?"

"Can't say. We all have our orders now." He stood. "Thank you, Dr. Botteneau. We need to be going."

≈ ≈ ≈

In the parking lot, Barbara took charge. "All right, guys, let's figure this out. We have to pick up some files and deliver them to Talpa. Supposedly Dima knows who has the package but not where."

"So, big brother, who might it be?"

"Who do I know that you would know where they are but I don't? What first comes to mind is that couple, the one I was . . . uh, assigned, in Upstate New York. They were investigating that cyber-attack on the natural gas pipeline. I don't know where they ended up, but I am now assuming you do. He was Jewish, right?"

"Yeah, and I do know where they ended up. We're going to have to book some airline tickets. It's way too long to drive."

"No tracking numbers, no electronics, remember?"

"Then we better go right back in and entreat the recently hooded Dr. Botteneau for a ride on his corporate jet."

≈ ≈ ≈

DB was not entirely surprised to see them return. He closed the fat file folder he was paging through on the conference table and stood. "Change of plans? Change of mind?"

"We need to do some traveling, international, with—what shall we say?—minimum attention. We were wondering if you might have a corporate jet we could commandeer."

"Why am I not surprised. Okay, for old time sake, I could make a plane and crew available, but where to?"

"Do you have a plane that can, say, make it non-stop to Europe? The Middle East?"

"Company owns a Gulfstream 650ER. I don't know the exact range, but I'm back and forth to Frankfurt all the time. And Suze and I have taken it to Hawaii from here. So, where are you headed?"

Arkady pondered for a moment. "Israel. You might as well know. We're running an errand for your old boss. Can you just put your crew at our disposal? We'll sort out the details with them."

DB's eyes narrowed, and it took several seconds to respond. "Okay. I assume this is important enough, but directly or indirectly, our old, er, 'friend' is asking a lot of us. Mission Impossible dissolving messages or not, we are not the IMF."

Dima laughed. "Maybe not. Maybe better."

≈ ≈ ≈

Ross showed them out for the second time, then returned. "Suze Kerchoff is still standing by."

"Yeah, thanks. Send her in. And return this to the librarian." He handed the file folder to Ross.

Suze greeted him with raised eyebrows that said it all. DB shook his head and said, "I really don't know. Something pretty big is going on, and I'm guessing it's all connected with the blackouts and the escalating tensions with the Russians."

"Why are we involved?"

"Why not? Industrial security is our second biggest revenue stream, and we're racing to deconstruct the Russian cyberweapon before anyone else does. I don't know whether Kaspersky has any insider advantage, what with being a Russian company, but you can count on all our competitors to be going flat out for the checkered flag."

"Not what I was asking. The Pohl brothers don't waltz in here to chat about anti-malware software. Dmitry and his ilk are a breed apart. They play for keeps."

"It's all for keeps, dear. And I have a past, too. I told you that I once had to kill somebody. I've never been able to get completely away from it. I have this weird feeling sometimes, that anyone who was ever connected with Richard Talpa is caught in an enterprise without an exit."

"That's depressing. Of course, when I got back from my last tour of duty in Afghanistan, I thought I was done with people shooting at me. But, you know, they just keep coming. As you said, no exit. Now I'm wondering how we and the Russians get off the dangerous merry-go-round we're on. Did you hear the latest? An explosion at a power plant outside Moscow, 'owing to a computer problem' it is said. Unlike terrorist attacks in the past, nobody is claiming credit for these cyber-strikes, but there are plenty of accusations being lobbed back and forth."

The knock on the door was Ross's signature tap. "It's Baumgarten. He has something to share from the Vault."

"Already?"

"Ask him."

Rufus Baumgarten had never outgrown tight jeans and band merch featuring little known groups and electronic music producers, but since being promoted to head the Vault, he grudgingly wore a sport coat over his tee shirts. Today it was a brown tweed over a black tee with the logo of Katahdin, a rising star on the EDM beats scene. He handed DB an SD card. "This copy is clean. Pictures of you two vacationing in Honolulu."

"What? How did he . . . how did anyone get pictures of us?"

"I don't know, but there they are. We isolated the worm and payload from the original card. It was easy, there was no attempt to hide or disguise anything. The code is straightforward and grabs some unique handles in the core of our own software. Obscure stuff that I wouldn't expect any outsider to even know about."

"What does it do? Do we know yet?"

"Yeah, as I said, it's straightforward. It turns our anti-malware packages into a covert messaging network with end-to-end encryption. It's pretty clever, hitching a ride on our software update push on the outbound and customer-side report-back on the inbound, with customer installation number as the forwarding address. I think the traffic would be all but invisible to even the most advanced nation-state monitoring. I mean, it's just anti-virus software and malware signature updates and infection reports going back and forth, not messages, with our own server farms functioning as the post office. Until somebody blew the whistle, no one would even think to look for it." He shrugged. "What do you want to do with it."

"Archive it for now, security level Executive One. Program a bot scan to make sure it's not already out there in the wild, and keep me informed. And keep this all on a need-to-know basis. Oh, yes, I want the original SD card back. I'm retaining physical custody myself. And don't put that in the log. Okay?"

Baumgarten scowled. "I don't know."

"I do. So just do it."

Baumgarten looked toward Suze. She nodded. "It's okay, Bumpus. You're covered. Just bring us the card." After he left, Suze walked over beside DB. "What do you have in mind?"

"I'm thinking this messaging malware might sometime prove useful under present circumstances, and I'm thinking that's exactly what Richard Talpa had in mind."

≈ ≈ ≈

The motel in a strip mall was a cheapy whose owner was more than happy to rent for cash with no entry in the guest register. Their car was legally parked on a side street, out of view of the office, so not even the license plate would be noted.

As they entered the darkened room that smelled liked the cleaning staff had made a valiant effort to smother the evidence of previous occupants, Dima stood in the doorway for a minute. "I hope you know what you're doing, wolf cub."

"I hope so, too. Talpa was rather cryptic with his directions."

Not with me, Dima was thinking. He was rather plain, but that does not necessarily mean he will get what he wants or when he wants it.

Chapter 14

THE GULFSTREAM, its taupe and cream interior outfitted for luxurious business efficiency, with wide padded leather seats, flexible work surfaces, and a compact wet bar and galley, was nearly empty. Its three passengers on the flight were matched by two pilots and a flight attendant. As the plane droned on at cruising altitude, Arkady reluctantly stopped typing on his laptop and reached to pull a power brick from his backpack. He plugged it into the outlet beneath his seat and connected it to his laptop. Barbara smiled at him from across the drop-down table between them. "You've been busy," she said, talking above the dulled rush of the rear-mounted twin engines. "You've been tooling away ever since takeoff. Whatcha working on?"

"Just stuff. I'm rusty. And this was never my strong suit. I'm going from memory and instinct, plus an article I read last year and some downloads I grabbed before we left. Fortunately, Sam Parsons was a good tutor." Dima, pretending to be asleep across the aisle, didn't stir.

Guessing it was something to do with the escalating cyber-attacks but knowing, after the mild brushoff, it was pointless to press for more detail, Barbara returned to her book. She stole occasional glances at Arkady, who kept typing away and scowling, with occasional glances up at the flight progress map displayed on the bulkhead. Suddenly, oxygen masks dropped down in front of them, and the plane started into a steep descent.

It was several seconds before the pilot came on the intercom. "This is Captain Emerson. We've apparently experienced a loss of cabin pressure. Please use your oxygen masks as instructed before takeoff. Your flight attendant will assist if you need help. We are descending to a lower altitude and figuring out what happened. Our aircraft is flying fine, however, and there is no cause for alarm."

"No cause for alarm." Barbara's voice was muffled by the bright yellow-orange mask that now covered her mouth and nose. "Easy for him to say that." Arkady nodded. He had elbowed Dima awake, and both were still adjusting their masks.

"This is Captain Emerson again. We have some indicator problems here in the cockpit—nothing serious—but just to be sure to get everything right, we have called in a pan-pan and requested an emergency landing at Stanfield International Airport in Halifax. Air traffic control has vectored us directly in, and we will be landing in just a few short minutes. Please stow any items you have taken out during the flight and tighten your seatbelts."

Barbara reached across the table and took Arkady's hand. "My first time on a private jet and this happens."

"Don't worry. The guys up there have it under control, I'm sure. Like they said, it's just instrument failure, lights not blinking right or something."

"So, what the hell is a pan-pan?"

Dima leaned across the aisle. "An emergency distress call but short of a mayday. Not an immediate danger to life or the aircraft."

"And you know this how?"

"I was a pilot, too."

"Is there anything you haven't done? What about the cabin pressure thing?" she asked.

"Not a biggy," Arkady answered. "That is probably just an instrumentation glitch, too."

She let go of his hand and pulled back. "Man, sometimes you infuriate me. Like, you just don't take these sorts of things seriously."

"Sorry. Of course, I take this all seriously. I'm just not worried, since . . . well, since there's nothing we can do. Those two up front know what they're doing, and right now they're landing us in Halifax. Ever been to Halifax?"

"No. And isn't that funny that you were asking me just yesterday about *sayanim* in Nova Scotia. There was one in Halifax I told you about."

"Life's full of coincidences like that."

Above her mask, Barbara's eyes narrowed.

Chapter 15

THE GENERAL AVIATION TERMINAL was all but deserted. After a perfunctory check by a Canadian Customs and Border Protection agent, the threesome caught a cab. Arkady gave the driver an address in a suburb, one that Barbara thought she recognized, but she said nothing. Dima maintained his stoic silence throughout the ride until after they had paid the driver and the taxi had pulled away. He grabbed Arkady by the bicep and spun him around. "Are you going to tell us what is happening? Because that was no emergency landing, and we are not standing freezing on this particular corner by pure chance. I thought our targets had made *aliyah* to Israel and that's why we filed a flight plan for Tel Aviv."

"You thought that because I wanted you—and everyone else—to think that. But let's walk while we're talking. It's rather chilly out here tonight." He set off down the street at a brisk pace. "Barbara almost figured it out from my questioning her about *sayanim* in Nova Scotia. The couple in question did make *aliyah*, all right, but they 'came up' to Canada, not Israel. They now live near Wolfville on the north coast. We're going to borrow a car from a *sayan* here and drive up to pay a visit. Then we'll drive back and resume our flight to Israel, with no tracks pointing to Wolfville."

"What about the plane?"

"What about it? It'll check out and be cleared by the time we get back tomorrow."

"How do you know? Oh, right, let me guess, because the plane is fine." He gave out a quick snort of a laugh. "You hacked it, didn't you."

"Bingo! I just made it look like things were going haywire. Look, white-hat hackers have demonstrated that you can hack into commercial aircraft and take control or disrupt the avionics. Sam Parsons and the bunch at the NTSB knew all about that. I figured a private jet would be even easier. The last thing for designers and engineers to expect would be some rich corporate dude hacking his own jet. Right? The hardest part for me was not the code but the timing. I had to be sure we'd divert to Halifax and not Bangor. I was watching the flight progress display, but it was still some guesswork. Anyway, here we are, this is the real address, which, of course, I would not give to the cabbie."

The place was a gabled frame house that looked like it could have been imported from New England in the 1940s. Arkady led the way up the brick path and reached for the door knocker. After a third try, a man in his fifties with a neatly trimmed gray moustache answered the door. "Yes, can I be of help to you?"

"*Ken, shalom,*" Arkady answered in Hebrew. "Yes, peace. Avraham and Sarah send their greetings."

The man leaned out and looked up and down the street. "Come in, come in. Quickly." He waved them in and closed the door behind them. "You are from the Institute?"

Barbara stepped forward. "No, not Mossad. I'm Barbara Delacroix, and my husband Abe Feingold would send his greetings, but his memory is a blessing."

"Oh, I am sorry about Abe. He was a good man, I hear. But

I'm afraid I can't help you."

"We only need to borrow a car, just overnight, then we'll be gone and there will be no trouble."

"Then I definitely can't be of assistance. My son was in line ahead of you. He has my car."

"Is there any chance you can, well, borrow it back?"

"Next week, yes, for sure. But if you need a car now, there is a Hertz over at the airport. It's only a short ride by taxi."

"Yes, we know, but you can imagine we have our reasons for not wanting to use a rental car."

"I can. And that's why you'll be wanting to look elsewhere. I'm not on the list anymore, not since my wife died, you understand, eh? We were working for them at the time. She shouldn't have even been along. I tried to tell them I was through, but I never got a response."

Dima stepped forward and glared at the man. "It's a lifetime commitment, being a *sayan*. You don't get to take it back. You don't get uncircumcised."

"I don't know who any of you are, but I'll tell you, I haven't been inside a synagogue for years, and I haven't been to Israel for decades. It's over for me."

"It's not over for Israel,"—Dima grabbed the man by his shirt—"and it's not over for me." The man cringed. "Now, get on the phone, and tell your son you need the car back, just overnight, but you need it." The man's eyes darted from face-to-face of his visitors, but he saw no allies among them. Barbara turned away.

"I'll call him. But you tell them in Israel that I am done with them. Tell them that, will you?"

"I'll tell them, but I don't think they accept resignations. Now, get your son here with the car. And if you give him even a hint about us or what is happening, we will kill him in front of you and then kill you. Do I make myself clear?"

"As clear as spring water. I'll try, but my son can be stubborn, if you know what I mean."

≈ ≈ ≈

It took some time for the *sayan* to persuade his son to leave the car overnight. After a tense half hour, during which the two men chatted in the living room in the serious but amicable style of Canadian disagreement while their guests anxiously listened in from the kitchen, the son left on foot. It was nearly midnight when Barbara finally backed the Ford Focus out of the driveway and headed toward the 101 highway north. "Would you have really killed them?" she said to Dima.

"Of course. That's what I do, eliminate obstacles. It would have been perhaps a bit messy—I have only the nylon garrote threaded in my belt, that and Arkady's never-sharpened pocket knife—but I've managed before with even less. And it certainly would have been inconvenient for our mission. But, yes, I would have done it and then hoped we could return the car and be airborne before the bodies were discovered."

Arkady snorted. "And you said you were through with all that."

"I did, but the world said I was not. My exit plans failed, so I am still a *kidon* for Israel, still a soldier-assassin. It is looking as if that will be my fate for as long as I breathe." He looked at his watch. "You do know, it will be the middle of the night when we get to Wolfville. Perhaps we should have waited until morning."

"By morning, I hope we are back at the airport, waiting for the aircraft mechanics to finish their unnecessary checklists. Let's hit the road."

≈ ≈ ≈

At the turnoff, just past a small wind turbine standing like an isolated sentinel, a carved wooden sign, visible in the light of the gibbous moon, announced "Gaudet Vineyards, Kat Gaudet and Len Bergen, Proprietors."

"I guess we can tell who wears the pants in that pair," Dima said. Barbara grunted her disapproval.

The lights were still on when they arrived at the house at the end of the access road. Arkady told the other two to wait in the car while he approached the front porch of the black-trimmed white farmhouse. Two motorcycles, covered in custom rain tarps, stood to the side. He could hear a baby crying inside, and, through the window, he caught a glimpse of a dark-haired woman pacing with an infant in her arms. He hesitated, then pulled the chain on the mechanical door chime. The porchlight went on and the front door was opened a cautious four inches. "Yes?" the woman said.

"You may not remember me, but I assume you still have the passports I gave you and Len."

"Oh, oh my God! Is it you? Ah, yes, uh, Agent Pohl, it was. Am I right? Come in, I suppose, do come in. I hope there's not, well, not some problem."

"Not a problem," he said, trying to be reassuring. "I have some friends with me. Is it all right? I know it's late, but we need to talk."

"Ah, yes, for sure. They can come in. Len's out back, working late on a compressor that keeps giving out. You get your friends and I'll get Len."

The baby she was carrying finally turned around from her shoulder, took one look at Arkady, and started crying again. "Never was a big hit with kids," he said.

"Oh, Simone is just not used to late-night visitors. I'll see if I can get her to give up for the evening and go back to sleep."

"And I'll get the others."

≈ ≈ ≈

It was several minutes of awkward standing around for Arkady, Dima, and Barbara before a bearded young man entered from the kitchen with a wary look on his face and one hand behind his back. "What's the occasion? I thought everything was settled years ago."

"And I thought Canadians were polite and welcoming," Dima said. "Is this any way to greet benefactors?"

"I don't know you. And I'm not Canadian, at least not yet. What's going on? What do you want? Look, there's two little kids sleeping in the house. At least one of them is. Maybe we should take this outside. Kat and I just don't want any trouble."

Arkady stepped forward with his hand outstretched for a shake. "Neither do we. We were just hoping you could help us with something, then we'll be on our way."

Len reluctantly shook hands. "Who are these people?"

"Sorry. This is my wife, Barbara—"

"Former agent Delacroix," she held out her hand. "We met in West Virginia some years ago. You two were rather in a hurry to head north on your motorcycles, if I recall."

"Oh, I'm sorry. I didn't recognize you."

"Well, I've put on a few pounds and taken off a badge since then."

"And this is my brother, Dmitry," Arkady said. "You never met, but he knows you—from a distance."

Dima stepped forward and shook hands with some energy. "I am so glad you seem to be thriving here."

"Well, we're above water on the mortgage, and we'll soon be releasing last fall's whites. I guess we're doing okay."

"May I ask, what you are growing? I . . . I've been in the wine business myself."

"Really? Well, our mainstay is l'acadie blanc, which is the

local superstar white varietal, but we brought in our first viognier in September. It's still in French oak, but showing promise."

"Viognier, a favorite. But, so far north?"

"The winters are getting milder and milder. We're planting for the long run."

"I was, too, but I had to leave the business. My last crush was also viognier, but slated to be unoaked, a zippy, fruit-forward summer white."

"I can appreciate that, too, but we're trying for some novelty and extra complexity with our viognier. And the l'acadie blanc. It's a trademark for us. Upfront punch, with a long, layered finish."

"Like his wife." The quiet voice came from the petite raven-haired woman who was descending the stairs. "He adds that afterthought when he's talking with the guys and thinks I'm not listening." She entered the room. "Simone is asleep, finally, but Andre is now awake and wondering what is happening down here, so let's keep our voices down and maybe retreat to the kitchen. I can offer you some of our last vintage, if you'd like to taste how we do wine here in the Annapolis Valley."

Dima, suddenly softened. "I'd like that very much." His smile broadened.

"Would you, now? Well, maybe we'll just have to open a bottle of our late-picked l'acadie blanc to celebrate visitors from the States. It's got a touch of spritz, full-bodied but well-balanced. Like me," she said. "This way, please." She led the way to the kitchen. As she passed Len, she whispered, "Give that thing to me."

≈ ≈ ≈

With Kat Gaudet clearly in charge, the wine flowed and the conversation around the painted drop-leaf table in the cramped kitchen roamed the landscape of viticulture and winemaking until she decided it was time to get to the bottom of things. "Well, not to put a damp towel on the evening, but perhaps we better talk about what really brings you here."

After a silence that stretched a few seconds too long, Arkady spoke. "It's about software, malware to be specific. I got to know you two well enough to figure you probably left the country with souvenirs. Or should I say an insurance policy. We need copies of the malicious software and the logs you recovered when you were working in Pennsylvania and West Virginia." He looked at Len. "I presume you have copies on your laptop or a USB stick somewhere."

Kat grinned. "He doesn't, but I do. What do you need them for? And what are you offering?"

Dima started to edge out of his seat, but Arkady restrained him. "We didn't come with a satchel full of Benjamins."

"But you did come some ways to track us down, now didn't you? It must be something important," she said, "something worth some, uh, compensation."

Arkady grinned broadly. "I remember now that spark of yours. Look, I'm not in a position to promise anything, but I will note that your lights are on, while our apartment in DC is still without electricity. If you follow the news, you know we're on the verge of outright war in cyberspace."

"You, maybe, but not Canada. As you said, our lights are on."

"If the whole grid goes out across the continent, do you think Canada will be spared? If the internet goes down, how will anything function up here? No, you're part of this, even if you are reluctant combatants."

Kat nonchalantly tilted her chair back. "So, you three seem to know something that's not in the news yet. If you want our help, we need to know what we're helping with."

Dima, disinhibited by the wine, slammed his hand on the table. "You have no idea who or what you're dealing with here."

Kat rocked her chair back upright and straightened her back. "No, perhaps we don't, but I would guess you can enlighten us. And I'm thinking you'd be wanting to do that."

Arkady put his hand on Dima's arm. "Trust me, she's a lot tougher than she looks, and right now she's a mama bear protecting her cubs. I wouldn't tangle with her if I were you. Besides, what chance do we have of finding the software without her?"

"None," she said. "And I don't take too well to threats. I think maybe you three should leave. Come back when you're ready to deal with an open hand."

Arkady stretched his arm on the table between Kat and Dima. "We can't come back. We have to leave tomorrow, with the files. There's no time. So let me remind you of who we are. Barbara put herself in the line of fire for you two in Pennsylvania and took a bullet for her troubles. Dima purposefully missed his shot for you. And me, I put my career on the line by getting you new passports and then letting you get away. So, I think maybe we already paid for the merchandise. What I can promise you is, after this, you'll be left alone."

"We heard that one before, yet, wonder of wonders, here you are. Look, we're just trying to grow grapes, raise kids, and make wine."

Dima bit his lip as he nodded. "I understand. More than you could know. But this is life-and-death. The putz presidents of two countries seem hell-bent to plunge the world into darkness and send us all back to scrambling just to survive. All-out cyberwarfare could end up not much better than nuclear war. And that's not off the table, either. We're trying to do something about all of this."

Kat laughed. "You are? An old dude and two former FBI agents? Right."

"We're not alone."

"Who else?"

"You know I can't say, but you can probably suss it out yourselves. You're smart."

Kat half covered her mouth. "Hint, hint, whisper, whisper. Clandestine services. Not the Russians or the Americans, obviously. Who else?"

"Work on the puzzle on your own time. Just give us the software you saved off. We'll get it to the people who can use it to try and stop this insanity."

Len, who had been silent for some time, spoke up. "Yeah, I get it. I think I know who you're working with. Israel, right? So, Kat, let's give them what they came for."

"Are you sure?"

He nodded. "Give them the whole damn laptop. It's hopelessly out of date and probably won't even boot anymore."

"The whole laptop?"

"Yeah, the laptop."

"Okay, I'll get it." She excused herself and headed upstairs. She returned a few minutes later with a bulky old Panasonic Toughbook.

"It's on there? All of it?"

"Everything that was saved off, yeah."

Arkady opened it and pressed the power button. "It's dead. You have the brick?"

"Not anymore. It fried itself not long after we arrived. Sorry."

"Okay, we'll try to get one in Halifax before we take off. We'll just have to trust you."

Len smiled. "And we'll just have to trust you. Seems like a quid-pro-quo."

"Or a détente."

"Either way, we're done here. I'll see you out."

At the door Len gave the brothers a funny look. "*Shalom, l'hitraot*," he said quietly.

Dima paused. "Peace, yes, but you won't be seeing us again. At least you should hope that."

"I'll take that as a promise." He turned his back on the three of them. As soon as they were down the driveway, he turned out the porch light. Inside, Kat was waiting, her hand resting on the side table by the door, not quite touching the pistol laying there.

"What were you thinking, Len? Do you know who these people are? Don't you remember?"

He hung his head. "Yeah. You're right. But now we have nothing, not even any bargaining chips."

"They got a laptop that won't boot anymore, with an encrypted hard drive for which they have no key. They got nothing. And now we can go back to raising beautiful grapes and beautiful kids."

"Maybe," he said. "What happens when they find out the drive's been encrypted?"

"They call up the crack troops, their code-cracking *wunderkinder*, who will do their best to save the world. We don't have the key, never did, since it was our friend Smitty's laptop that he left here when he took off to see the world. Maybe even he doesn't remember the passphrase. We're out of the loop."

"Maybe. Or maybe we're under the train wheels. In any case, I'm keeping this handy for now." He slipped the pistol into the back of his pants.

"You are such the macho American dude, Len Bergen, and

the amazing thing is, I still love you." She pulled the pistol out of his pants and stood on tiptoe to stash it on the plate rail, just out of sight and out of reach of the children.

Chapter 16

THE BLACK STONE-FACED SLAB that bridged the entryway to the campus of the *Millî İstihbarat Teşkilatı*, Turkey's central intelligence agency, was a billboard of foreboding. Black-uniformed guards in deep red berets stood, feet spread, with their Heckler & Koch MP5 semiautomatic rifles at the ready in front of the sliding steel gate across the entrance. As a tall mocha-skinned man in a business suit approached the national intelligence headquarters on foot, his pace was just fast enough for the guards to react with a subtle but noticeable increase in muscle tension.

The man held out his newly acquired ID, and the lead guard in the center, armed only with his holstered Yavuz 16, a Turkish knockoff of the popular Beretta 92 handgun, took a step forward. After a perfunctory examination and a quizzical look, the guard waved him on. In foot-high letters, the red digital clock at the top of the check-in booth displayed the time: 6:47. Even after two weeks, the visitor felt he was still fighting jet lag from a seven-hour time difference, but he was determined to be punctual. Inside, he was given a more thorough vetting, including a pat down and cross checking of both his MİT badge and his passport against a list of "special visitors."

The guard in the booth called ahead to the office listed as the authorized destination. "I have Yilmaz here to see you.

Shall I send him up? He needs an escort."

The voice on the other end was sharp enough to be audible to everyone. "I'll send someone for him."

Yilmaz was getting used to this ritual that repeated without variation on a daily basis. He did not look Turkish, and he spoke little of the language he had been struggling to learn, but his passport was real, and he was, by virtue of his Turkish mother, a citizen of Turkey. The only irregularity was that he had taken, on petition to the courts, his mother's surname, which was not only a common one in Turkey but held a meaning of special significance to him. Yilmaz meant fearless fighter. It was a reminder not of who he was nor where he came from, but of who he was determined to become.

≈ ≈ ≈

"Ah, here is our engineer," General Arslan greeted him. The General, once handsome but now with sagging jowls and a belly that strained to escape his uniform, dismissed the national police escort and accompanied Yilmaz through the outer office and into the inner suite. Gathered at a conference table were the team, a mix of baby-faced youngsters just out of university and gray-mustached oldsters with years in Turkey's clandestine services. The exception was Bedia Tekın, the only woman in the room, a middle-aged analyst who was proving to be a hidden treasure within the group. Her face, always framed by a loose gauzy head scarf, carried the serene but strong beauty of distant Persian ancestry. Even in a room full of other women, she would be a magnet for attention, not only for her looks and quiet bearing but for the words of unexpected insight that she spoke when she did speak. After the customary handshakes all around that began every meeting, Yilmaz took his seat and glanced again her way. She reminded him of his mother. As he looked her way, she lowered her eyes in a subtle acknowledgement of an unspoken connection.

"Coffee, tea?" Arslan asked.

"Coffee this morning, please. *Orta*. With sugar."

"With sugar, then." He signaled an assistant. "Our coffee takes time for one to appreciate, but eventually you will be asking for it *sade*, without. I hope you will forgive us for beginning without you, but it was just the morning briefing . . . on other matters. You understand."

Yilmaz understood. He understood that he was an outsider, an important member of the team, but still an outsider. To General Arslan, he had been one of many contacts in a loose international network of experts in cybersecurity. Now that he was here, his fresh Turkish passport meant nothing in a world that was based on connections tracing back generations and where trust was built only very slowly but could be withdrawn in an eye-blink. "That's only to be expected," Yilmaz said. "I am ready when you are, General, to continue our work on our project, our *kıvılcım*."

"Yes, our spark. Your pronunciation is good. Also your ideas. And the code samples you brought with you, as well. But please, we have been working together on this project now—for what—nearly two weeks? Turks are not big on titles. Please. I am Ismail, Ismail Arslan."

Yilmaz lowered his head in the Turkish manner of nodding yes. "Of course, Ismail. I trust it is time we start planning for the next of our 'sparks' in the night."

"Most definitely. And your thoughts?"

"Timing is everything. It is a gigantic clockwork. We must use small nudges at the right moment to keep the pendulum in motion. Too little, or too much at the wrong time, and the pendulum slows and stops its swing."

A lieutenant entered the room and handed the general a

manila envelope. Arslan dismissed the lieutenant, opened the packet, and read in silence. He tapped on the table as he finished the dispatch. "Well, it seems one of your missions has failed. The South American appears to have slipped the surly bonds of his fate to be on his way to Israel with two companions."

"What? That's impossible."

"But true, nevertheless. We have a direct report from an informant in Nova Scotia. Even now, his plane is overflying the Mediterranean and about to leave Turkish airspace."

Yilmaz stared into the distance as he thought about what might be on board the flight to Israel. "We must take them out." He turned to Arslan. "You need to scramble your fighters."

Arslan scowled in surprise. "Is this about our mission, or is this something more personal?"

"Both. Preventing them from reaching Israel is crucial to our plans."

From the middle of the table, Bedia Tekın spoke to the general in quiet but rapid Turkish. The room erupted into a heated exchange. Yilmaz could follow none of it, but finally said, "*Bekleyin!* Wait, this is not the time to debate our way to consensus. This is a time to act, while we still can."

"Very well. Let me see what I can do." The general reached for a secure telephone.

Chapter 17

DIMA, WHO COULD SLEEP anywhere but never slept on planes, was now sitting facing Arkady, staring out the window down into the lightening clouds far below. From the dimpled cloud cover, two specks emerged, quickly growing in size without changing relative position; they were on a collision course. "Arkady! Arkady, are you awake?"

Arkady shook his head. "No, not yet."

"Don't joke. I think we have company heading our way."

"Who?"

"It's still too far to tell, but from the direction, I'd say it's coming out of Turkey."

"Not to worry. Turkey is a NATO ally."

"Ally or not, they're closing on us."

Dima got up and headed forward toward the flight deck. The flight attendant in her blue and green Scenaria uniform, was reading in the rest bay. She looked up. "Do you need anything?"

"Yes, I want to talk with the captain."

"I can get him on the intercom."

"No. Look, I'm a pilot. I just want to chat."

"I don't know. Let me check first." While the attendant was picking up the intercom handset, Dima was already rapping on the door to the flight deck. It opened almost immediately.

"We're kind of busy up here," the first officer said. "Can it wait?"

"What's up?"

"The Turkish air force is claiming we are an unauthorized overflight and are violating Turkish airspace. We aren't, but they're sending up an escort and want us to follow them down to land at a military airbase. And here they are now." A Turkish-built F-16 fighter jet with extra wing tanks and a full loud-out of missiles pulled abreast on the left and waggled its wings. Over the radio, the captain repeated their duly filed flight plan. "Looks like they've checked our tail number," he said to Dima, "but they're still claiming we're violating Turkish airspace. We may have no choice but to follow them down and sort this out on the ground."

"Where's the other one?" Dima looked around. "I saw two approaching."

"Looks like he's probably hanging back aft—in a shooter position."

"Captain Emerson." Dima's voice had taken on a note of urgent command. "I don't think they really want us to land."

"Are you serious?"

Dima pulled an ID from his back pocket and flashed it too fast for the pilot to even see what it was an identification for. "I'm serious. They want us dead, not down. My guess is that, any second now, the guy here is going to pull away to let the one hanging back use an air-to-air missile." Even as he spoke, the fighter to port rolled away. "I'd say that confirms it. By any chance were you military before becoming a Gulfstream jockey?"

"Yeah, Naval Air, I flew F-18s in Iraq. I also spent time stateside training against F-16s in what they call dissimilar air-to-air exercises, so I know what those things can do."

"Okay, use what you know, as long as you remember you're in a Gulfstream."

Emerson paused for only seconds. "Okay, we can't outrun them, and we can't pull nine-gee maneuvers, but we can make it a little harder for them if they really want to fire a missile." He eased back on the throttles.

First Officer Grantman turned. "We're going to make it easier to catch us?"

"No, we're already caught. We're going to force the guy on our tail to keep slowing in order to drop back far enough to safely use his missiles. I don't think he's going to use his cannon. If our passenger is right, he is going to want to be certain to obliterate us, not just fill us full of holes. We should also lose altitude, as if we were complying with their demands that we land."

"I think I get it, yeah. But are you sure about this?"

"Worth a try. Switch frequencies to Guard. There's plenty of air traffic in the area, we want people listening in."

The First Officer reset to 121.5 megahertz and started calling an emergency. "Mayday, mayday, mayday. This is Capitol Air Services Two-One charter out of DC in route from Halifax to Tel Aviv. We have Turkish Airforce on our tail ordering us to land and threatening to shoot us down. We are descending through 29,000 feet attempting to comply."

"Good. Now, we keep dropping altitude and slow to approach speed. The F-16s should go into a racetrack pattern overhead. As soon as prudent, flaps down, minimal, as if we were serious about coming in. Keep them guessing."

"I think I'm following you," Dima said.

"You better get back belted in. I'm going to take a hard left toward the coast first. Then hold on."

Dima took the front-facing seat in the first row, buckled

up, and leaned into the aisle to be able to watch the action in the cockpit.

"What's happening?" Barbara said. "Why are we dropping down?"

"We got company. The Turks. Hang on."

As the lead F-16 slowed and dropped with them, now trying to keep to the rear and follow them down, Captain Emerson shouted, "Hold on, everybody!" He banked right, away from the coast, pointed the nose sharply down, and pushed up to full-throttle. Without being told, the co-pilot started the flaps retracting. With the controls nose down and the engines dollying up, the plane was in a steep dive, approaching vertical. The plane shook with increasing violence as it pushed past its official maximum design airspeed and crept up toward Mach 1.

Above them, the lead F-16 overshot past them and started to bank to circle back, but its heavy wing tanks reduced maneuverability just enough that the circle was wide, and the fighter pilot, not expecting combat tactics from the G6, momentarily lost track of his target. Without target lock, he couldn't fire his missiles. His wingman radioed that the G6 was now below and behind him. The wingman rolled into a steep diving turn to follow the target down and take it out.

Captain Emerson gritted his teeth and held the descent until what he judged was the very last second. With the glassy, sun-spattered sea rushing up at them, he edged back on the yoke, ever so gently easing the plane's nose back up as the copilot simultaneously began easing off on the throttles. "Flaps down, ten degrees."

"We're still over-speed for flaps, Bud."

"Not by too much, I hope. Do it." The plane shuddered as the flaps extended. The drag helped the G6 steadily drop airspeed while maintaining lift, and it finally leveled out at less than two hundred feet. "All right, flaps up and flat out for Cyprus."

"Since when were you a stunt pilot, Bud? Next thing you know you'll have us doing loops and barrel rolls."

"Not this flight, I won't. And we're not home yet. It all depends now on how badly they want us and what missiles they might try to use with us surfing the waves, but they don't seem to be on our tail anymore. Just in case, we are going to stay right down on the deck all the way into Cyprus. Have them vector us in to Larnaca. And warn them we may be coming in hot."

"It looks like the Turks have given up and backed off. Your evasive tactics must have worked."

"Just pulling a Crazy Ivan. We were lucky. I'm pretty sure once they got their wits about them, they could have shot us down, but now we're too low and too close to Cyprus for them to risk some very messy consequences, so my guess is they've been called back."

"Okay, ATC now wants us to land at the nearest airport, Paphos."

Chapter 18

ON THE APPROACH TO PAPHOS, a combined military and civilian airport on the west coast of Greek Cyprus, Captain Emerson called for flaps twenty-degrees.

"They're not extending. We must have damaged them in our aerobatics."

"Any other bad news? Nope? Let 'em know."

"Paphos ATC, this is Capitol Two-One. We're making a no-flaps landing. We're going to need all the runway we can get."

"Capitol Two-One, this is Paphos ATC. You're cleared for immediate landing on runway 11."

"More bad news, Bud. We have a gear-up condition. I can't get them down and locked."

"Great, a worse-case combo with no flaps. You did try the alternate landing gear extension, right?" He thumbed the mike on. "Paphos, this is Capitol Two-One. We are going to climb and do a go-around while we try to get our landing gear down and locked."

They ran through the checklist twice, ruling out an indicator failure, but they still couldn't get a green light that the gear were down and locked. If the gear were partially down or down but not locked, they would collapse on hitting the tarmac and the plane would be doing a belly slide.

"Five years with Capitol Air without incident, and now a

pan-pan and a mayday on the same run," Emerson said.

The co-pilot thumbed the intercom. "Okay, people. Looks like we drew the short straw today and could be doing a belly-landing. Fire and emergency crew are standing by. Keep your belts firmly tightened and brace yourselves. But don't worry, we're going to be fine. Bud Emerson can land anything. He used to land F-18s on a carrier deck."

"Thanks for that reminder, Lew. But I don't think they have a tailhook cable waiting to keep us from sliding off the end of the runway. Okay, we're lined up for a fast, shallow landing."

Seconds later, tires screeched as the underwing gear touched down almost at the start of the runway, but the gear did not collapse. They immediately deployed the spoilers and thrust reversers as the captain gingerly settled the nose and the plane screamed down the tarmac. They were almost out of runway when the plane slowed enough to turn off the active runway in a drunken wing-tipping swerve.

As they taxied toward the terminal, Dima called forward. "What was all that about? I thought we would be skidding down the length of the runway."

"I thought so too. Something screwy with the controls and indicators, maybe left over from the mess on the first leg. Halifax maintenance said they had to reboot and reset everything, almost like we'd been hacked or something."

≈ ≈ ≈

With the crew spending the day arranging for repairs and dealing with Cypriot and corporate paperwork over the incident, Dima, Arkady, and Barbara hired a local to drive them to Larnaca for the hop to Tel Aviv. There were flights directly from Paphos to Israel, but Dima and Arkady agreed that it was better to make their trail harder to follow by breaking up the trip. Despite a plethora of commercial options, including on El Al,

Dima insisted they find a private operator in Larnaca who would do the two-hundred mile flight for cash. After hours of looking, the best deal he was able to find for a one-way flight on short notice was from a solo pilot who called himself Zorba and was willing to take them in his vintage vee-tailed Beechcraft Bonanza for $5,000.

"You realize, we can fly El Al for less than $100 apiece," Dima said.

"Then fly El Al."

"Over and back in three hours. What can the fuel cost? Look, here," Dima pulled out his wallet. "Make yourself a quick $600 and still be back in time for dinner."

"No, not worth the hassle. I gotta pay my co-pilot and landing fees and—"

"You're full of crap. There's no copilot on a Bonanza. You—"

"Well, I don't know you, and I don't want to, so it's $4,000 or take a boat. I figure you have your reasons for not wanting to fly commercial. Reasons cost extra."

Dima flipped him the Brazilian fig and stomped back across the tarmac to where Arkady and Barbara waited.

"So?"

"Unless we can come up with several thousand American, we're stuck flying the regular flights, which will break our radio silence."

"Maybe it's already broken. It's damned hard to stay below the radar these days. But all three of us have new passports. Let's hop the next flight. I checked. We have our pick of Aegean, Arkia, El Al, or Cyprus."

"All right. But at least let's fly with the good guys." He took out a coin from his pants pocket and flipped it. "Heads it's El Al, tails it's Arkia."

≈ ≈ ≈

"I do not have a good feeling about this whole trip," Barbara said, as they waited for takeoff. "And now we're flying in the open and exposing our new passports again. To whom? What is this about? We're just mules, couriers carrying contraband. And for what?"

Arkady took her hand. "To stay alive, maybe?" he said quietly. "Maybe to keep the lights on."

Dima slipped out of his seat across the aisle. "I'll leave you kids to your tête-à-tête. I'm going to hit the head and maybe hit on that black-haired beauty of a flight attendant before we taxi and it's too late for either." He grabbed something from the overhead and started up the aisle just as the flight attendant was headed toward the rear taking her passenger count. As they passed, Dima leaned in and said something to her, pointing back toward his seat. She nodded, and both continued on.

Arkady and Barbara, tired from too little sleep, had both drifted off. When he realized they were already airborne, Arkady looked across the aisle. Dima wasn't in his seat. He gently stroked Barbara's arm. She opened her eyes and gave him a sleepy look of inquiry. "Dima's gone," he said. "He's not in his seat."

"Again? I swear that man is losing it with his bladder. Either that or he's hitting on that flight attendant again. He'll be back."

"But the seatbelt sign is still on and we're still climbing."

"Chill. Your brother can take care of himself. Didn't he say he was a pilot once? Maybe he's up on the flight deck, swapping stories with the pilots. With him, who knows?"

"I don't. Look, I'm going to wait until the seatbelt sign goes off, then I'm going to go scouting."

"Scout all you want, but we'll be landing in"—she checked

her watch—"maybe less than a half hour. I mean, where can he go on this little plane? What is it?"

"An Embraer 195."

"Right. He's up front schmoozing with the crew. I'll just bet."

≈ ≈ ≈

In Be'er Sheva, General Barg knocked but didn't wait for an acknowledgement before pushing into the room. "Looks like your threesome have had some misadventures along the way. They're now on an Arkia flight from Larnaca on Cyprus bound for Tel Aviv. I thought they were supposed to stay off the main highways."

"Threesome?"

"Yeah, the two brothers and the ex-FBI woman."

"Definitely not according to plan. Something must have happened. I just hope they have the files. Have them met when they land."

Chapter 19

NICOSIA WAS FAMILIAR TO DIMA, not because he had been there before but because cities at crossroads and on borders were the favored playgrounds of his kind. It was the divided capital of a divided country, with the UN-patrolled Green Line between, a stark reminder that realities on the ground and official definitions of countries do not always align. A little like home, he thought. Greeks and Turks, Palestinians and Jews, claims and counter claims. The street signs in Nicosia were a different mashup of languages than those in Israel, but it was known territory.

At the Ledra Street Crossing from Greek Cyprus to the northern portion controlled by the Turkish military, Dima stood in the short mid-morning line at the checkpoint, letting conversations in several languages drift past. There were Cypriots speaking Greek and Turkish, young Israelis on excursions talking in animated Hebrew, and an older couple traveling on shoulder-season bargain tours speaking in loud, American-accented English. In his black fisherman's cap and faded sweater, for which he had paid his driver too much, Dima was neither tourist nor quite native, but he was unremarkable as he shuffled along, listening. Besides multilingual eavesdropping, invisibility was one of his best developed survival skills. It had served him well of late.

On board the plane in Larnaca, while the flight attendant had completed her count, Dima had hung around momentarily at the front, flipping through magazines, checking his watch, waiting for just the right moment to slip into the toilet, reverse his jacket, and put on the pilfered ground-crew badge. He trotted down the exit stairs as if he were just doing his job just before the woman returned to initial the passenger list and close the door. Years of practice in acting as if he belonged backstage enabled him to slip past the ground crew and back into the gate area without drawing so much as a look. Between his money belt and the billfold he had lifted on the way out of the lounge area, he figured he had enough for the next stage of his assignment. It was a longshot. The territory ahead was vast and his was only a wild guess about the quarry, but he had a history of being right about wild guesses.

Once out of the airport, Dima had quickly found a driver who would take him from Larnaca on the southeast coast to the capital. Nicosia was in the middle of the island in more than one sense. The Greek side was a city of optimism. Crowds of early-season tourists from around the EU sipped coffee and nibbled pastries at local cafes or shopped for bargains in pocket stores that crowded the thoroughfare.

At the Turkish-run checkpoint, Dima showed one of his passports and was given a stamped slip of paper by a border guard who had opened and closed the passport with only a lazy glance and whose mind might have been on anything but his job. On the other side of the checkpoint, the city changed. The steeples of Greek Orthodox churches were replaced with the twin minarets of mosques, and the atmosphere of bustling optimism gave way to a quieter stoicism. Storefronts wore more grime and, unlike on the Greek side, no Starbucks or McDonalds intruded among the cafes. He was now officially in Turkey, confident of having entered the country without leaving an electronic trail at the crossing. He was back in his comfort zone, flying below the radar. A crossing to the mainland on a fishing boat would keep him below. Then where?

Ankara.

Chapter 20

THE CLASS IN BEGINNING TURKISH had gone long, and traffic on the street had begun to thin. Tankut detoured to pass through the *pazar*, a market still busy with after-work shoppers grabbing something extra to take home for dinner. He stopped at a vegetable stand and looked over the neatly stacked produce.

"Not that one," a voice from behind him said, as he reached for an eggplant. "They're not in season. Who knows where that came from or how it was grown." A woman's hand reached past him and pointed toward a hanging bunch of shrunken vegetables, browned flesh banded by stripes of purple-black skin. "Use the dried aubergines. I can show you how to fix them."

He turned to face Bedia Tekin, who greeted his look of annoyed confusion with a warm, closed-mouth smile. "I didn't know that you . . .," he said.

"You didn't know that I what? That I live near you? See, I know where you live. It's my job to know, especially to know who I'm working with. We take these things more seriously than you Americans."

"That was then. Now I'm a Turk."

"A Turk who speaks little Turkish, and that with an American accent."

"I am learning, taking classes."

"Yes, I know. That too. What I do not know is why. Why are

135

you here? Why are you suddenly so invested in your mother's country in place of your own."

"Returning to my roots."

"A short answer, but it was an essay question. So, buy the dried *patlıcan* and come with me. I will teach you to cook like a Turk even if you cannot speak like one. Of course, the men here never cook, except for those who live alone, and they do it very badly."

"At home . . . I mean, back in America, I really was quite a good cook. My mother taught me."

"Yes, I know about your mother, but just how good the son might be remains to be seen. So, join me for dinner. I will teach you how to make *dolmas* with the dried *patlıcan*. You can be my sous chef, and we will see just how good you are in the kitchen." She gave him another warm smile, followed quickly by a demur downward glance.

"I don't know."

"But I do, as I keep telling you. You are surprised by my manner, so forward, no? See, I live up to my name, Tekın, the only, unique. I am a Turkish woman with a Parisian soul. My years in the service in France . . . but that is another story. After dinner. Now, come this way, through that store. There is a man following you, and we can lose him through a passageway I know. Come." She took his hand, a move so bold that he almost pulled back, but there was no arguing with Bedia Tekın, as he was beginning to understand.

≈ ≈ ≈

Dima Pohl watched the pair duck into a small store opposite the vegetable stand, but he didn't follow. He had noted the briefest glance his way, half hidden behind the woman's pale lavender scarf. She was good, too good, too professional to be a mere casual acquaintance bumped into at random on the street. Who was she? For the present, he didn't care. He knew the man.

He chose not to follow them. Better to let them think they had lost their tail. In any event, he now knew where to look. This general neighborhood, of course, but also the stretch between here and a gated and guarded campus with a foreboding black entrance.

Tomorrow. The next day. Soon, he thought. I have found you. You, at least, are no pro. You are, at best, an amateur enthusiast in this game. You learned what little tradecraft you know seated at a desk, swapping stories with others seated at their desks. It will be simple to find you again, and you will not even know I am there until it is time, a time of my choosing, but soon.

≈ ≈ ≈

On arrival, it quickly became clear to Tankut that Bedia lived alone. Her apartment was small, reached by separate outside stairs rising from a short alleyway at the back of a well-maintained building that nevertheless showed its age. She opened the door, stepped in ahead of him, then turned back to say, "Hoş geldiniz. Welcome, please come in." Hanging her scarf and jacket on pegs beside the door, she added, "My home is yours."

Tankut turned slowly, taking in a room that interwove the old and new. The window facing the alleyway, the only one in the room, was closed with slatted green shutters. The floor was covered in a tiling of small Oriental carpets in patterns of disparate cultures but sharing a common aesthetic. The walls, save for the one presenting an enormous television screen, were hung with tapestries showing a similar eclecticism but with a subtle visual link and a strong preference for blue. On a low round brass table in the center of the room rested an inlaid chess board set with tall pieces carved from blue and white stone. "Do you play?" He gestured toward the table.

"Only in life. That set was a gift from a lover in France, at a time we were playing in Nice. In the end, I liked the shape of the chess pieces better than I liked his." She noted his quickly suppressed surprise at the disclosure. "It was many years and a lifetime ago," she said. "As you are beginning to see, we each have a past that does not completely match our present."

"And I see that you did not invite me here just for learning how to cook dolmas with dried aubergines."

"No."

"Then why? What is on the menu for the evening."

"That we will find out. But first we eat, and for that we must cook. Follow me, my man of mystery, and let me show you how to make small bites of heaven with fire and spice." She cocked her head playfully as she led him into the kitchen.

He was thinking of fire and spice as a versatile metaphor and wondered just how far it might stretch.

Chapter 21

BINI DOUBLE-TIMED down the service stairs to what the younger team members were calling The Pit—a temporary operations room set up in the basement emergency shelter of the building. It now had secure dedicated fiber optic connections directly to Headquarters outside Tel Aviv and to the military base in the Negev. Bini had reluctantly accepted that the arrangement was a necessary expedient. Unit 8200 could hardly allow a bunch of civilians, especially the likes of Talpa or the Pohls, to be running around a top-secret military base.

Despite the somewhat awkward setup, the pressure was on to produce results. After the DC area blackout, Moscow had experienced two more outages in forty-eight hours. Then another massive blackout in the American West plunged Silicon Valley and most of California into dark chaos along with forcing the massive server farms scattered throughout the region to turn to backup generators.

The press was peppered with posturing and blame-laying from both sides, but both also denied responsibility. Polls in the two countries reported plummeting public confidence in their leaders. The UN was convened in emergency session, with France and Germany calling for brokered negotiations between the Whitehouse and the Kremlin. In Washington, the government was having trouble staying on message, with the president vacillating between badmouthing Russia and blaming the utility companies for failing to properly protect the infrastructure. Although the internet had not yet gone down completely, online sales had plummeted as response times stretched from milliseconds to minutes, and the American economy rocked from the indirect impacts of lost productivity. The heartland had yet to experience power outages, but ripple effects were beginning to impact farms and manufacturing throughout the Midwest.

All this was on Bini's mind as he approached the room, with its blast door now fitted with a secure lock. When Bini held up his ID, one of the two armed soldiers guarding the door nodded and waved him in. Across the room, Roni looked up from her machine and smiled. "Bini, we have something interesting here."

He stood behind her as she pulled up a series of graphs. "We've been using Wolfram Language to do some digging into details of backbone network traffic at various intervals before and after each of the blackouts, looking for patterns, and—"

"I thought you were supposed to be doing target analysis, hacking into the actual systems that were hit."

She scowled up at him. "And I thought we were following the trail wherever it led. Besides, everyone in the world is looking into the malware itself. Kaspersky, Scenaria, Norton, McAfee—they're all working on that angle, and, of course, we know exactly what is going on with them. That's what 8200 does."

He paused for a moment in thought. "Okay, point taken, but then I want at least one of you to pull together everything we know from all that civilian work and to look for holes or clues that maybe they're missing. Now, what do you have?"

Her smile returned. "A pattern. Internet traffic around the

Mediterranean has its usual randomness and overall daily cycles, but look at this. If we plot traffic by packet type, we get a different picture. See? Dips in some types, peaks in others. It's small but significant and"—she typed another line of code—"if we superimpose the approximate times of the events in Russia and the States, as well as those in Brazil, we get this: almost a perfect match."

"Except for there." He reached past her to touch the screen and highlight one of the waves in the plot. "There's nothing with that little one."

She brushed his hand aside and typed another line of Wolfram. "I'm not even sure that's real, just a blip." She tapped enter. "Wow."

Everyone gathered around the two of them nodded. "That's our blackout, the one just before Passover," Bini said. "And I thought this was between the Americans and the Russians, but somehow we're in the game."

"Do we dare ask the next question?" Roni said.

"Ask away."

"On which side in the game? And how many sides are there?"

"That's what the dependency model was supposed to tease out." A note of impatience had crept into his voice. "How are we doing on that?"

"We've been working with the Professor, but it's hard to follow what he is getting at. The programming's not that difficult. In principle, it's just a systems dynamics simulation, but none of us can make sense of it, and every time we ask for help, we get a lecture. And then he tells us to make it right. I don't think he understands how we do things around here. I think he is used to working alone or telling other people to do his work. So, while you were in meetings, we kind of set his model aside to work on this instead. And look, now we have something."

"But we still don't know what it means," Bini said, "not even who's behind it. Okay, we'll play from our strengths and go with your code and stats approach for now. See what happens if you keep drilling down into the captured traffic. Be creative. Try stuff." He patted Roni's shoulder and her hand reached upward for an instant, unnoticed except by Bini. He pulled his hand back, but as her monitor timed out and went to a screen-saver, he saw her face reflected, looking at him, locking eyes.

"All right," he said after an awkward moment. "I'm going to see if we can get some extra resources to help with the social systems modeling. Maybe Mossad has something or someone with ears to the ground. I don't know. I'll talk with the General. And I'll see if I can get Talpa to be more, uh, collaborative. I know he can be a nudge, but we need what he knows and what he can do. I've worked with him before, and it pays."

As he left the room, he glanced back at the team, now gathered around Roni's workstation. She looked over her shoulder, expressionless but not without a message. What now, he thought, what now?

≈ ≈ ≈

Richard Talpa rose from the desk in his temporary office. "Welcome to the Negev." He came around and walked up to Barbara. "Arkady and I have worked together before, but you and I haven't had the pleasure." He shook her hand. "Of course, your reputation precedes you." He turned to Arkady. "Look at you, still fighting trim." They shook hands.

Arkady took a step back. "Wait a minute, something's different. Ohmygod, you're standing. You've had an operation or something."

"Biomechanical legs. I'll show you in due course, but first to the business at hand. You two are no doubt a little travel weary.

And I hear you, uh, lost somebody along the way."

"Yeah, Dima disappeared in midair somewhere over the Mediterranean. He boarded with us in Cyprus but was gone by the time we disembarked in Tel Aviv. But then, you know Dima, always pulling fast ones."

"Not even the legendary Dima Pohl can pull off a D.B. Cooper on the way to Israel. No, he's either here or there. But, not to worry. You're here, that's what counts. Do you have the package?"

"You're eager. We just arrived."

"And we are on the clock. We need those files."

"We."

"Israel. The free world. It's a joint operation."

"I'd ask who exactly is the free world, but I'm guessing that's on a need-to-know basis."

"Just give me the files." He looked Arkady squarely in the eyes. "Please."

"Barbara has them. We pulled the hard drive."

Talpa reached out his hand.

Barbara stared at it a moment. "I suppose we've no leverage, no room to bargain." She reached into her backpack and handed the drive to him.

"You don't need to bargain," Talpa said. "You're already on the team." He walked with the hard drive to the open doorway. "Oh, hi, Bini. There you are. Did you want to see me? Your timing is perfect. Here, take this and get what you can from it."

Arkady spun around. "Bini? Bini Markham?"

Bini ducked his head in the door. "Well, look who finally made it to Israel. Are you at last ready to make *aliyah*?"

"I don't think so, but it looks like Barbara and I are here for this project anyway. What's it really about?"

"Keeping the lights on. We're trying to stop the superpowers from wiping out each other's power grids along with maybe everybody else's."

"And how do you propose to do that?"

"We're working on that. Speaking of which"—Bini turned to Talpa—"we need to meet with Dan and maybe Yishai. I need to bring in somebody. We're hamstrung in the social and political science area. The team is getting nowhere with the social system modeling." He noted the expression on Talpa's face. "Someone besides you, someone who can work more fulltime as part of the team, down at their level."

"I see. No worry, I'll get Dan to call somebody up."

"Not somebody. Marwa."

"I don't know about that."

"You've worked with her before. You've seen how we work together, a regular Dynamic Duo."

"Yes, but that was Stateside, Batman. Robin is big over there. Here in the desert, not so much. This is the heart of Israeli military intelligence. You understand what I'm saying."

Bini tensed. "No, I don't. Spell it out."

"She's Muslim."

"And you're what? I've never been quite sure what you are, but you're not Jewish, and you're not an Israeli citizen. She is."

"And this project is of the utmost importance and at the highest level of security. Outside of this facility, only a handful of people even know it exists. No, we . . . they are not going to authorize her participation." His shoulders slumped visibly. "Actually, I tried. I really wanted to reactivate the whole team from Operation Hedgerow. What you did—what we all did—was absolutely amazing."

"And we can do it again. Marwa has a way of seeing things that none of us numbers-and-functions people seem to be able to pull off—or even to fake."

"No. I'm sorry. My hands are tied.

"Okay." Bini handed the hard drive back to Talpa. "Then I'm going directly to Shapiro. And Barg."

≈ ≈ ≈

"Yishai Barg? This is Bini Markham. I need to talk with you."

"Then talk away." The sound of voices at the Unit 8200 headquarters outside Tel Aviv could be heard in the background.

"Not over the phone. This is not a secure line."

"Take it up with Dan, then. General Shapiro reports directly to me."

"I already did. He says it's out of his hands."

"Well, can you tell me in broad terms what this is about?"

"I want to bring Marwa in. You already know her by reputation. You hear her quoted on some cybersecurity issue or another almost every day. We need her expertise and special perspective."

"I can try to get someone with the right skillset."

"I don't want someone, I want Marwa."

"I appreciate the domestic dedication, but we don't make allowances for that sort of thing, Markham, not on a project like this. Surely you understand. It's impossible."

"Then I'm out."

"You forget, you're on active duty. You are under orders."

"And in the IDF, there are grounds for refusing direct orders."

"Picking your platoon mates is not one of them. At least it wasn't the last time I consulted the regs."

"You want this operation to succeed. Without her, it's not going to. We've been running in circles. We need what she brings to it."

"We'll find somebody."

"Okay, listen, uh, Yishai. Just look at her Wikipedia page—or the bio on her faculty profile at the Technion. You find somebody with the equivalent of that résumé, and I'll shut up. I'm not saying the collaboration will be quite as easy, but I'll do my best and I'll stop complaining."

"Look, Bini, I know your family and what you all have done for Israel. And I know it hasn't always been all strictly by the book, but it has always been more than asked and the best that can be given. So, with that in mind, I will commit to getting someone with that résumé. You have my word."

"Okay, best to the family."

"And to yours."

≈ ≈ ≈

Bini was called into General Shapiro's office three hours later. "Well, they found somebody or other with the qualifications you were asking for," the general said. "They're being escorted down here by military transport. Should be here by morning." Bini did not hide his disappointment.

"Hey, you got what you needed and damned fast. I'm not sure what story you told HQ or what strings you pulled, but somebody in some high place must be on your side. Beats me."

"I wasn't pulling strings, just trying to get what is best for the project."

"Spare me the team rouser, Bini. Just tell me what you have so far? What about the files that our mole-friend had us reach halfway around the world for?"

"The hard drive is encrypted. So far, we haven't been able to break the code."

"Well, better get cracking." He snorted a laugh. "A good pun is forever."

"Forever worth a groan."

"And the hard drive? What is it worth?"

"We honestly don't know yet. Talpa wants something off of it, but we don't know what. We're waiting to hear from Crypto about what they could get from it."

"Okay, keep me posted. And remember, I'm heading this operation. Talpa may act like he's in charge, but he's a contractor, nothing more. I hope I don't need to remind any of you which side you are on."

"You don't," he said, but he was thinking of Roni's question about sides. Who wins in a chess game played on an invisible board with an unknown number of players?

Chapter 22

LIFE IN ANKARA had quickly taken on a new rhythm for Tankut, with days spent at the Center in meetings and teamwork mapping out strategy and putting pieces into position for the next move, and evenings spent exploring with Bedia. Like him, she was nominally Turkish but did not belong. Her field assignments in Paris, Nice, and Brussels had transformed her into a chimeric creature, a Turk and a Western European, a Muslim and a heretic, a calculating professional and a romantic. She had sensed in him a fellow traveler on a road leading somewhere else.

"I still don't understand why you came here," she said one night as they shared an after-dinner coffee. "You arrive armed with gifts, like others before you, and with a personal agenda that we accepted gladly even as we did not believe it. A rekindled patriotism for a country you never knew? Pshaw. Righteous anger over how the West is treating Muslims? A deep hatred of Israel and what you see as Jewish hegemony in world affairs?"

"All that is real."

"Real, perhaps, but that's another story and not the full story. There is something else that drives you, some spark, some *kıvılcım*, that ignited the fire now burning in you and that may yet consume you. As I am beginning to know you, I am guessing there is someone, someone you have not told me about: an enemy, a friend, or perhaps a lover."

"Maybe all the above."

"Who was she?"

"She? She was a friend become lover. He was an agent, an Israeli, an assassin who killed her for nothing, nothing except to send a message to me, a message I received and ignored, because I was too immersed in what I thought was a good cause and too painfully wounded to see how I was on the wrong side, fighting beside the Jews when I should be fighting against the Jews."

"This side of you I have seen at the Center," she said, "this hatred that flares while others are merely talking tactics and countermeasures. A flame so bright can blind you."

"Or it can light the way forward. With the help of the Americans and the Russians—and our real allies, those in *our* world—we will end an evil, a blot on the Middle East and on the world."

"And you will get personal revenge, or so you hope."

"My revenge is merely fuel, but the fire is righteous."

"I don't know. I'm a Turk, but I am also a person of the world. I have no love for the Jews but also, I confess, no hatred."

Tankut took in a deep breath and held it. "Then you are as bad as the others," he said, the words exploding from his mouth. He clenched his fists.

She took a step back and shook her head, side-to-side, in the Western style. "Then perhaps it is time that you leave."

"Perhaps not." He took another step toward her.

As he advanced, she retreated until her back was against a tapestry hanging on the wall. The silence between them dragged on. "I understand now," she said, "but I also understand that this"—she held her hands opened upward as if in prayer—"this cannot continue. I will work with you, because, whatever else I am, I am a Turk, loyal and professional. But . . ."

As he advanced toward her, she reached behind her and withdrew a small pistol from a niche hidden by the tapestry. "Leave," she said. "Now."

"You wouldn't."

"Oh, I would. And not for the first time."

"You would never get by with it. At the Center, I'm the new-found Atatürk, hero of the republic."

"And I am the esteemed old heroine. What do you think it took for me, a woman, to rise to my position in such a man's world? Connections, influence, and the agility to dance gracefully to whatever tune is playing."

"What would you tell them?"

"A story, a good one. It's one of my talents. And not one of yours. You lie well enough but have little skill at weaving your lies into stories. So, go, and trust that your truth is safe with me—safe as long as you continue to serve my country and our agenda."

His eyes shifted between hers and the pistol in her hand and back to her eyes. It was the same message from both. He picked up his hat from the peg beside the door and left. As he trotted down the stairs, she open the shutter a crack to watch him retreat. With her free hand, she wiped her eyes.

≈ ≈ ≈

As Tankut hurried down the back ways toward his apartment, he burned with inner fury: anger at Bedia and anger at himself for trusting, for opening up, something he had vowed would never happen again. Trust no one, he had told himself on that first flight to Istanbul, keep to the chosen path and see it to the end. Let them use you, but remember that you are using them. They are instruments, nothing more.

By contrast to Bedia's, his apartment was in a thoroughly modern building with an elevator. As he reached the end of the hall on his floor, he was deep in thought, rehearsing how he would act at the Center the next morning. "Remember who you are," he told himself out loud.

"Sam Parsons." At first he thought the quiet whisper was his own imagination, then it came again. "Sam Parsons." He was not imagining it, but he pretended not to hear as he turned the key in the lock and reached for the door handle. "Sam Parsons." This time the voice was so near his ear that the plosive of the surname kissed the back of his neck with a pulse of warm breath. He turned slowly to face a weather-beaten face a foot from his own.

"Aren't you going to invite me in? We have much to talk about."

In mangled Turkish, Tankut said, "I Tankut Yilmaz. You have mistaken."

The man laughed, then replied in accented but flawless Turkish. "I see you are learning the language. We have never met, but I am Dmitry Andreevich Pohl."

"I know who you are," Tankut said, switching to English. "And I know your work, your very messy work. I've seen your picture and studied your face."

"Have you now? Well then, open the door and let's go beyond faces and changeable names, Tankut Yilmaz, née Samuel Tankut Parsons. We can talk over a coffee. The coffee here is almost as good as Israel's, but then there are so many things shared by the countries around the Mediterranean. Have you learned how to make Turkish coffee?"

It was Tankut's turn to laugh. "On my mother's knee, I

learned, long before I ever saw this country. I hated the taste of it as a boy." He turned away and unlocked the door. "I suppose you might as well come in, but I can offer you only tea."

"Tea will be fine," he said, reaching past Tankut to push the door open and give the room a quick survey before entering. "This is a nice place. They must be paying you well." He gestured for Tankut to go ahead.

"The apartment comes with the job."

"Which is? Tell me what work you are doing and for whom." He sat down on a sofa and casually spread his arms over the backrest. "Ministry of Aviation? Do you still investigate plane crashes, like when you were with the NTSB? Or is it something to do with some other part of your on-the-job training? Maybe in cybersecurity?"

Tankut, playing along, turned on an electric kettle in the kitchenette and set out cups on a tray before returning to the sitting room. "So, we are talking about work. And yours? Is it going well? What exactly do you do, Mr. Pohl? I've always wondered."

"I'm a consultant, a solver of problems, much as you, I imagine."

"And what brings you to Ankara?"

"I could ask the same of you?"

"And we could dance in circles of questions until we are dizzy and tire of it."

"I'm already tiring of it. So, I'll tell you that I am here as a recruiter, looking for someone with special skills for a special client."

"I already have a position, a good one, working with good people."

"The Turks."

"Obviously."

"Good work?"

"Obviously."

"What if I asked you to come back to the team you left in Washington?"

"To work with the Americans?"

"Not exactly. To work with the same team, though: Talpa, the Scenaria people, the young Markham—and my brother."

"If not the Americans, then who?"

"Israel."

"Jews." Tankut spat out the word.

"We're not all Jews."

"Might as well be."

"Look, whatever your feelings about Jews, this project is critical to more than just the Jews. I can't go into detail, of course, but it's up your alley. It's about cybersecurity and infrastructure vulnerabilities."

"What a coincidence, exactly what I am working on."

Dima held his breath.

"I think our tea is ready? How do you take it? English style or with a cube of sugar?"

"Black, thank you."

Tankut left for the kitchen, fussing over the tea out of sight. When he returned, he was concealing a loaded Yavuz beneath the tray of the tea set. He stopped in the doorway. The sofa was empty. He looked to the side just as Dima finished fitting the suppresser to his Beretta and raised it in both hands.

"A standoff, of sorts," Dima said, nodding toward the tray, "except I have the advantage of aim. Let me make my job offer clear. My orders are to recruit you or . . ."

"Or?"

"Fill in the blank."

"Then I guess I'll have to give some serious thought to your offer. Shall we have our tea?"

Chapter 23

Talpa opened the door to his room and turned on the light. He tried not to register his surprise at the guest who had been sitting in the dark. "Dima, how the hell did you . . . ?"

"Tradecraft." He stood, grinning. "No, I entered the country on a passport that I knew would guarantee I was met by Mossad and no one else. Old loyalties and old rivalries run deep. And they provided transportation. At any rate, the Technology Park itself is not a secure facility, and once you're here it's easy to get around. I thought you and I better meet and talk in private before I rejoin the rest of the team. Aren't you going to welcome me and ask for my report?"

"Welcome." Talpa lowered himself awkwardly into a chair. "My new legs." He tapped a thigh with a denim-dulled thunk. "Still getting some of the moves properly programmed. So, give me your report."

"Terse, to the point, just like your original orders. Six words on dissolving paper: 'Find Sam Parsons. Recruit or neutralize.' Not a lot of ambiguity there, but what a lot of room to improvise."

"You're here. Mission accomplished?"

"I wouldn't be here otherwise."

"I take it by the fact that you're alone, that you didn't recruit him."

"Your greatest strength and biggest liability: a fast mind. You are jumping to an unwarranted conclusion. He's just not with me right now."

"So, you did recruit him."

"In a manner of speaking. It might be more accurate to say he recruited himself."

"So when does he arrive?"

"Never. He had an accident, a tragic fall from the balcony of his fourth-floor apartment."

"Look, I've had a long day, and I am not in the mood for word play or a round of twenty questions. Just tell me what the fuck happened."

"Ask me where."

"Look, dammit, you report to me. Just fucking tell me what happened."

"I did report to you, once, then we undid the whole unit. These days I am what I once so disdained: a freelancer, a hired gun. You may be my client, but you are not my commanding officer."

Talpa shook his head and sighed. "Okay, okay. What do I have to do to find out what happened."

"Ask me where it happened and I'll tell you."

Talpa gritted his teeth. "So, where?"

"Ankara."

"Turkey? So what's the story?"

"That's it. I just told you. That's the whole story. In a word. Ankara."

"You fucker!" Talpa tried to stand quickly to lunge at Dima, but his battery-powered legs wouldn't cooperate, and he ended up tottering, knees bent, half risen. "Shit."

"Look, Richard, sit down—if you can, that is—and relax. If you can. I'll give you the details, but if you're as smart as you always claim to be, you should be able to put most of the details together from just my one-word answer."

"You always were a tricky bastard. Your brother plays the intellect and bills you as the muscle, but . . . Okay, I'll play." He lowered himself back into the chair and sat for a moment, deep in thought. "My guess would have to be *Millî İstihbarat Teşkilatı*, Turkish central intelligence."

"Your pronunciation is atrocious, but you get bonus points for knowing the name in Turkish. Yes, he was working for Turkish intelligence. On what exactly, I couldn't extract from him, but that, too, we can guess from his background."

"Airliner hacking? Bringing commercial jets down?"

"Possibly, but I don't think that was in his immediate job description. Think earlier. Where did he start at the NTSB?"

"Gas transmission pipelines, if I remember. Energy Infrastructure. Oh, I get it, he was in demand for his knowledge about infrastructure hacking."

"Bingo!"

"The Turks want to protect their grid from . . . from attack by the Prancing Presidents?"

"I don't know. Our conversation didn't last that long before his defenestration. Does it count as that if it's over a balcony railing?"

"You?"

"He made a break for the balcony, maybe to try to get away, maybe to the balcony below. I added to his momentum, neither entirely by accident nor purposeful. I wish we could have talked longer. I did learn that he has a personal vendetta against me, which is part of the story. He thinks I killed his sweetheart. It was actually the other guy on the HaVered wet team, but that may be just an irrelevant detail. At least it was to him. As far as he was concerned, all of Israel and the Jewish people killed her, end of story. End of his story."

"Too bad. I think we could have used him."

"We still can. He gave us a lot. We know Turkey is on the playing field. That means something. And we can make some guesses about their playbook. It has chapters and appendices supplied by Parsons."

"Damn, that means the contents of the disk you three brought over are probably worthless. We can assume the Turks now have the same material, code and all."

"Too quick on the assumptions again, my Richard. In fact, we have good reason to believe that whatever he gave the Turks and whatever our motorcyclists took with them to Canada are quite different."

"Yeah, he could have had stuff on the airliner hacking cyberattack; the West Virginia kids left for Canada before that. So, it's also possible that the Turks have even more than we do."

"Or not." Dima stood up from his chair. "Don't get up. Let your battery recharge. I'm tired from all this travel. I'll see you in the morning. Have a badge waiting for me."

Chapter 24

THE COLONEL INTERSECTED the new arrival and her escort, a young soldier in fatigues, just as they arrived at the security desk in the temporary operations center. "I'll take over soldier," he said. "She's in my charge now."

"My orders are to . . ."

"The silver leaves I'm wearing means that your orders are now to release this woman into my custody."

The soldier hesitated, but handed the colonel a large manila envelope. "She's supposed to be—"

"I know, soldier. I'll take good care of her. I know how all this works."

"Yes, Colonel." He saluted smartly.

"Bag the salutes, just get on with whatever else you have on your list."

"I have to return to Haifa, sir."

"I don't care if you have to return to Timbuktu, carry on."

The young soldier turned and left. As her new minder slipped her papers from the envelope, the woman studied his face. "You look familiar, but I don't think we've met." He continue to flip through the stack of papers. "I'm Marwa, Marwa Markham."

"I know." He fluttered the papers toward her.

"And you are . . . ?"

159

He continued to ignore her as he finished speedreading the papers and slipped them back into the envelope. Then he smiled at her.

"The face is all wrong, but I recognize the lukewarm smile from somewhere," she said. "Wait, you're Arkady Pohl's brother, right? Dima, is it?"

"Dmitry. The Opposite Pohl, as they used to call me. Let's get our badges from this patient soldier here and head for The Pit. Don't you love the name? They're waiting for us."

"You really are a colonel in the air force?"

"Was. Retired. It's not Purim, but I figured I might as well come in costume and look the part if I'm going to be back in the land of the living. I've been a ghost for more years than I can count. This was the only uniform left in my old closet. You realize, it's been decades since I was home in Israel. It feels right and all wrong at the same time."

"I think I know what you're talking about. I've spent more than half my life in other countries, yet . . ."

"Yeah." He took a deep breath. "Well, let's get on with it and join our teammates."

≈ ≈ ≈

It took several seconds for the multiple conversations in The Pit to slowly mute as knots of people turned toward the two who had just arrived and stood inside the blast door.

"Marwa!" Bini was at a loss at what to do. He wanted to run to her and sweep her up in his arms.

Dima glared at him. "Give her a damn hug, and then let's all get back to work. I need to brief you all on developments on the Turkish front."

Arkady crossed the room to stand in front of Dima. "All love and warmth with you as always, big brother."

"Your department, wolf cub." He threw his arms around

Arkady, then pulled back after a perfunctory back pat.

"What's this about Turkey?" Bini said.

"Need to know basis."

Arkady gestured around the room. "We need to know. Inside this room, this is an open op. Outside this room, we don't exist."

"You always loved the dramatic language, Arka."

"And whose life is drama?"

"Hmm. Wouldn't know. But I do know shit when I smell it, and we are swimming in an overflowing two-holer. So tell us where things are at here, and I'll tell you what I picked up in Ankara."

≈ ≈ ≈

In the cafeteria that had been commandeered to serve as a mess hall for the project team, Dima, Arkady, Barbara, Bini, and Marwa took a table in the corner and unloaded their trays. "It's no Michelin star facility," Arkady offered, "but the shakshuka is good and the shawarma is very good."

"You don't know what you are talking about," Bini said. "Until you've had Marwa's Palestinian-style chicken shawarma, you've never had shawarma."

Dima held up his hand. "Enough," he said, keeping his voice low. "We're not here for foodie debates. I figure we may have a few minutes to talk before Talpa shows up or one of the team saunters over and asks if they can join us. So, everyone, what was not said at the briefing this morning?" There was silent headshaking. "All right, I'll start. I was improvising in Turkey, but I was under direct orders to find Parsons and either onboard him or eliminate him."

Marwa looked puzzled. "Orders? Aman?"

"Talpa."

"Who the hell is Talpa to be calling the shots?" she said.

"My former commanding officer."

Bini mimed being startled. "What the f—?"

"Complicated. Full story later, film at eleven."

Bini persisted. "If we're being on the up-and-up here, we need the full story now."

"As I said, we have a few minutes, so I'm going to have to prioritize the recent stuff and leave the relationship archeology for later. Parsons was on some big operation in Turkey."

"You said that in the briefing."

"What I didn't say was that it was an official op. Turkish intelligence. He approached them and convinced them to launch something. It had to be big, and it must have been something in his old bailiwick. They were no doubt using him, and he was using them to advance his personal crusade against me—and my people. Meaning us. He thinks I killed his girlfriend, which I mentioned this morning, but there was more. Once I got him to talking, he was like a maniac, a fanatic. He babbled about destroying Israel, about the New Final Solution, about the elimination of all the Jews in, quote-unquote, the entire Islamic world."

"We've heard that one before, but here we are. Still."

"I know, but this was different. He kept hinting at something new, a spark. He kept using this Turkish word, *kıvılcım*, a spark, like to ignite a fire."

"So, what is the operation? What is it about?"

"We never got that far. Suddenly he stopped talking, and said he needed some air. We stepped out onto the balcony of his apartment and the next thing I know, he's trying to vault over the railing. I grabbed for him but only managed to help him along. I don't know. Maybe it was no accident. I saw him as the worst sort of traitor—and the most dangerous kind. He knew things, had his store of secret weapons, and he was driven. I . . ."

Marwa leaned toward him from across the table. "You wanted to use the time. So, let's use it, brainstorm about the Turkish connection: what it might be about, what he knew that maybe they didn't, what his 'spark' might have been about. And let's get somebody fluent in Turkish working on their social media. We can plug that all into our model and start trying to make sense of it."

"I'm with Marwa," Bini said.

"We all know that," Dima chided.

"No, I meant in broadening our remit, including Turkey and Turkish intelligence in our surveillance and analysis."

"Right, of course. So, ideas? Let's just throw out random inspirations and see what we come up with."

Across the room, Richard Talpa did his studied walk into the cafeteria, accompanied by General Shapiro. He pretended not to notice the intense conversation at the table in the far corner. He took his time getting his falafel and tabbouleh, then made a beeline for the table and balanced his tray on the corner.

"Here," he said, pulling a small harddrive from his shirt pocket and placing it in the center of the table. "This is an unlocked forensic clone of the drive recovered from the Canadians. See what you can make of it. I got nothing." He picked up his tray and walked away.

They were still staring at the drive when Roni Zimro came over with her tray. "All right if I join you? Or is this a private conversation?"

"There's no privacy around here, in case you hadn't noticed," Barbara said. "Grab a chair."

Roni squeezed in next to Marwa and held out her hand. "I know we were introduced at the briefing this morning, but I just wanted to say 'hi' in person. I've read your papers and know about your work at the Technion. Me, I'm an electrical engineer and power systems programmer, but I really admire what you do, turning social media analysis into a science. I've been experimenting with some of your techniques. I think we all have so much to learn from you."

Marwa's grin broadened. "Well, thanks. You should say that again so my husband can hear you." She nodded toward Bini, who shrugged.

Roni looked from Marwa to Bini and back. "Oh, right. Of course."

Across the table Bini watched, completely confused about what had just happened.

≈ ≈ ≈

Bini helped Marwa stow her things in the hotel room they had been reassigned to. "It's not exactly the Meredith in D.C., but at least it's not a military base. If we were on base, I'm not sure this would be allowed." He closed the closet door.

Marwa came up behind him and put her arms around his waist. "I don't care. I'm here, maybe just in time."

"Yeah, we have really been floundering in the whole social systems stuff. We need you." He pivoted in her arms to face her. "Talpa fancies himself the world's greatest at modeling social systems, but he is not good at working with others, not like you."

"I wasn't talking about the work. I was thinking about another sort of social dynamics."

"Like what?"

"Like you and Roni."

"Me and Roni? What about me and Roni. We work closely together on this team. She's a systems engineering geek like me, although I think part of her is interested in stepping into your world."

"Stepping into my world, all right."

The frown on his face intensified. "I don't know what you're hinting at, but there's nothing . . ."

"I saw how she looks at you."

"Maybe. I don't know about how she looks at me. You are always telling me that we males are all members of the same clueless clan. But what counts is how I look at her, which is as just another soldier, a fellow geek who knows what she is doing."

Marwa chewed on her lower lip as she shook her head. She closed her eyes and tears squeezed from them. "I . . ."

Bini held her in silence for long seconds. "I don't know what's happening with you right now, but nothing is happening with Roni Zimro. And nothing has happened."

"What's happening with me is that I'm scared. I'm scared about you, about all this. I'm feeling vulnerable. And I'm pregnant."

"What?"

"Yeah."

"Pregnant? For real? For sure?"

She leaned back in his arms and looked up into his eyes, half smiling through her tears. "For real."

"Ohmygod, that's wonderful. How long have you known?"

"Since Passover. I wasn't sure until just after you left . . . and, well, you suddenly had so much on your plate. I wanted to tell you at the right time."

"Wow!"

"Yeah, wow. I just don't know about the timing, like whether this is a good time to be bringing a baby into the world."

"It's a good time. It's our time."

"But . . ."

165

"No, not but anything. We're going to get through this, and we're going to have a baby. God, that is so . . ." He started kissing her. "So . . ."

"Don't stop."

≈ ≈ ≈

They lay awake, talking afterwards. "I still don't know," she said. "About you, I know; about the rest of the world, not so much. Everything, everyone, the world seems so divided."

"Parallel lines of opposing signs," he said, quoting.

"Yes, like the song."

"If you call that a song. Maybe more like screaming rap. What was the group? Algal Invasion?"

"Blue-Green Algae Invasion. And it wasn't screaming. They were just trying to make a point about voices being lost."

"Yeah, 'the voices of the many all murmur a dream. Too subdued to be heard above the slogans and screams, the words and whimpers of those in midstream are lost in the chaos of the stubborn extremes.'"

"See, you do remember."

"Of course. It was the first new music you introduced me to, and it seems more than ever like an anthem for our times. The divides seem to only get wider and deeper with every year."

"You know, the two leads are touring again. Chaim Hassan and Abdullah Sirhan must be in their fifties. They sing under the name Innervasion. I heard one of their songs, 'Don't Look Down.' On the Alt-Israel feed."

"More of the same? Or are they doing something new?"

"They're still singing about what ails the world, if that's what you mean, and the world is certainly more of the same, but their style is, if anything, more eclectic and hard to pin down than ever. You wanna hear it?"

"Sure. You going to sing it for me?"

"Not likely, but I downloaded it from YouTube." She reached for her phone.

The piece started in close *a capella* harmony between Gershon and Sirhan, with a quiet finger-tap tattoo played on the *darbuka* in the background. The rhythm and feel was more 1960s folk-rock than rap-metal.

> Like a river through the desert, mountains rising from
> the sea,
> Do you remember what you promised then, when you
> promised me?

"What the . . . ? What is this?" he said, talking over the music. "What are they talking about?"

"Shhh. Just wait."

> Like the earth above the treetops and the air beneath
> the plow,
> Do you remember how we wondered then, when we
> wondered how?

Then, with a percussion flourish, the rest of the band hit with a blast of synth and fuzz-heavy electric bass and a shout from the backup singers launching the pounding rap that had been the original group's signature.

> DON'T LOOK DOWN!
> A dark ravine, a screen unseen, lying in between us.
> —DON'T LOOK DOWN!—
> But we don't know how to bridge it,
> standing far apart so rigid,
> angry echo from the frigid
> hidden waters below.
> And we neither of us know it,
> how and why we would still fear it,

but the spirit arching bright across,
a line of life too quickly lost
in deepened gloom, without the room
for passing or returning
in a stomach-churning yearning
on a span that seems too narrow to be crossed.

They listened in the dark as the lyric intensified and built to a final shouted crescendo.

—DON'T LOOK DOWN!—
Take a step!
Take a step!
AND DON'T LOOK DOWN!

They held each other for long seconds without speaking. "They're right," Bini said. "As the Rabbi said, it's all a narrow bridge."

Chapter 25

KAT GAUDET SLOWED her BMW F800 yellow and chrome motorcycle, leaned into the turn at the wind turbine, and sped down the long drive toward the house. Rounding the last curve, she could see through the stand of red spruce that an extra car was parked behind their van, blocking the way. Not very neighborly, she thought. Then she noticed the license plates. Quebec, not a neighbor. She quickly surveyed the yard, then throttled back, turned off from the drive, and pulled into the trees. Earlier, when she left to run over to talk with the people at Gaspereau Vineyards, Len had been out with the kids in the play yard. Now there was no sign of them.

Ever since their night visitors, Kat had been on hyper alert. With time, Len had shrugged it off and had begun to tease her about worrying too much. No such thing as worrying too much, she thought, not when you had little ones and not when men with guns show up in the middle of the night.

Once in the grove, Kat gently laid her bike down so its bright colors would be less obvious through the trees. She reversed her jacket to hide the magenta shell and made a wide detour to come in from the vineyard side of the grounds. Taking advantage of her short stature, she crouched and ran through the budding rows of grapevines. As she neared the house, she could hear voices, two men, then a sudden cry, a loud little-boy cry from Andre, followed by a shout from Len. Her every instinct screamed for her to run to their rescue, but she knew that could be a terrible mistake.

Taking advantage of the distraction of Andre's crying, who was now joined in chorus by his little sister, Kat did a tuck-and-run straight for the back porch and stepped carefully, trying to avoid the creaky boards still in need of replacement, keeping as close to the wall of the house as possible. She could now clearly hear a man's voice with a foreign accent.

"We understand the drive was a bust. We were told it was encrypted, then it turns out to have been carefully curated, with anything of possible importance permanently deleted and the free space on the disk wiped so it couldn't be recovered. You jerked them around good. Now, tell us where you have the real files and we'll leave you and your sweet family alone."

"That's what your buddies said." It was Len. "And here you are."

"Buddies? Look just give us what we want."

"I don't know what you want."

"Sure you do. You and your enterprising little wife helped crack the gas pipeline attack. That's what we want: the records, the logs, the source code, whatever. Just give it to us and we'll be gone. Okay?"

"I told you, we don't have anything else. Smitty . . ."

"Who is this Smitty?"

"Just a guy."

"Look, we got all day. We don't want to hurt you or your kids, but we aren't leaving until we get what we came for."

On the porch, Kat winced at the sound of a hard punch inside. She thought about retreating and dialing 9-1-1, but it would take time for the police to get out this far and there were too many ways for things to go badly. What do I have, she thought. Len's pistol was stashed on the plate rail by the front door. Could she get to it without them knowing? Not without a distraction. She needed tools, weapons.

Kat tiptoed off the back porch and forced herself to walk away from the house where her husband and two young children were being held at gunpoint. She headed for the barn where Len kept all their construction tools. Something. There'll be something there I can use.

She returned to the house in a few minutes shouldering her weapon of choice. She had thought about the nail gun, but it would be short range, not very accurate, and of little use against any decent handgun. She had thought of using what she carried directly on the two gunmen, but had rejected the idea. She wasn't even sure it would work on people, but she had another plan. She just had to trust that Len would have the right instincts when the moment came.

She rounded the corner to the front of the house and looked up through the open bathroom window. She had to move around to get the angle right. By standing on tiptoes, she could just see through into the hallway at the top of the stairs. She spotted her target, the white disk on the ceiling with its reassuring little green LED glowing. How glad she was that they had been prudent in upgrading the old wood frame house when they had expanded the winery.

She opened the legs on the tripod, sighted, and turned on the laser level, now angled acutely upward to shine through the window and onto the ceiling in the hallway. She could see she was a little off target. She gently tapped until the bright spot fell right where she wanted it. Then she headed for the front porch and waited.

Minutes passed. Maybe the beam wasn't powerful enough.

After all, it had to be eye-safe for use at a work site. She was almost ready to give up and fall back on her riskier plan B when the ear-splitting screech of the fire alarm started. She scrambled onto the porch, opened the door, and leapt to grab the gun from the plate rail. In the living room, Andre was screaming with his hands over his ears as the two men looked around, trying to figure out what was happening. The taller of the two spotted her in the front hall just as the sprinkler system finally cut in. Blinded by the downpour, he fired wildly in her direction.

"Go, Len!" she screamed as she calmly took aim and squeezed the trigger. She wasn't prepared for the recoil from the .38 police special, but her aim was true and the man dropped, exposing his partner to her line of fire. At the same time, Len scooped up Simone and Andre, one under each arm, and darted for the kitchen.

Before she could get her aim and fire again, the man fired at her. This time, the shot didn't go wild. She knew she'd been hit, but it didn't hurt as she had always expected it would. It made her think of times when she had wiped out on her bike and the moments before the hot pain of road rash cut in. She dropped to the floor just before he fired again. As the red began to spread from her shoulder, she stretched out and struggled to restore her aim. Her shot came a fraction of a second ahead of his. She didn't know if she had been hit again, but she kept aiming and squeezing the trigger until the last of her six rounds had been fired. She watched as water from the sprinkler system spread blood over the living room carpet.

Above the hiss of falling water and the continued pulsing scream of the alarm, she called out. "Are you okay, Len?"

"Yes. You?"

"Mostly. You got the kids?"

"They're here, safe. Scared. Let's get out of here."

"There's no place to go. The fire brigade will be here any minute. And the police. We can't run." She tried to push herself up to check the damages and get to the kitchen, but her arm wouldn't work. "I think you better help me. Make sure those two are . . . taken care of first. I hear the sirens. What's going to happen to us when they arrive?"

"I don't know." he said, as he stepped carefully around the two bodies. "You're the Canadian. You tell me." He reached down to help her stand.

Chapter 26

PUSHING PAST THE GUARD at the door, Barbara stormed into Talpa's office and pounded on his desk. "You fucking lying monster. Now you have gone too far. How the hell do you sleep at night, the way you work."

"What in hell are you talking about, Barbara?"

"The Canadians. Those two kids, Kat and Len, and their babies. You sic'd your goons on them, threatened to kill them, terrified their kids. And now they're in jail, facing multiple charges. Illegal possession of firearms, murder, accessory to murder. Their kids have been taken away from them, put in protective foster care. How could you? Didn't you get enough from the laptop drive? What does it take?"

Talpa's expression was unreadable. "I have no idea what you are talking about."

"I told you what I'm talking about. An old friend at the Bureau who works with Canadian authorities called me. She knew I had been on that West Virginia case with those two. She was wondering if I had any leads, any guesses as to what's going on and who's behind it."

"And you said what to her?"

"I told her I'd look into it. Now I am looking into it, looking straight into your ugly lying face. I don't know who you are, and I don't know why I ever tagged along with Arkady on this crazy-ass secret project. I don't know about social system modeling or Wolfram code or open-source intelligence, but I know the bad guys when I see them, and I see one of them right in front of me. I'm out. And as soon as I tell Arkady about this, I'm sure he'll be out, too. His brother, I don't know about. Let's just say Dima's sense of morality may be quite different from ours."

Talpa sat in silence and waited. "Are you through?"

"Oh, I'm through. And on my way as fast as I can pack my bags. And I certainly intend to get back in touch with my friend at the Bureau."

"You can't leave, not like this. With what you know, the Israelis would never allow it. So calm down. Think. And listen to me. Have a seat."

"I'll stand, thank you. It reminds me of your moral inferiority."

"Whatever. Anyway, I was telling the truth when I said I didn't know what you are talking about. You and the Pohl brothers are the only ones I sent after those two. Somebody else is involved. I'll put people right on it, and we'll get to the bottom of it. And, I'll go one better, because, whatever happened, I know people in Canadian intelligence. I've worked with people at CSIS. I can maybe get this thing with those two straightened out."

"Is there anyone you haven't worked with?"

"Lots. I'm very selective about my clientele. You don't have to believe it, but I have a fine-tuned sense of morality. Why do you think I helped neuter HaVered?"

"I figure it's because they were after you, and you figured that the only way to keep your own ass safe was to take them out."

"You're right, they were after me, but only because I was after them first. They had finally gone too far. I knew it was time to pull the plug, and they knew my sentiments."

"Pull the plug? A convenient metaphor in these times, but usually it implies that someone in the first place put the plug in."

"Hmm, perhaps. At any rate, let's get the Canadians out of jail and back with their kids, okay? I can get things started on that right away. Meanwhile, chill. And don't do anything rash that could bring down lightning bolts on your parade, if you get the reference."

She stood, blinking, unsure what to believe and uncertain about what to do next.

≈ ≈ ≈

Talpa waited until he was back in his room. He turned on the shower and left the bathroom door open before undressing. Standing behind the door, he pressed firmly on one of the bolt heads on his left thigh, holding it until he felt the faint click. He opened the panel and extracted the satellite phone from its compartment. Israeli intelligence were the best, and Unit 8200 was the best of the best, but he was Richard Talpa. They had no idea who they were dealing with or how far he could go. He powered up the phone, thumb-typed an encrypted text message, held the phone out the window to send it, and powered down immediately. Even if they were monitoring him—and they probably were—the activity would be nothing but noise on an unexpected frequency. As he had said to Barbara, he had worked with many intelligence agencies—or they had worked with him. There was always an alternative channel when one was blocked.

He knew he would have to hustle to get Barbara and Arkady to trust him again, but he had already set the wheels turning on that. The tough one would be figuring out who had targeted the Canadians and why. It was implausible that someone else had independently figured out what they had, so it had to be a leak. That seemed almost laughable considering their current circumstances, leaving only the Turkish connection by way of Parsons. But did Parsons know? What had he given the Turks? What were they after?

It was time to tug at some old ties. But how? From here inside, it would be nearly impossible to work any sustained side operation. He knew he was good, but so were the Israelis. No, the only way to pull this off would be right out in the open, right under everyone's noses.

He would use the evening to work out the details. In the morning, he would tell the team that he had a connection inside Turkish intelligence who might prove useful. He could picture her in Nice, her dark beauty, her poise, and her ability to dissemble. She had used him, of course, and disguised well her contempt for him physically. Did she still have the chess set? Probably. It would reinforce her sense of superiority.

"Time to renew our acquaintance, Bedia Tekın," he whispered to the mirror covered in steam. "And time to turn off this bloody shower before it shorts out all my electronics." He restored the satellite phone to its hidden compartment next to another tool of his trade.

Chapter 27

THEY HAD BEEN LOVERS before they had been partners, and now Ismail was her boss, her superior, not only at the agency but on Knight's Move, the project within the project, the umbra at the shadowy core. The general did not look up when she entered his office and sat in the upholstered chair across from him.

"So, Bedia, you couldn't string him along until we were finished?" He finally looked at her, raising one eyebrow. "Now we have the lover, rejected by the Oriental beauty, throwing himself from a balcony."

"If that's what you believe, Ismail. Or if that's the story you want believed. We both knew he was a dangerous and unstable commodity. We knew that from the beginning."

He tapped on the thin stack of folders at his side. "But he brought us useful goods and fresh ideas about how to best use them."

"He was a fanatic who became a patriot for the sole reason of acting out his fanatical fantasies. For him, it was about revenge and little more."

"But you were charmed by him, Bedia, admit it—this handsome exotic man with his, as you say, fanatical fantasies. You let yourself be played. Is it possible that your judgment is clouding over—or that you are perhaps finally becoming a romantic in your middle age?"

"I was a romantic when you knew me at university. Then I grew up. Since then, I prefer to be useful. And alone. I was not the one under the spell of his charm. I still cannot believe you ordered our fighters to shoot down a civilian aircraft at his request. It was insane. The international repercussions would have been—"

"Would have been minimal," he said, interrupting, "as they were, in fact. I ordered no such thing, not at his behest nor at anyone else's. You think I'm that foolish? Or senile? The pilots were told to fake an attack, to engage but never fire. I wanted to secure the allegiance of our 'fearless fighter' and to put our adversaries on notice. Along the way, we learned a great deal. We learned about their persistence and their determination to deliver something to the Israelis. And eventually, we were able to track our travelers' dog-legged journey back to a source and a reason."

He smiled in grim triumph. "And it seems your mixed-race lover was not completely forthcoming after all. There appear to be more files, no doubt vital, that the Israelis thought worth such a high price."

"A high price, yes. We lost two agents in a clumsy attempt to get at those same files."

"One agent. The other is in intensive care in Halifax. Of course, we shall have to lose him, too. Pity. Eyman was a good man. I went through training with his father. However, neither he nor his father ever had what I had. And now, we must let him go. We can hardly risk any word or omission on his part tipping our hand, not at this point, what with the action drawing attention that will be hard to deflect or smother."

"You are a cold-hearted jackal, Ismael."

"And you are not? We are two of a kind. Perhaps we should have married when we thought that looked like a good idea."

"It never looked like a good idea to me," she said, standing up and adjusting her scarf. "I prefer to sleep at night. Married or not, had you ever perceived me as a threat, you would have eliminated me without so much as a tittle of remorse."

"More than a tittle, my Bedia. I thought you were good in bed, as I imagine you still are today."

She tilted her head way back in a resounding Turkish no. "Imagine away, my dreaming general. Right now, we have an operation to complete, and with Yilmaz gone, we need all the resources we can get. Without official sanction, we are short-handed and short of lira."

"When we are successful, that will be remedied, and we will be the heroes of the Republic and the entire Islamic world."

"Just what I have always wanted," she said as she opened the door and let herself out of his office.

The lieutenant standing outside the office looked in. General Arslan gave him an angled shake of the head, urging him to follow her.

≈ ≈ ≈

The next team meeting was nearly over when Bedia once again used her quietly commanding voice to get everyone's attention. "We should target one of the Arab states, otherwise soon it will be suspicious that Israel has been the only nation in the Middle East to suffer the blackouts. We don't want the intelligence services to turn their attentions away from Russia or from the Americans and begin poking around too much in the Mediterranean for sources."

The general looked unconvinced. "Such a diversion could be smart, but these are our friends."

"Some more than others. We probably should pick a target that fits the America versus Russia narrative. Or at least that keeps everyone guessing and looking elsewhere."

Ismael stroked his chin, feigning deep thought. "And which ally who is not an ally would you suggest, Bedia?"

"Iran, perhaps. I would make it costly and extensive enough that it will help ensure that in the aftermath they are poor contenders to fill an ensuing power vacuum."

"I would think Syria might be a better target. They will suffer more. Russia will blame the Americans for attacking a proxy state. The Arab world will start to blame Israel. It will be a wonderful free-for-all."

Bedia nodded in deference, knowing that he had played into her hand by opposing her. "Yes, a wonderful free-for-all. I'm persuaded." As she was gathering her things and preparing to head for her own office, a text message arrived, unencrypted, on her personal phone. In the hallway, she managed a quick glance at the few words contrived to resemble spam:

> Chess? Click on the link and select blue or white:
> playnice.ly/g51fsx99/

It could not have been spelled out more plainly. She felt her heart skip. Analytical as always, she wondered whether her reaction was more out of fear or anticipation. Neither, she concluded, it was excitement. If Richard Talpa was playing, the match was suddenly far more interesting and engaging than she had thought before. One text had changed the name of the game for her. It was more complicated, which she liked, but, coming after the exchange with Ismail, it also got her thinking about her own exit plans.

Chapter 28

Be'er Sheva, Israel

THE TEAM IN THE PIT watched as the software mashup finished its trace of the gimmicked text message, drawing a jagged line from the middle of the Negev to the middle of Turkey. Marwa pointed in triumph. "Now we know. Your contact got the message. He's in Ankara."

"She's in Ankara. It's Bedia Tekın," Talpa said. "Can we identify the nearest cell tower?"

Roni grinned. "Can we light candles for Shabbat?" She typed a command and a city map appeared onscreen, with a blue circle gradually contracting to a small area.

Talpa pretended to be indifferent. "Çankaya, the Ulus quarter. I know it. Looks like Tekın may have actually taken the message inside the National Intelligence campus itself. And she's still using the same old personal cell number. I always suspected she was a romantic at heart." He looked around at the curious faces. "I told you, I knew her. We were working Paris at the same time." And we played in Nice, he thought, that too.

Marwa did a quick Google search for a picture. "Don't bother," he said. "Tekın is a spy, after all. But she should be in the Aman files."

"I don't have access," Marwa said.

Bini typed a query with two-finger speed. "There she is.

182

Not bad." Marwa gave him a look.

"That's an old photo," Talpa said. "Today? Who knows."

Dima leaned in. "I do. She's still a looker. And still fast on her feet. Parsons was with her when I first got on his trail. That suggests she is definitely connected with whatever is going on over there."

"Now what?" Roni asked.

"Now we wait," Talpa said, "see if she takes the bait."

"How about we track her phone," Roni added.

"You can do that?"

"Do we eat matzohs on Passover?" She typed a fresh command line, backspaced over part of it, retyped, and hit enter. "Erp. I can't hack her GPS—it seems to be turned off—but we can use cell tower triangulation to keep rough track of her whereabouts. As long as the phone is on." As she was typing, a flashing message appeared in the upper right corner of the screen. "Damn. It's almost as if she's listening. The network is no longer getting handshaking. She must have turned off the phone."

"Of course she did. She's no dummy. She would assume we got her. But by turning off her phone, she has sent me a message without sending a message that could be intercepted. I'm going to have to approach her in person."

Bini gave him a look of deep skepticism. "I don't think you should do that, Talpa. Frankly, I don't think you can. Think about it. You are a rather slow-moving target that can be spotted from miles away."

"We need somebody to try and reach her."

Dima stood up. "I know her and where she hangs out. I mean, besides at Turkish Intelligence. I'm the one who should go. I'm not much good here, anyway. I'm not in the same league as the rest of you. But, I do speak Turkish."

"Why didn't you say so," Roni said. "We've been waiting for our Turkish expert to show up from Tel Aviv. They have an intensive program in Arabic languages for new recruits with an aptitude."

Dima sneered. "Turkish is not an Arabic language."

"Well, Middle Eastern."

"The Turks consider themselves part of Europe."

"Whatever. But—"

"But I'm the obvious candidate to go instead of Talpa here. I slipped into Turkey unnoticed before; I can do it again. We don't have a lot of time. The latest news is that Syria is now suddenly without power, and we have no idea what's going on. That's your job, here. Figure it out. I've got my job. I'm going to Ankara to be the Professor's RemSAAR."

Roni scowled up at him. "RemSAAR?"

"Remote Semi-Autonomous Ambulatory Robot."

"Is that what it's called?"

"How should I know? Not my area of expertise. I just made it up. Making stuff up is my expertise."

Arkady's laugh was forced. "You were always good at that, big brother. One of these days some of your improvs are going to come back to haunt you."

"One of these days, wolf cub, we'll all be haunted. Or haunting. For now, I'm off to pack." He started for the door, then stopped and faced Talpa. "I'll need some tools. I assume that either you can supply them or can get the great powers of Unit 8200 to cough up."

"Sure. Make a list. I'll see what I can do."

"You make the list. I'm going to be the robotic you, the avatar of the cyborg."

Bini slapped Talpa on the back. "That's you Professor, our resident cyborg."

≈ ≈ ≈

Talpa handed Dima the small khaki-green duffle.

Dima hefted it. "You didn't get everything."

"No, not everything, but it should be enough, although how you are going to get all that into the country is anybody's guess."

"I'm resourceful. You know that. And you know enough not to ask how I do my job."

"Or even sometimes what your job is."

"Smart man." Dima stared past Talpa. "I keep thinking about us. We go a lot further back than most of these kids around here realize."

"And we'll keep it that way."

Dima took an extra deep breath and expelled it in a puff. "Ever want to get out? Ever make any exit plans?"

"All the time. All the time. To both questions. Dreams are that, though: just dreams. Be careful, Dima."

"You, too. I don't think even you have everything figured out." He strode to the door, then stopped with a hand on the doorjamb. "Thanks for the briefing about Bedia. And thanks for the trust."

"Trust is easy. In our world, it's always counterfeit currency. It's like ante in poker. I meet your trust with mine, because we have no choice about it most of the time. We just put it in the pot, even when it's fake."

"Fuck, you are something else, Talpa. And people call me the philosophical one."

"You are. Me? As you say, I'm something else."

Chapter 29

As she turned the corner into the *pazar*, Bedia sensed she was being followed. She had been expecting it, but she also knew it couldn't possibly be Talpa. This man was playing her, letting her know she had a tail but never giving her more than a fleeting glimpse and never showing his face. After the text message, it had to be someone sent by Talpa. Was the man ever going to make his move? Should she take the initiative? She wove her way among shoppers and racks of dresses and shirts. She took the opportunity to look over her shoulder, more boldly than usual, and collided with the man walking in front of her. "*Affedersiniz, çok özür dilerim,*" she said. "I'm so sorry."

"You should be sorry," he said in Turkish. "Ramming into people on the street, like a chess piece taking out an opponent."

"You are . . .?"

"Blue. And you are white. Your king is in check."

"The game isn't over. There are still many pieces on the board." She pretended to ignore him and to be interested in the head scarves draped over a small handcart.

"But the pieces are scattered and their strategic value is, shall we say, hard to calculate. The Mole sends his love, by the way. Would you like to finish the game? Do you have a set?"

"In my apartment. It's just—"

"Down the block and around the corner. Or we can duck through this next store and come out in an intersecting alleyway."

"You seem to know the neighborhood very well," she said, a little surprised.

"Only the neighbors I've met."

"Would that include a certain fearless fighter?"

Dima didn't answer.

"We have a saying. Silence speaks with the clearest voice. Now I understand what happened."

"My turn to be sorry. It was not my intention at the time."

"Nor mine, if we are still talking about fearless fighters. Yet, I was ready to end it much the same way. A little different timing, a few more words—or fewer—and it would have been me pleading to you that it was not my intention. It's the game we play, Mister . . ."

"Pohl, Dmitry."

"Of course. I'm impressed. Twice now you slipped in without our notice. Only after you are gone do we know we had a visitor. Should I be flattered? Or frightened?"

"I wouldn't know. For the present, I am the alter ego of Richard Talpa, who thinks you know him well."

Her fingers stopped in their exploration of a hand-woven headscarf. "What does he want?"

"We should get off the street before our conversation goes too far."

"This is my neighborhood, in my city. I know every face, veiled or not." If it were not strictly true, it was at least in the vicinity. "If I were being followed, I would know. But there is no reason to be followed. I am trusted."

"All trust is manufactured."

"You do sound like Rick. Are you really his alter ego?"

187

"If not, the closest he'll ever come to it. I've known him more years than I care to count."

"Likewise. How is he?"

"So, you ask the question, the key question that shows interest. And the answer is . . . Is what? I don't know. No one but Talpa knows how he is. He's still around, which is an accomplishment in itself. He has new legs. Bionic, amazing. He wants to know how you are. Maybe he wants to ask you for help."

"So, after all these years, he thinks I would become an asset to the ever elusive Mole. I don't think so."

"I don't think so, either. I got the impression he was thinking of something more . . . more involved. More like a partnership."

"Then he's as crazy as ever."

Dima nodded assent.

"You're blunt, even when you're short on words."

Dima nodded again.

"You know, even though your Turkish is good enough for no one to take notice, your western-style nods give you away. I think we better do as you suggested and go to my apartment."

≈ ≈ ≈

It was well into the small hours of the morning and they were still talking, each still jockeying for position, playing for information, even as the conversation became more real, more personal.

"I don't know, but I think this is as far as we should go," she said suddenly. "I'm not used to this. I mean the hour. And I rarely drink. I'm Muslim."

"A Muslim who knows and appreciates French wine, and keeps a well-stocked cabinet. Do you also know the wines of the New World?"

"If you mean the over-priced, over-oaked wines of California, no thank you." She took another sip.

"No, I was not thinking of North America, but of the other America, where the wines are both more interesting and more affordable. You know, I own—once owned—a winery myself. In Brazil. We made some wonderful wines in a refreshing, fruit-forward style."

"Like the new wave of the younger Californians."

"No, like the Brazilians. We—"

She interrupted him by placing a finger to his lips. "Enough. Enough for tonight."

"I'll go."

"No. At this hour, if you are noticed, it would not be good for either of us. You will have to stay the night." Before he could say anything, she pointed toward the couch. "There. Make yourself at home. As you can. But I'm sure you've had experience to draw on." She leaned over and kissed him, a light, chaste kiss on the lips. "Good night. The morning sun this time of year can be harsh, more than you might expect, but it clears the head and puts things in perspective." She left him looking at the couch, which was a foot too short for him.

≈ ≈ ≈

He awoke to a snapped command. "Now," she said, "before people fill the alleyway but with the main streets already crowded. Go."

He was awake and alert the moment he stood. As he reached for his jacket she stopped his hand. "Tonight, after work, in the *pazar* in the next street over. Find me there, not here. We have unfinished business, a dangling conversation, as the Americans say." She gave his hand a squeeze. "Count thirty after I leave, then go."

And then she was gone, leaving Dima more confused than

he had ever been. By the evening, he would have to report in, and he still had no idea what he would report. Perhaps, "Contact made. Details later." There was always a way to say something while saying nothing. Wait and see, he told himself, wait and see. And remember who you are and why you are here.

"Who am I?" he said, as he finished counting to himself and ducked out the door. A piebald cat looked up at him with sleepy eyes as he hurried down the outside steps from the second floor.

≈ ≈ ≈

The second night, they sat on pillows on the floor and talked about childhood. The very wariness that linked them gave the conversation its forward momentum. "I grew up in privilege," she said, "with a father who told me I was beautiful and brilliant and told my mother she had become an ugly and stupid sow. He was a professor at the Middle East Technical University here in Ankara, where I later matriculated." She savored another swallow of the wine she had spent her lunch hour looking for. It was an Argentine Torrontés that Dima admitted was quite good, especially considering that it was the only South American wine she was able to find in the city. "By the time I was studying at the university, he had been purged—too liberal, too outspoken with his criticism of the government. I was lucky."

"How so?"

"Had he still been teaching there, I would have killed him. He was the one who introduced me to sex, taught me that sex was something to be endured, something to be used, a means to an end. Had I killed him, I never would have gotten into this work, which he helped make possible."

Dima considered responding with sympathy, but thought better of it. Sympathy was another devalued currency, and it could be taken as a sign of weakness. Instead, he went for the heart. "You like it, this using your power."

She looked pleased. "Yes. I do. Surely you understand how women are treated in this part of the world. I live alone, needing no man, and do work I love, for which I am well paid, even if not so well as if I had a penis. It's a good life." She paused, swirled the wine in her glass, and inhaled. "Such flowers, such spice. You rarely get anything like this from France—maybe never."

"There was an unspoken 'but' after the good life bit."

"You have an ear for the unspoken."

"As do you. It's a prerequisite for what we do. So, what is the 'but' of your good life?"

"English is fun for puns and plays on words. I had forgotten. But. The butt. Okay. It is all the rest, everything else, the things I don't have and never will. In that, I am no different from anyone else. We choose A and then B is gone, and thereafter we long for B. All of life is this way."

"True, but there are specifics within those lost universes that each of us regrets."

"Okay, you brought it up, so you go first. What is it you long for?"

Dima stared at her, licking his lips, trying not to speak and yet trying to force the words to his tongue. "Stability. Comfort, maybe. Some semblance of security—though who really ever has that?" He laughed again. "Talk about illusions!"

"Easy answers, those. What about the hard ones?"

"Is this some kind of recruitment test or an audition for a role in an art film?"

She looked hurt. "I . . . I was serious."

"I know. And . . . I was scared. Okay, I'll say it: someone. That's what I want. I won't even call it love." He looked upward to stare at the ceiling. "And I almost cannot believe I'm saying this. But, yes. Some other person with whom I can just be who I am. My younger brother comes closest to that, I suppose, but he has his own life, with its own choices, and even there, we both have to be guarded, at least to some degree. I just want someone, sometime, somewhere to . . . to just be, without being always on stage, always in role, always making it up as I go along. There, I've said it. You are good, very skilled—no, amazing—and I am beginning to see what it was that might have ensnared Talpa. You wrangled the secret out of me, and now, as they say in the films, I shall have to kill you." He forced a laugh, then regretted being so flippant. "In truth," he said just above a whisper. "I keep looking for an exit sign."

Bedia was not laughing. There were tears in her eyes, and she turned to the side, away from him. Her voiced cracked when she forced the words out. "Also me."

They sat side-by-side, rocking slightly, for several minutes without speaking, both lost in their own private worlds.

He broke the silence. "There's no exit for people like us. I thought I had it all worked out, I had plans, exit plans. You know what they say in the military about plans, how everything can go completely according to plan right up until the fighting starts. Well, the fighting started—again—and my plans got shredded. And here I am, still looking for the next move in the game, ready to sacrifice a bishop to save my queen."

"What does that mean?"

"How the hell should I know. It's not my specialty." He chuckled and let himself fall over with his head in her lap. She stroked his hair and bent over to gently kiss his ear. He let his hand reach up under her dress.

"No," she said. "It would not be what you think it would be, not for me. Can we just hold each other? I . . . I've never done that before."

"Neither have I. I guess we're both virgins . . . of a sort."

≈ ≈ ≈

It was only one night, and a night with almost no further words, but it was enough to convince Dima to change course. Meeting at her apartment had been a risk he would not normally have taken, but it was a risk that would pay off—for both of them. There is always another way forward, he reminded himself. There is always another way.

Perhaps it was all an act, her manipulating him. He didn't know. He wasn't even certain about himself, how much was real, how much the game played so long and well that it had become second nature. But it almost didn't matter at this point, because either way, he could see the path ahead.

Chapter 30

TALPA WAS FURIOUS. He paced his office with all the tense energy he could manage through his prosthetic legs. "I trusted him, and now he wants us to help exfiltrate the target, bring her here. That's crazy. What the fuck good is she here? We need somebody there, on the inside. Fuck."

General Barg was down from Tel Aviv, trying to find out in person why the blackouts were continuing and why nothing definitive was coming out of Operation Floodlight. He was losing his patience with Talpa and the way the entire operation was going. "I don't understand this whole distraction with the Turks. I thought we were dealing with the Russians and the Americans, trying to dodge their bullets and get them to chill out."

"We are, but that means we have to be ready to adapt, change course as needed. The road now leads to Ankara."

"You came to us, Talpa. You said you had an inside track to head this off, reminding us of how big a stake we had in this silly faceoff between presidents with outsized egos."

"Well, you do. Don't you read your own damn PR? You're the Startup Nation. No economy in the world is more dependent on the internet infrastructure than yours. And none is more vulnerable to attack if you run out of power."

"Fine words, great arguments, but what have you delivered? A bubble chart that only you seem to understand and a request—a demand—for help in exfiltrating a Turkish national and a renegade ex-Mossad agent of uncertain loyalties."

"Dmitry Pohl's loyalty to Israel is beyond question. If you look at what he has done for the—"

"What about you, your loyalties?" the general interrupted. "I don't even know why the hell you are here or why certain old guard in the intelligence community, even older than me, are willing to trust you. I thought I knew who you are, now I don't even know what you are. What the fuck are you doing here?"

Talpa bristled but tried to contain his temper. "You have no idea . . ."

"You bet your sweet ass I have no idea. So why don't you tell me."

"One thing at a time. Bedia Tekın is important because she has intimate knowledge of what the Turks are up to in connection with the blackout battles. She's already been vetted by Pohl. It's not just the Russians and the Americans. Turkey—or some of the Turks, maybe independent operatives—well, they have been pulling levers. We don't know exactly which levers or how, but Tekın does. We need to get her here to fully debrief her. Unless Mossad has some deep-cover assets in Ankara they are not owning up to, she's our only 'in' at this point."

"What about this talk going around that your Dmitry has a thing for her?"

"Just talk. Inevitable. I know Dima. He's the consummate professional, all business all the way."

Barg narrowed his eyes. "You better be right, because I'm going to have to put my ass on the line for you. I want to keep this strictly in-house, which means getting a field team from our own combat intelligence assigned to this op. I've listened to you before, Richard, and I've been glad I did, but this time I don't know, I don't really know."

≈ ≈ ≈

Except for his pug nose, freckles, and boyish good looks, Bradley Pomerantz looked the part of a special forces commando. An American who had played football in high school and made *aliyah* as a teenager after his prominent parents split in a spectacularly public divorce, he had distinguished himself in the IDF as a Lone Soldier who was both brainy and physically tough-as-nails. He now led one of the small combat intelligence teams of Unit 8200. "Sir," he said to General Shapiro, "I don't think you understand the parameters. Ankara is not on the coast; it's in the middle of the fuckin' country. We can't just chopper in. An amphibious approach is out. It's over 300 kilometers from the nearest point on the Mediterranean. It's actually closer to the Black Sea, but how the hell are we going to come in from there?"

Shapiro glared at him. "Mossad extracted people from Rome. That's not exactly a port city."

"We're not exactly Mossad, either. No, wait. I didn't mean that the way it sounded. I'm just saying this is something different, not the sort of forward SIGINT we are usually involved in. It's going to take a lot of legwork and a lot of planning. We can't just charge into Turkey and grab this woman. If it was someplace like Cyprus, then we would have better options."

Talpa perked up at that. "Cyprus? You could pull this off from Cyprus?"

"Yeah, for sure. I was just saying. Cyprus has a lot of unwatched coastline, lots of Israeli tourists, and fairly lax borders. I think we could find a way."

"Then stop thinking and start finding. Assume the subjects are in Cyprus, in the Turkish-controlled north. We'll worry about exactly where as we get closer to the go date."

"When is that, sir."

"Oh, cut it out. Don't 'sir' me. I'm a civilian."

"But when is the go date?"

"Next Friday."

"Shit."

Chapter 31

ISMAIL ARSLAN WAITED in the bar, nursing his tall glass of orange juice. Part of him was flattered, even as the bulk of him was deeply suspicious. Bedia had a reputation, but to the best of his knowledge, she had never messed around within the service. The brief affair in their youth had come before either of them joined the organization. Her involvements since had always been on assignment—or instrumental. And now, over the course of several days, he had picked up signals from her, ambiguous at first, but progressively clearer. The warming trend was a surprising turn after their recent argument over the black Turk. He assumed it was a ploy of some sort but was confident in his own ability to outplay her—and get some good sex on the side.

For Ismail, she would not be the first, but Bedia Tekın was special. She was classy and intelligent, with some potential for more than a weekend. The others had been dalliance, breaks from the tedium of his marriage to a wife who had grown fat and disinterested in equal measure to his own increasing weight and waning interest. When he told her he had to spend the weekend on a military exercise in Cyprus, she might not have believed him, but she did not seem to care. To her it would also be respite. It would mean she did not have to put up with his restless prowling around the house for another tense and boring weekend. He had no idea what she would do with herself, but he, too, no longer cared.

Bedia had told him to trust her to make the arrangements. Within the intelligence community, trust was a cheap and malleable word, but he also had no interest in arranging hotels or flights. That was work for women. Bedia was good at such things, at details. She was smart but not threatening. She was easy on the eyes. And if her reputation was accurate, she was a virtuoso in the bedroom, which could not have been said of their fumbling affair in the beginning. All in all, this long weekend in Cyprus was looking better and better. Maybe he would even let himself drink something stronger than fruit juice.

≈ ≈ ≈

With the last sliver of moon not yet risen and only scattered onshore lights to guide them, Pomerantz and his team used their night-vision goggles for the long but uneventful paddle from the Greek-flagged small freighter owned by a shell corporation. They beached their rubber boats two hours after dusk at the landing zone, a stretch of gravelly sand beach on the southern edge of Cape Greco, its name made ironic by now being within the Turkish controlled sector. Dmitry Pohl was supposed to rendezvous with them there, but Pohl was a no show. The team's orders were to give priority to getting the woman out. If necessary, Pohl was to be left behind, on his own.

The team pulled their boats ashore and hid them in the brush. After a ten minute wait, they prepared to set out along the shoreline toward the hotel, which was déclassé enough not to be busy this time of year. It had been chosen for its quiet isolation and proximity to the landing beach which, in turn, offered straightforward access by sea from Israel.

Pomerantz turned to his team: six of his regular men plus

one woman, a young soldier on temporary assignment from Aman headquarters. She was the only one among them who spoke Turkish. She had completed combat training but not yet advanced tactical, and she was a recent graduate of an intensive language program within Aman based on the Israeli-developed *ulpan* immersion model. Pomerantz did not like having to take along someone so green, but there seemed to be a current shortage of translators, particularly for Turkish.

"Okay, you all know the drill. And you"—he pointed to the translator—"you are behind me, never in front, and you follow my orders. No improvising."

The team advanced toward the west, doing their best to dodge floodlit stretches of beach adjacent to the resort between them and the hotel. They were within sight of the hotel, when a man walking the beach spotted movement in the shadows and challenged them.

"What did he say?" Pomerantz whispered to his translator.

"Uh, like, who is there, what are we doing here. This is, uh, private property," she whispered in his ear. "I'll talk with him." Before he could stop her, she stood up and started to cross the beach toward the man. She was wearing civilian garb intended to help her pass as a young Turkish woman, a student. She strolled casually toward the Turk. "Who are you?" he said.

"Asli. At the hotel, I stay with my parents." Trying to keep from shaking, she drew on as much vocabulary as she could muster under the pressure of the moment, sticking to the present tense and hoping that her pronunciation would pass. "It is warm. My Yusef and I, we walk."

"Why are you talking this way?"

"This way?"

"Like you were—what do they say these days? Are you deficient or something?"

Suddenly inspired, she feigned embarrassment. "My father says I am stupid girl. Pretty but stupid."

The man tried to look past her into the gloom near the water. "Where is this Yusef? And what is a young girl doing out with a boy and no one to chaperone?"

Out of the darkness up the beach, a man wearing a fisherman's cap and a heavy blue-black sweater marched toward them. "And who are you to be bothering my daughter?" he said. "Now move on, and leave her and Yusef alone. Yusef is her brother, but it's none of your business."

There was a silent stare-down for a long moment as the two men considered their options. Finally, as the Turk walked away from the beach muttering insults in Turkish, the newcomer whispered in Hebrew. "Where are the others?"

"Who are you? Wait, I mean, 'Has the moon risen yet? I cannot tell.'"

"It has, behind the clouds," he answered.

"Now that we've settled the passphrase, where were you? You were supposed to be at the landing zone."

"I was. Watching, keeping an eye on things. Good thing. Now, who are you and where are the others?"

"They're hiding, down at the water's edge. And I'm their translator, Shoshana Markham, military intelligence."

"Markham? Not Bini Markham's kid sister, Shoshi?"

"Yeah, that's me. How do you know Bini?"

"For another time. I don't know what the hell you're doing on this detail, but let's collect the package and get out of here."

She signaled to the team that it was safe to come up.

Pomerantz glared at her. "I thought I told you to keep behind me."

"How the fuck am I supposed to do my job, pretending to be a Turk, while I'm hiding behind a man dressed all in black and wearing a balaclava. Think about it. Now let's get this done. The target is on the ground floor of the new wing. I'll go in first and signal when it's clear for you to come in. If I don't signal, you wait for me to come out with the subject."

Dima laughed. "She's a Markham, all right. You better listen to her, soldier, if you value your ass."

"I lead this team, and I'm in charge of the mission."

"And I outrank you. I set up this whole op. Now do your thing and let this soldier do hers, and we'll all get out of here in one piece."

Before Pomerantz could argue, Shoshi was off trudging through the sand toward the hotel. Inside, she located the room. A do-not-disturb tag hung on the door handle. It was an agreed-upon code that the woman was not alone in the room. As Shoshi started back down the hallway to signal for her team, a security guard rounded the corner. Shoshi, pretending to be a little tipsy, pulled a key card from the pocket of her jeans and waved it in the air. "I look for my room," she said speaking Turkish, "and . . . oh my, I think I am in the wrong hall."

"What room number are you looking for?"

"Uh, three something. No two. Oh, I don't know. I think I go to the front desk and ask them who I am. Uh, where I am."

The guard, not much older than Shoshi, smiled warmly. "I'll take you to reception."

"You don't have to do that. I can—" As the team stormed into the hallway from both ends at once, the guard reached for his handgun. Shoshi drew hers from under her loose top, but Pomerantz already had the red dot from the laser sight of his Tavor in the middle of the man's forehead and dropped him with a single shot. He held up a finger as everyone froze and listened to see if anybody might have heard the shot despite the custom-designed suppressor on the rifle.

"We're clear," he said. "Collect the package."

Two of his men positioned themselves out of sight on either side of the door while Shoshi inserted her doctored keycard into the slot. The lock winked red. She tried again. Same result. "They must have the lock turned on the inside," she said.

Pomerantz signaled and another commando stepped forward with a wedge-shaped tool the size of a walkie-talkie. He slipped the slim end into the card slot, then rocked a switch. A two-second rising whine was followed by a sharp crack of electricity as the tool shorted out the electronics in the lock. He twisted the door handle and pushed with the toe of his boot. The door swung open.

Bedia Tekın, dressed in jeans and a sweater jacket, stood facing them with a palm facing forward and the index finger of her other hand to her lips. Behind her on the bed, a naked, open-mouthed man with a belly like an exercise ball, lay snoring. Bedia motioned everybody out.

"Quickly," she said in the hall. "He's drugged, but he still might wake up."

Dima pointed to Pomerantz. "Go with him. Now." To Pomerantz he said, "I'll clean up and meet you at the landing zone. Go."

Shoshi and the commando assigned as sweep were the last ones out. They were almost to the exit when a second security guard rounded the corner at the other end of the corridor. He looked around, glanced at the body of his fellow guard, then drew his handgun. "*Dur!*" he called. "Stop!"

Dima dropped to a crouch and popped off a round as the guard fired toward the fleeing figures. Shoshi stumbled and the commando grabbed her, dragging her through the doorway. Dima's second round hit the guard in the chest, and he fell forward.

Dima looked around, scanning the carnage. "What a fucking mess. There is no way to clean this up to look like a robbery or kidnapping gone bad."

Awakened by the gunfire, the naked man staggered into the hallway, his belly bouncing. "Who the—" That was as far as he got before joining the two guards dead on the carpet.

Dima slammed through the exit and sprinted down the beach. He caught up with the team near where the boats were stashed. Pomerantz was supervising as one of his men wrapped a compression bandage on Shoshi's arm. He looked up at Dima. "This is what happens when we have to work with fucking amateurs."

Dima laughed to himself as he positioned his foot carefully. Pomerantz rose from his knees, turned to take a step toward the nearest boat, and face-planted in the sand. He stood again and wiped wet sand from his face as he pointed with menace toward Dima.

Dima's smile broadened. "What? Let's just get the fuck out of here before something else goes wrong. That's the problem of working with fucking amateurs."

Chapter 32

"SO WHERE THE HELL is she?" Talpa's voice hovered at the edge of shouting. "You sent word the package was collected."

Dima ignored the tone of voice and shrugged. "Mossad, I presume. We were met. They insisted on debriefing her. It's an interagency issue, now. Aman, Mossad. They're both claiming jurisdiction."

"And what are you claiming?"

"I have no claims to make. I was once with Mossad, so I am still of them. Now I am with Aman but not of them. And at the moment, I'm just telling you what happened. It was a cluster fuck from the moment your crew entered the hotel. Now the Turks will certainly know that somebody has targeted some of their key players, and it won't be that long before they have intelligence to guess who that somebody was."

"They were not my crew. It was Aman, 8200 wanting to show off their own little special forces team. In any case, the woman is ours. This was our operation. You know what Mossad means by debriefing. If they work on her first, we'll never get her onside, which we have to. You don't know this woman. Once she closes up, nothing is going to break through."

"I do know this woman, and I agree. At least she's not in the hands of domestic intelligence. I wouldn't want to see her after a Shinbet interrogation."

"They save the worst for the Palestinians, I'm told."

"Scant comfort. Do they distinguish between Palestinians and Turks? There must be some way we can intervene quickly, before we lose too much ground with her. I am telling you, she was absolutely ready to come over. Almost eager."

"Really?" Talpa's voice was finally back to its usual controlled growl. "I admit I'm surprised that she still . . . well . . ."

"Don't flatter yourself, Richard. You were just a stepping stone, as I imagine she was to you. No, this is something different, something outside principle or national agenda."

"You?"

"I don't flatter myself either, but . . . well, maybe, in a way. But none of this is relevant at the moment. We need to get her out of Mossad hands and into ours. Asap."

"Okay, let me see whether I can call in some markers."

"With Mossad or . . . ?"

"Yeah, the 'or' part: a breach in the wall between Aman and Mossad. We're all tribal. When official channels are no good, you turn to blood ties. Yishai Barg has a daughter highly placed in Mossad. Let me see if we can work that angle."

≈ ≈ ≈

Dima, Talpa, and General Shapiro watched from their 4-by-4 as the helicopter approached the helipad at the technology park. "She is going to be pissed," Dima said.

"She should be grateful to see our smiling faces," Shapiro countered.

"Perhaps, but she'll be pissed, trust me on that."

The look on her face as she was escorted toward them told the story, and Dima knew it was going to take some time to repair the damage inflicted in Tel Aviv. She stood at stiff attention in front of the three of them as her escort handed papers over to Shapiro, unlocked her handcuffs, then trotted back to the helicopter.

Ignoring Dima and the general, she stood toe-to-toe with Talpa. "Look at you, Rick," she said, "standing tall with the rest, like a real man. I heard you had gotten some new accessories. But, of course, the accessories don't make the man." She landed a punch to his solar plexus that should have doubled him over, but he barely reacted. "Still keeping in shape, I see."

"And still staying a step ahead of you, Bedia. I saw that coming. Now let's get over to our facilities and get reacquainted. Dima here says we have a lot to talk about."

"We'll see just how much we have to talk about now that Dima has shown his true colors."

Dima reached toward her, but she pulled back. "I had nothing to do with what happened after we landed," he said. "That was Mossad. We are working with Aman, military intelligence."

"I know what Aman is." She turned to Shapiro. "These two I know well, perhaps too well. And you?"

"General Daniel Shapiro. I'm in charge here."

She laughed, sucking in the hot dry air, and breaking into a cough. "That's what just about everyone I meet seems to think, or at least what they tell me. This is a whole nation of people in charge."

"Well, I am, for real, at least until I'm relieved of my command, but I'm going to turn you over to these two, who claim to know you better and claim to know what they're doing."

She laughed again. "That's what I was told in Cyprus, but then I was treated to a blood bath of operatic proportions and hauled away the moment the chopper from the ship landed on Israeli soil. My first visit to your country and such an enthusiastic welcome. And the welcoming committee continued the celebration with much enthusiasm for hours. And hours."

"I'm sorry about that. It wasn't our doing."

"Never is, General, it never is." She looked toward the car. "Well, are we going to get out of the sun or stand here making small talk for the rest of the day?"

≈ ≈ ≈

The rest of the day might as well have been spent in small talk. There was no grand tour of the facilities for Bedia and no introduction to the unit's mission. She was neither an ally nor an enemy. She was a defector whose arrival was timely yet ill-timed. Dima insisted they delay any debriefing until she could settle in and recover some from the more aggressive interrogation in Tel Aviv. This left the entire team in a holding pattern for the day, during which, back in Tel Aviv, Mossad continued to play coy with their IDF counterparts about what they had learned. Bedia knew they had learned nothing.

After a sullen private dinner during which even small talk was sparse, she was escorted to a modest hotel room newly fitted with bars on the window and with an armed guard posted outside the door. She laughed. "And, Dima, do you think any of this would matter if I really wanted to escape or pull off some sabotage?"

"Of course not. It's just another form of security theater, but we have to do it to be able to say we did our best and followed military protocol."

"Of course." She lowered her voice. "Does protocol allow you to stay with me tonight?" She permitted a look of vulnerability to flash on her face for an instant.

Dima held her eyes as he whispered, "No." He walked away.

≈ ≈ ≈

It was sometime after midnight when she sensed a presence in the room. She reached under her pillow for the weapon that wasn't there, then felt his weight as he slipped into the bed beside her. "I thought . . . ," she whispered.

"Shhh, sleep." Dima put his arm around her and closed his eyes, focusing on the rhythm of her breathing, waiting for the tremors that told him she was falling asleep again before letting himself drift off.

Bedia, who had feigned going to sleep, listened and pondered and planned as he snored on. When he slipped away shortly before dawn, she finally willed herself into genuine sleep for the few hours before her day would begin, a day that she knew would be filled with questions, questions for which she would have to have good answers.

≈ ≈ ≈

Shapiro was not happy with the course of the next day and a half. "This may not be a military base, but this is a military operation," he said, tapping his desk for emphasis, "and I am concerned about the way we are taking this woman into our confidence. You may have your methods, your open collaboration, Talpa, but there are limits."

As Talpa sat considering how best to deal with Shapiro and the command structure, Dima stood up and looked at Shapiro. "Permission to speak freely, sir?"

"Don't pull that officious crap on me. We always speak freely in this unit. That's what gives 8200 an edge."

"Well, then, I suggest you shut the fuck up and get out of the way of those of us who know what we are doing." Dima ignored the general's reddening face and continued. "This woman, as you call her, has to see us opening up to her before she will open up to us. And if she is going to be of any real use to us, she has to know what we know and don't know, what we can do and can't do."

"But, what if—"

"If? If? Well, then we manage the if. Look, she knows how

all this works and exactly what the price would be for fucking with us. She bought a one-way ticket out of Turkey. Nobody is going to come to her rescue and get her out of here, and there's no place else for her to go. We're her only option now."

Shapiro looked from Dima to Talpa. Their expressions were the same. "Okay, but Roni Zimro, who knows the grid and the control software as well as anyone, says the country is a sitting duck for another attack despite all the new measures recently put in place. And you saw what happened in Syria. We don't have time for trust walks and song circles. If this woman knows what is going on, she had better start telling us damn soon or we're going to have to pull it out of her."

"Dima and I both know Bedia well enough to know that nothing you can do to her would break her. Call me Hobson, Dan. It's your choice: our way or nothing."

Shapiro looked unpersuaded, but he nodded. "Then just get it done, because this thing is spiraling out of control. Manhattan is in its third day without power, and Israel Electric is screaming that they can barely keep up fending off the cyberattacks on their network. We're on the clock, gentlemen."

"We're doing our best," Talpa said. "We're having an all-hands session in an hour. You're welcome to come, of course. As long as you keep your mouth shut."

"If you weren't a civilian, Talpa"—Shapiro spoke through clenched teeth—"I would have you hauled up on charges so fast it—"

"Then, aren't you lucky I'm not under your command? And you still talk like an American." He stood and signaled to Dima. "Let's get set up for our big meeting. As the general keeps reminding us, we're on the clock." He looked at the Breitling on his wrist. "Well, what do you know, tempus fugit. Thanks for the reminders, general. I don't know what the team would do without you. You are such a valuable player."

Shapiro put his hands on his desk and started to rise as Dima almost dragged Talpa from the room. In the hallway outside the office, he turned to Talpa. "What was that all about? Why provoke the man?"

"Because I want him off balance, caught up in his emotions and his habitual responses. Then he becomes predictable and won't be a problem to us."

"But what if he goes up the chain-of-command and we end up on the outside—or in a cell?"

"Won't happen. The chain-of-command is Barg, and Yishai and I have . . . let's just say, some history. So, don't worry, we're in this for the duration, whatever the outcome, which is why I'm not playing this by their playbook or deferring to Shapiro or anyone else."

"You act as if you really were in charge."

"Of course, I do. That's how it works, Dima. You of all people should know that."

Chapter 33

SUZE GAVE DB A LOOK so sharp it bordered on being a deadly weapon. "This is wrong-headed and just plain wrong. You're risking the business and who knows how many of our customers for what? A hunch?"

"It's not a hunch. I told you. I got an encrypted message from Bini Markham. I would trust that kid with my life."

"Well, maybe that's what's at stake. Have you thought about that?"

"A lot. But I'm also seeing the Doomsday Clock inching toward midnight. What do you think will happen? Do Donaldson and Petrov turn out the lights and shut down civilization before or after they turn in desperation to the nukes? Look, maybe we're already dead, but I'm not going to sit on my hands until I find out." He opened his tablet computer, plugged in a USB dongle to connect to the company's internal wired network, and slipped the SD card in the slot on the side. "Here goes." He tapped the power button on the tablet.

"There's no going back from this, DB." She held her breath as she kept glancing toward the fluorescents overhead.

"It's not an on-off switch, Suze. It'll take days for the worm to permeate the customer base, but it will start with our highest priority, most sensitive customers whose systems are designed for continuous check-in. And besides, it's not going to effect the lights, except it might help us keep them on."

As if on cue from a perverse stage manager, the overhead lights flickered but then held steady. "This is getting to be so regular that nobody blinks anymore," he said, hoping to reassure her. Then he noticed the flashing icon on his tablet. "It's Talpa. Already. He must have set an alarm to alert him when the messaging system got installed and activated." He tapped the icon. A text, obviously prepared in advance and sent automatically, painted itself on his screen."

> So, you finally decided to chance it. Things must be getting desperate. Or you are just learning prudence. In any case, an update will follow as soon as I can prepare it. Sit tight. RT

Suze read over his shoulder. "It looks like Talpa has your number—in more than one sense. And I would bet he really does need you."

"Us."

"We'll see about that. But now that we're in the lifeboat together, I'll row as hard as I can right alongside you."

≈ ≈ ≈

It was several hours before the messages started arriving, a string of lengthy texts from Talpa and Dima, followed by an unexpected one from Bini Markham.

> Send details on customer base for Scenaria PowerShield installations worldwide, starting with Turkey and Russian Federation. BM

DB sighed. "We'll need the whole team on this. I can't do it alone."

"Are you sure? The more people we drag into this, the riskier it gets."

"We are not talking about the next quarter profits or even

corporate survival. This is life and death for all of us. Supporting Talpa and his team is our best shot at coming out the other side."

"Okay, I'll trust you. Let's do it."

≈ ≈ ≈

Conference Room B was packed. In addition to DB and Suze, Maude Girard, Ed Idris, and Dune Huang were joined by Inez Coreirro from Customer Relations, and Rufus Baumgarten had brought Lynette Wesley, his second in command in the Vault and a hotshot new industrial security specialist. Only sales and marketing were not represented in the room. DB had decided he did not want to have to deal with their predictable resistance.

He looked at Baumgarten, then nodded toward Wesley. "Are you sure? This is supposed to be limited to the core team."

"We need her expertise. And besides, I'm grooming her to take on my role when I retire next year."

"Retire? You never said . . ."

"Well, now I'm saying. The stress is getting to me, and my wife says—"

"Your wife? I . . . I didn't even know you were married?"

"A lot you don't know up here. But that's understandable. We eloped during the first blackout. It's a long story, but if this is an emergency meeting, maybe we better move on from gossip to the real game."

DB opened his mouth to speak, but before he could say a word, Suze had her hand on his arm. "He's right," she said. "Let's get to the heart of the matter."

DB gave her a sideways glance before beginning. "First," he said, addressing the group, "nothing said here today goes beyond this room. Second, after I introduce what we are talking about, if any of you want to opt out, I'll accept your immediate resignation with very generous exit terms in exchange for a permanent non-disclosure agreement. So let me tell you this is about what the press, ever in quest of alliterative click-bait, are currently calling the Power Plug Ploys. Also it's about the special—possibly illegal—role that Scenaria will be, or is already playing in trying to keep the lights on. So, if anyone wants out, speak now or forever bite your tongue."

The room was silent, with all eyes on him. "Okay," he said. "Truth time. This morning, acting solely on my own, I installed malware in our own system that propagates throughout all installations of any version of Scenaria antimalware software and turns it into a clandestine encrypted instant messaging network." He scanned the table, but no one reacted.

It was the newcomer, Lynette Wesley from The Vault, who spoke. "Yeah, we know. We monitor all that shit. We already have a removal tool, should that become necessary. But, we assumed you had good reason. At least that's what Bumpus told us."

"Us? The whole Vault knows?"

"Yeah, pretty much," she acknowledged. "Noel is out sick, so he doesn't know yet—unless he decides to log in from home on the VPN and access the internal event logs."

"Shit. So much for security and secrecy."

She opened her hands. "That's what we do. It's our job to know these things and take pre-emptive action."

"Your job." He smiled at Baumgarten. "You picked your team and your successor well, Bumpus. All right, everybody. Here's the state-of-play in this world-cup match." He outlined what he knew from the updates from Israel in a rapid-fire delivery peppered with 'ands' and 'buts'.

"So," Maude Girard said, drawing out the vowel. "You need details, including access keys, for all installations of our software in Turkey and the Russian Federation. Or is it just in the power industry?"

"All of them, but flag the ones in any way connected with electric power, even if they're not subscribers to PowerShield."

Correiro pursed her lips in thought. "That's still not big numbers. The Turks don't trust us, and the Russians favor Kaspersky."

DB looked to Girard, then Baumgarten. "Is there some way we can get access to Kaspersky's customer base?"

"Are you kidding?" Baumgarten said. "Is there any way they could get access to ours? Think about it. No way."

Ed Idris raised a finger. "There might be a way, from the inside. I left myself a VPN backdoor before I left Kaspersky." He held up his hands at the looks of surprise and disapproval. "I know, I know, but what's done is done. They might not have found it. Could be worth a try."

There were raised eyebrows around the table. "You'd do that?" DB said. "You're more of a sonofabitch than I would have guessed. I'll remember to have you strip-searched and to shred your hard drives when the time comes for you to move on from here."

"I wouldn't expect any less from you, DB. But, like you said, we might be facing the end of the world as we know it. Melo-dramatics aside, the stakes are pretty high. In any event, I know a lot about how their system is set up. Maybe I can work with the Vault and find some way to get access."

"All right. This is the game plan. We want to be able to look into every power plant and grid in the world and all the man-agement and corporate networks directly or indirectly con-nected to them to find where there is implanted malware that could be responsible for the blackouts here and in Russia."

"Don't forget South America. And now Israel. And Syria."

"Right."

Baumgarten was shaking his head low over the table. "No way. If we had months, we couldn't pull that off. Not for the whole world."

"Not that long," Ed Idris said. "We could—"

He was interrupted by Lynette. "We only need to know where there are systems infected with specific malware. So far, every outage seems to have been triggered by slightly different malware, but there has to be a common link. We've been fighting the last war, developing signatures and removal tools for the last blackout. We need to find what amounts to the operating system of the series of injections."

DB nodded. "Good thinking. But even if we do develop some signature or snapshot of this 'malware OS',"—he made air-quotes—"we can't send some bot looking at every damn system in the world. We need a list of possible targets. We need—"

Dune Huang, who had seemed to be meditating, spoke quietly over him without waiting to be recognized. "Let us imagine we know what we are looking for and where to look. What then? What do we do next?"

DB finished his sentence and looked toward Dune. "It's above our pay grades. We, the whole of us, are like a service function, quartermasters to a combat unit."

"So, the Israelis are in charge? I thought we were beholding only to our shareholders."

"And to society. It's in our charter. But I am talking about our shareholders. Richard Talpa is in charge. Yes, that Richard Talpa. Although he is long gone, it turns out he still holds, through various mechanisms and intermediaries, a majority of our stock. Talpa is running the show. Literally."

The faces around the table were full of misgiving, but DB

didn't wait for further discussion. "That's it, people. You all know your assignments. Let's compile those lists and get them to the big boss."

Chapter 34

THE BARE CONCRETE WALLS of The Pit had been brightened with band and concert posters put up by Marwa, but the air was rank from too many bodies working too many hours in a windowless bunker that was never designed for long-term occupancy. Bini wiped his brow with the sleeve of his tee-shirt before returning to the spreadsheet on his screen, flipping rapidly through pages of rows, then skipping to the end. "This is no good, Talpa. Tell me this isn't all you got from Scenaria. This can't be half. Roni, can you get a quick ballpark on the number of power plants in Europe, the Americas, and the Russian Federation?"

"Already done," she said. "According to Google, *The Washington Post* reports there are 62,500 in the world. It says there are 9,719 in the U.S., nearly 800 separate generating units in the EU." She typed a few lines. "Looks like maybe some 1,300 in Russia, maybe 1,700 plus in China. I don't trust those numbers pulled from multiple sources. Give me a few minutes more digging, and I can probably pin it all down."

"That's okay. It's clear we're way short of what we need. A partial solution is no solution at all. My simulations say we need to have access to at least ninety-three percent of the generating capacity in the U.S. and Russia, and seventy plus in the rest of the world."

Marwa, who had been busy at her own workstation, spoke up. "That's an engineering answer. We need to look at the social systems questions. How much has to change for the players to decide they can't keep playing the same game?"

"For instance . . ."

"Turkey, for instance. Now that we know they are the provocateurs in what amounts to a double false-flag operation, we can make moves on them. Like, what happens if Turkey gets their grid knocked out for a couple of days?"

Talpa looked interested. "Have you updated the dependency models to include players in Turkey? Can we probe the models, run new simulations to play around with different scenarios?"

"We have already," she said, pointing at the screen of her own computer, "at least as far as we can, given that we know so little about the group that Sam Parsons and Bedia were part of. Bedia had a lot to say about the head of that team, but he's out of the picture now, and we don't yet know for certain who his replacement is. And even Bedia doesn't know who sanctioned the operation or how it is embedded in the government as a whole. It could be a completely rogue op, or it could go all the way to the top. They were very compartmentalized in Ankara. No one could see anything outside their own silos."

"That's the excuses. Did you learn anything from gaming with the models?"

"Nothing much so far. We calculate that an attack on Turkey is about as likely to nudge them to push the button as to get them to back off for a time. Or they could just ignore any attacks on their own infrastructure and stick to the original game plan, whatever that was. We don't know the timetable—if there was one. There are so many ambiguities and uncertainties that you change one number here or a connection there and you get completely different predictions."

"So much for the predictive power of soft-systems methods," Bini teased her.

"And tell me, what is the margin of error in your numbers, Bini? We're all feeling our way around in the dark. And we'll all be doing that, literally, if we don't make some progress real soon."

Bedia Tekın, who had pulled her chair to the side and had been listening with her elbows on her knees and her chin in her hands, spoke quietly. "I don't know anything about social modeling or soft-systems methods, but I do know people and politics, and I know the politics of the people I worked with. Unless you outright stop them, completely eliminate their offensive capability, they are going to keep going. It's not a game for them. Our leaders have fantasies that Turkey will move in to fill a power vacuum and become the new leaders and defenders of the Muslim world. Once Israel goes dark, it will be all out war, swift and deadly. You—"

"We can always turn the power back on," Marwa said. "A blackout would be an inconvenient setback, not a defeat."

"Roni," Bedia said, "you're the local expert in this area. Tell them what you know, what everybody in Israel, including, it seems, everybody in this room, seems to ignore. What is special about electric power in Israel?"

"Well, for one, it's one long stretched out corridor rather than a normal grid, which reduces the options for rerouting and makes the whole grid less resilient."

"And how much of the country's generating capacity is thermal power?"

"Nearly all of it. Renewables, mostly solar, is less than five percent."

"And what does that mean, thermal generation?"

"Turbines, mostly natural gas and coal-fired."

"Rick,"—she turned to Talpa—"remind them of what happened at the Tricorn Power Station."

Talpa shrugged. "Tricorn was a coal-fired power plant in Utah that was shut down by a cyberattack a decade or so ago."

Marwa looked confused. "I wasn't there, but couldn't they just start them up again?"

Bini jumped in. "I was there. Well, indirectly. I helped hack the grid later to head off more widespread damage. Those mothers are so heavy that they have to be kept slowly rotating, even when they are not generating power. If they ever stop, the shafts start to sag, and the unit is destroyed. That's probably what happened more recently at the Comanaugh plant in the States during the first big blackout. In principle, almost all of Israel's generating capacity could be completely wiped out with the right sort of coordinated attack on the plants themselves. And it would take a long time to repair or replace the generators— years, maybe, even under normal circumstances. With the world manufacturing and supply chain in chaos? Forget it."

"Exactly," Talpa said, "which is why I coined what the experts now refer to as the Third Law of Cyberterrorism. Anything with a rotating shaft under computer control can be destabilized or desynchronized under computer control. Of course, you know all about that after what Unit 8200 did to the Iranian centrifuges at Natanz."

"And that," Bedia added, "is what Operation Lightning Bolt intends to do to you all amidst the chaos of a cyberspace shootout between the Russians and the Americans. However quickly that is resolved, your country will be permanently crippled, and, in the hopes of many, soon erased."

"I don't see it," Roni said. "Our grid is the most secure in the world. We have the latest and best security software there is, beefed up by our own programming tweaks and extra layers of homegrown software and . . ."

"And what happened here in mid-April?" Bedia said.

"That was a fluke. Besides, we had a fix and got the lights back on in a few hours. I know, because I did the analysis and part of the coding."

"It was no fluke. It was Lightning Bolt, and it was intended to be easily found and easily fixed. And you here have exactly the same blind spot shared by nearly everyone in the world who works in cybersecurity. The more layers and monitors and firewalls you add, the more complex the system becomes. More software and hardware means more undiscovered flaws, all the more holes to be found and plugged up—with what? More software, more hardware. An impenetrable system is an impossibility. In any case, there was also more to that attack before your Passover holiday. There was the part that was not so easily found or fixed. After you all thought you found the problem you stopped looking, just as we intended."

"Tell us about it."

"I can't. Tankut knew all about it, ideas he brought with him. I just knew the general concepts. Nothing much I can tell you, except to say it's now there, in place, waiting. Tankut called it the ultimate Trojan, only this time from the Turks."

"Then it's our job to find it and neutralize it." Talpa chewed on his lip. "That's a more focused and separate task addressing only the power-related systems inside Israel. I'll get our glorious general to organize another team within 8200 to take that on. That'll also give him something to do other than hand-wringing and hanging around us. Then we can concentrate on the big picture."

"Have him find a way of working with my colleagues back

at isGrid," Roni said. "They're good at this stuff. And I know one guy at Israel Electric who is particularly good. Get Bruce Latham. Tell him I said hello."

Talpa was nearly to the door when the explosion shook the building and the lights flickered out.

Chapter 35

FOLLOWING PRE-PLANNED PROTOCOL, the group in The Pit waited for a military escort, talking by the light of the workstation screens, each powered by its own UPS. When the lights came back on, Talpa took matters in his own hands. "I don't think it was this building, whatever it was. Let's go check this out ourselves." The exit was no longer guarded, and they encountered no one as he led the team up the stairs and out of the building. "Almost as if they suddenly forgot us," he said, as they reached the ground floor, "or want to pretend we aren't here."

Outside, the brick plaza at the center of the circle of buildings was controlled chaos, with firefighters, military and local police, and knots of waiting and watching civilians. Smoke poured from the corner entrance of the farthest building opposite. Its entry lobby was now concrete, glass, and rebar rubble, leaving the upper stories at the corner of the building precariously cantilevered over the smoldering destruction below. Bodies lay on the ground outside, and emergency medical personnel from *Magen David Adom*, Red Star, were attending to several of them.

Talpa herded his team to one side, where they were quickly joined by a military escort with Aman patches on their uniforms. He cocked his head toward Dima and spoke quietly enough not to be heard above the shouts and the hiss of fire-hoses. "That was the only one of these buildings not commandeered by our group. Either they had flawed intelligence and targeted the wrong building or they just took out the easiest target."

"You're saying this was an attack? On us?"

"And you think it wasn't? Come on, Dima, it should be obvious, at least to us old timers. The youngsters will do their careful analyses and reconstructions and figure out just what happened and maybe who did it, but you and I, we're not above jumping to conclusions. We already know the story. I would have thought our by-the-book General Shapiro would have done a better job anticipating possible threats. I'm going to get him to clear that building, too, and cordon off everything we are using, establish a closed perimeter that includes the hotel."

"I think he was trying to draw as little attention as possible to our operation. We're not supposed to exist. Put up razor wire and checkpoints, and suddenly it's obvious that what was once just a random corner of a technology park is now a high-value target."

"I don't think we have much choice. Somebody is after us and somehow blew up a building in the middle of a city in the middle of the desert. Oh, there's our General. Let me go talk with him."

Talpa pushed his way across the crowded plaza, stepping over hoses and debris to approach from behind. "Shapiro, we need to talk."

The General didn't turn until he finished his conversation with two subordinates. "Not now, Talpa. We're a bit busy, in case you hadn't noticed. Stay with your team and get yourself back to your bunker. We're under attack. I'll give you an escort." He signaled to two soldiers, snapping his fingers and pointing to Talpa. "Escort this man and his people back to the temporary command center in the basement of Building Gimel, and keep watch over them until you're relieved or I send for them."

Talpa put up his hand. "We won't need an escort, and we're not going to be kept under guard until it's convenient for you. You knew how this worked when Yishai spelled out our remit. You were told in no uncertain terms to give us all the help we need and to stay out of our way. You're in our way. Tell your soldiers to give us protection but free rein."

The two young soldiers looked confused by this rather unmilitary exchange, but Shapiro nodded to them. "Keep them safe, but give them what they want."

≈ ≈ ≈

Dan Shapiro stood outside the blast door and took a deep breath before telling the two guards on duty to let him in.

The entire group was huddled around one workstation. Talpa looked up. "Well, if it isn't General Dan Shapiro. What's the occasion to honor us with a visit to our dank catacombs?"

"I thought you might like to know what that was about."

"That. You mean the explosion. Sure, tell us."

"At first we thought it might have been—completely improbably—a drone attack, but that was quickly ruled out. It now appears to have been—only slightly less improbable—a suicide bomber. This is the first on Israeli soil since the 2016 attack on the bus in Jerusalem. I think it's the first here in the Negev since that shopping center bombing in Dimona in, what, 2008?. No one is claiming credit yet, and we may never identify the young woman who carried it out, but our sources suggest it was neither Hamas nor any of the other usual suspects. I was told she might have been Bedouin."

"Really?" Dima said. "The Bedouin certainly have no love for the way they've been treated by the State of Israel, but so far they have also not been a major threat."

"Until now, at least."

"Do we have any idea why that building?" Talpa asked.

"Yeah. There were eyewitnesses who saw her approach Building Gimel, this building, but she backed off when she saw the soldiers stationed at the entrance. Apparently, she targeted the other building for no reason other than she could get in. One building, another building, what difference did it make to her. But it does suggest that somebody knows we are here and maybe what we are about."

Talpa snorted. "Anyone who hangs around the technology park would know we are here—or that somebody is here and something important is going on."

"I don't think you understand how ordinary life works here in Israel. There are always soldiers everywhere, and enhanced security at some buildings is not that uncommon. No, I think this was something targeted at Floodlight or at least at the Floodlight team, which means someone somehow knows or has some inkling that this is a special operation." He stretched to look past Talpa. "I wonder how that could have happened? At any rate, from now on I don't want the Turkish woman in the command center again. I'm taking her into custody. And I'm restricting all of you to the hotel and these two buildings. Everyone will have an IDF escort at all times, twenty-four-seven. Understood?"

Talpa shook his head and exhaled sharply. "You don't get it, Shapiro. You just don't get it. Go ahead. Escort Bedia back to her hotel room. We'll get her back here faster than you can say chain-of-command."

"I don't know what you have going with General Barg, but I intend to protest with all diligence about having civilians trying to assume command over military personnel. These are my men and women, and this is my base of operations."

"Dan, Dan. That's how it works in a democracy. The civilians are always ultimately in charge." He grinned like a kid who had just made it to the next round in a spelling bee.

"Whatever." Shapiro signaled to his aid, who approached Bedia.

"Ma'am, I've been instructed to accompany you to your hotel room."

"Have you now?" She looked toward Talpa. "Your bravado is impressive, Rick. If your actual performance were as good as your bragging, it would be even more impressive, but I have my doubts." She stood. "Escort me, then, young man," she said to the soldier. "And perhaps you can escort me back someday soon. Maybe then I can help everyone understand about the suicide bomber."

≈ ≈ ≈

Bedia sat up from the bed when she heard the commotion at the door, followed by a light tapping.

"Come in," she called. "It's not locked from the inside."

Dima entered and handed her a jelly donut. "*Sufganiyot* are not exactly in season, according to custom, but still a treat," he said. "A peace offering from me and the whole crew."

"Did you and the whole crew feel a peace offering was in order? I thought we were on the same team."

"We are. We just thought . . . I just thought you might like some dessert and some company."

"I thought I was confined to quarters."

"You are, for the time being, while the big guys argue it out. But you aren't in solitary confinement."

"I might as well be." She accepted the donut and took a bite. "Good. I thought you only made these for Christmas."

"Hanukkah. No, you can get them year around now. How

are you feeling?"

"Unwanted. What did I expect. I don't belong here. And what happens after? Where do I go? It's not like there's going to be some witness protection program here for ex-spies. This is such a tiny country. I already feel claustrophobic."

Dima looked around the small room with the bars on the window. "Not surprising, considering. But Talpa is working his legerdemain, feeling around for the rabbit he keeps hidden somewhere in that vast, dark hat of his. You'll be out by morning."

"Out. And then in The Pit. And then . . . I don't see a future for me here. Ever. I don't speak the language, I don't follow the religion, and I don't look the part. And now I am thinking that my exit plans need an exit plan."

"And you're telling me."

"Yes, I am. We are two of a kind who have spent a lifetime as inside-outsiders. We don't belong, but we're very good at playing the part of neighbors or teammates or even best friends."

"It's not always a role. Sometimes . . ."

"We shall see." She turned to stare out the barred window. "We shall see."

Dima rocked onto his heels and studied his toes. "I, uh, have to go. Talpa has called for another all-nighter. We're working on a fresh angle to get this operation moving forward."

"Really? What?"

"I can't say." He was clearly embarrassed. "But in the morning, when you're back . . ."

"When I'm back. Right." She walked up to him and placed her hand on his cheek. "You are a man of dreams. And hopes. You learned one lesson from Brazil but not the other. Go. I'll see you when. Or if . . ."

Dima looked into her sad dark eyes and swallowed. He started wondering about Brazil. He had been targeted, and he still didn't know by whom. Did she know something he didn't? Of course. She knew a lot of things that none of them knew, which made it all the more important to get her back in with the team. And he wanted to ask her about Brazil. Instead, he just said, "It's going to be all right. Trust me."

"There's that word again, and that's your problem: who do you trust?" She looked away. "You were set up. By your own. Parsons walked away with files, remember. He was able to track down and reactivate part of a cell in South America. He relished the idea of using Jews to do his dirty work, the thought of you dying at the hands of your comrades. Of course, he underestimated you, as so many do."

Dima said nothing. It was if she had been reading his mind. He turned and tapped on the door to be let out.

As he walked down the deserted hallway, he glanced up at the lighted green sign ahead: *yetzi'a*, exit. Yes, it really is time, he thought.

Chapter 36

"WE NEED HELP," Talpa said, scanning the gathered group for emphasis. "We can't turn to the Americans, which would be the most natural for us; they're part of the problem. The resources of Scenaria are useful but inadequate. We need an army, a whole fucking army. And, yes, I know all about Israeli pride in its vaunted IDF, but we need an even bigger army."

The room stayed quiet. He noted the odd way people were paired. Bedia, newly released from her private purgatory, was seated with Marwa, their postures communicating some unspoken connection. Was it because they were Muslims among Jews or was it something else. Bini was with the red-headed kid—Adam something-oh-witz—who was a fellow quant and statistics soul brother under the skull. The Pohl twins had resumed their familial united front, with their postures perfectly mirrored. Barbara, who had yet to define a clear role in the group, was seated next to Roni, each of them in their own way looking like the odd-woman-out. And so on, throughout the entire team, now grown to nearly two dozen. And into the ark they went, he thought, two-by-two. He smiled grimly into the room full of tired faces fighting to hold back a new deluge. "Thoughts? Anyone? Anything?"

Marwa half-smiled back. "You said army. I have a question for you. Who has the biggest army of cyber-troops, the best state-sponsored offensive cyberwarfare capability in the entire world?"

"You're not thinking of the Chinese, are you? Unit 61398 of the People's Liberation Army?"

"I am. I know it may sound crazy, but you were looking for something on that hard drive we got from the Canadian couple involved in those attacks on the gas pipelines. Wasn't there a China connection of some kind?"

"Nothing definitive, and nothing for public consumption, but . . . Anyway, none of the code or material we were hoping for was recoverable from the drive."

"Weren't your friends at Scenaria involved in that caper, too?"

"They were."

"Then let's talk with them. We all know you have some kind of real-time messaging pipeline set up. Let's use it."

Talpa hesitated for a minute, then walked over to Roni's machine, one of the only ones in the room with a direct internet connection. He launched the Scenaria Security Control app and typed smokesig into the help search box. A popup with a flashing cursor appeared. He logged in, then typed: 99-00004-aaa-1. "That's me, or the Scenaria main account, home office, now sitting on the CEO's desk. This thing uses the installation serial number as the address." The confirmation displayed "Scenaria Baseline Installation – Botteneau."

Talpa tapped a Y, and a prompt appeared. He began his message:

> LOCAL: We are considering getting help from the Chinese.
> Advise.

He waited. "Maybe they're not in yet, or maybe he's not at his machine." A line appeared.

> REMOTE: Why?

Talpa started typing again.

> LOCAL: They have their fingers in everything, highly skilled,
>   disciplined, not party to dispute, and have stake in stopping
>   escalation. Big time.
> REMOTE: What do you want from us?
> LOCAL: Help making contact. Can't go thru official channels.
>   Obviously.
> REMOTE: I'll look into it.

Talpa swiveled in the chair. "Let's let them do that. I think we need a break. Go get something to eat, people, catch a nap, workout—whatever. Come back at two, refreshed and ready to get this thing into high gear."

The pairs shuffled and sorted themselves somewhat on the way out, with Marwa and Bini back together as usual. As he pushed past to catch up with Talpa, Dima bumped Bini's shoulder. "Oh, I meant to tell you, I saw your sister."

"My sister? You saw Shoshi? Where?"

"On the exfiltration op. She was the team's translator. I was impressed, she was very resourceful and didn't complain even after she was hit."

"Hit? She was wounded?"

"Upper arm. I don't think there was a lot of damage. They stopped the bleeding before we hit the boats, and they did field surgery on the ship. She was chipper by the time we landed and couldn't stop talking about the op. Got into a big argument with this red-head kid who was leading the team, and last I saw, she was winning. Takes after her mother, from what I understand, and tough, like the whole family."

Bini's shoulders slumped. "I was afraid of this. She ends up in forward reconnaissance. Thank the IDF in its wisdom and efficiency."

"Hey, she seemed to be enjoying herself. And she was good. Faked her way with her newly acquired pidgin Turkish and took charge as if she were the squad leader. Like I said, very impressive. You should be proud of her."

"Yeah, I should," Bini said. "I should."

Chapter 37

DB AND SUZE HAD COME into the office early to try to make some progress in the backlog of administrative work. Now he stared at the screen. "Hmm. Wasn't expecting that."

Suze looked up from her screen. "What's up?"

"Just got an IM from Talpa via the SmokeSig conduit. He wants to get help from the Chinese."

"What?"

"My thoughts exactly. Apparently, between what we delivered and what the Israelis have, they don't have enough of the field covered. Or maybe they don't have enough hands on deck. I don't know."

"Why does he think we would know anything or be able to help?"

"Dragon Wind. The gas pipeline attacks. We helped point the finger at the Chinese Army, but I don't think we ever took any action after that. Rumor has it that the government took over and sent some kind of convincing back-channel message to the Chinese not to fuck with our energy infrastructure. I would guess the action was from some part of the U.S. Cyber Command."

"Well, given that they are probably part of the current faceoff, I wouldn't expect Talpa to be looking to them for help."

"But he's always been rumored to be deep inside the NSA, I

don't see why he can't call on them."

"Maybe some rumors are just that," she said. "I have never been able to figure out Richard Talpa, and even my old buddies at Saltmarsh have never been able to pin him down. There's the early years, up until he left Scenaria, and then almost nothing. No definitive traces, only these infrequent sightings. Now he is purportedly in Israel working with Military Intelligence at Unit 8200, but there's no trace of that, nothing showing he ever left the States or set foot in Israel, and Saltmarsh says its sources over there know nothing of the man."

"Claim to know nothing."

"Okay, I know how this stuff works," she said, "but it's all about patterns and the weight of evidence. In this case, the pattern is the absence of data, and the weight of evidence is that the man doesn't exist. Maybe Richard Talpa is nothing but a persona that various people have adopted when convenient, a kind of shared *nom de guerre*."

"Except I've been in the same room with the man on multiple occasions, and he's altogether real."

"Or played by real people—more than one."

"All of them legless Viet Nam vets? Right."

"Okay, let's leave it at that. Nobody knows for sure about him. And we're being asked to help him and the Israeli's in some Hail Mary act of desperation to save their asses and ours—and maybe civilization."

"Your metaphor is so wonderfully mixed. I picture a group of Hasidic Jews fingering rosaries, saying their Hail Mary's—in Hebrew." He laughed and Suze joined him.

"Okay, enough joking around," she said. "Let's see if we can help Talpa. Do we have anything in the Vault that might help us, any records or artifacts from that operation. What did you call it? Dragon Wind?"

"Yeah, from some Chinese expression or something embedded in malware code. Let's get Baumgarten up here. And Dune Huang. I'm not sure, but I seem to remember he knows some Chinese—the language and maybe some people. Let's get Maude Gerard in here, too, the whole crew from that era."

≈ ≈ ≈

Maude smiled when she entered the office. "Looks like old home week for the Vault. Hi, Dune. Hi, Rufus. What's the occasion, DB?"

"The current crisis. And we're looking into some possible Chinese connections from the Dragon Wind era."

"Because?"

"Because Talpa wants to explore what role the Chinese might play with the Blackout Battles."

"He doesn't think they're involved, does he? I mean, it doesn't make sense."

"No, it doesn't, which is why he is interested in them as a somewhat disinterested third party. He thinks they might be able to help." DB turned to Dune Huang. "You remember Dragon Wind?"

"Of course. That was before I came out and changed my name to Dune. I was tired of being Sami Huang and tired of being in the closet. It was bad enough being stuck in the Vault." He smiled softly. "Yeah, I remember it all too well."

"So, is there any chance you—or any of you—might know of some point of access or way into the Chinese government or military or, even better, the army Unit 61398?"

"Maybe," Dune said. "There was a name embedded in the malware code."

"Rufus, do we have archival copies of that in the Vault?" DB said.

"Of course. We never throw anything away. Give me a couple of minutes, and I'll have it for you." He started to rise.

Dune put out his hand. "No need. I remember it now. We thought it was the name of an American at first. Deming. It's a Chinese given name, maybe Mongolian. I never knew the family name, but I seem to remember something about some officer in Unit 61398 being reprimanded just after the incident. Two others ended up before a firing squad, so I figured they were junior players and Deming was the officer who got a slap on the wrist."

"All right, that was quick. I'll pass all this on to Talpa and let him run the rest of the way with it."

Chapter 38

THE CALLING NUMBER SHOWED the +86 country code of China, but the voice on the phone spoke clumsy Mandarin. "General Zhang. Am I speaking with General Zhang Deming?"

"Who is this?"

"Richard Talpa." The caller switched to English. "Do you know the name?"

"I do not think so. How did you get this number?"

"Perhaps you know Scenaria Security Systems. Or do you remember *long feng*, dragon wind?"

"I'll call you back." Deming hung up and sat, staring at the phone. The call was a painful and totally unexpected reminder of a dark chapter in his life. He had fought his way back up the ranks from disgrace, but it had taken years. And now the past had called his personal phone. What should he do? By the rules, he should tell his superiors about the call. Perhaps they already knew. In either case, it would become a waving flag, and, once again, his loyalty and competence would be questioned. He had been given a second chance, but the People's Republic of China was not known for giving third chances.

Or, he could follow up himself, perhaps expose some unknown threat to his country and go from the tolerated former sinner to hero of the people. After memorizing the calling number, he powered down his phone, extracted the SIM card, and put it in his pocket. From a filing cabinet, he removed a phone he should not have, a simple flip-phone purchased in Hong Kong years before, along with several spare SIM cards. He was not even sure if it would work, but having taken his regular phone off-line, he was already committed. He tapped out the number.

The other party seemed to be taking forever. Just as Deming was ready to disconnect in panic, the call was answered.

"Talpa here. Can we talk now?"

"Zhang here. We can talk," he said in English.

"To begin, I know your whole story, and I can tell you details about the *long feng* malicious software that will prove my bona fides."

"That won't be necessary. Whether you are who you say or not is not yet of consequence. It depends on why you called me and what you want."

"I know what you did and did not do, what you and your unit are capable of. However, I do not know how much you can do on your own, as opposed to having to go further up your chain-of-command or all the way to the Party, to the Central Committee. I am prepared to work with you either way, so long as we can work quickly."

"And what is the urgency."

"Keeping the United States and Russia from wiping out their electric power grids and taking the rest of the world with them."

Deming listened to the silence, thinking ahead, wondering how far he could go, how far he was willing to go. "Continue, please."

"I will outline the threat and the problem as we know it, which I assume China has also already figured out. That way you will know I'm an insider, not just some random citizen or a journalist. Then you can decide if you want to take the next step, whether on your own or through channels. If you decide to proceed, I'll tell you how you can demonstrate your sincerity in cooperating."

Deming's heart was pounding like a drum at the New Year. "Please continue."

The call lasted more than an hour, broken up twice for Deming to change to another SIM card and relocate to a different building. The caller understood, and each time supplied a different number to call, each with a +86 country code. Deming assumed these were faked, but at least he would not appear to be making suspicious international calls. Just suspicious calls.

Chapter 39

TALPA WAS STARING into space when Bini entered his office. "Am I interrupting?" he said/

"No. I just got off the phone with the Chinese."

"And?"

"I think they are on board to help. We can start thinking in terms of multiplying our resources and how best to use them."

"That's great. We've had a breakthrough too, which probably dovetails with using the Chinese. The talk about needing an army got us thinking, going back to square one. If we couldn't get our fingers on all the vulnerable systems out there, the much smaller Turkish team certainly couldn't. So how did they do it? They didn't. They piggy-backed on work already done for them. The Russians had invaded the U.S. grid and the Americans had penetrated the Russian grid. The Turks must have found a way to get access to the command-and-control networks set up by the Russians and the Americans to manage their malicious plants. Our guess is that Sam Parsons delivered a sample or two that showed them what to look for on either side. What they did was still pretty hairy, but it wasn't as hard as figuring out how to penetrate thousands of different systems mostly running customized, one-of-a-kind industrial control software."

"Makes sense, but where does that leave us?"

"We play follow the leader. The Turks already have their fingers on the levers. We are just looking where their fingers are pointing. Once we find the levers, we can trace down to whatever the levers connect to, et cetera."

"Still sounds hairy. And time consuming. Time is something we don't have."

"Less hairy than you think. It's all automated. We already have bots out doing the work and putting together a massive database that we feed to machine learning algorithms. And it accelerates. The more data the bots send back, the better and faster the learning. Then an AI actually generates code to counter the embedded code and so on. The idea came from Bedia."

"From Bedia? I didn't think this kind of stuff was her forte."

"It isn't, but Marwa kept asking her what she did remember of the talk among the software engineers on the team. One of the things Bedia said they kept referring to was something about poets, poet routines, automatic poet routines or something like that. Then the lightbulb lit up: autopoietic. They were talking about self-defining, self-generating code, code that adapts and writes itself. We figured if they could do it, so could we. And we did."

"Well, your artificially intelligent system better be doing its thing really fast, because we could be facing a hard deadline."

"When?"

"We should know by the end of the week, so finish your database building and your code generation and be ready to roll."

≈ ≈ ≈

The Pit was drenched in tension. Talpa and the team watched the news feed in silence. From time to time, Dima or Bedia would translate something for the group. Then the streaming video feed flickered, broke up, and went dead. After nearly a minute, the picture returned with a static message posted.

"In case it's not obvious, it's apologies," Bedia said. "It says they are having technical difficulties and will resume the program shortly." A cheer went up in the room. She held up a cautionary hand. "Not yet. We need confirmation. Wait until they are broadcasting again." A talking-head reporter finally appeared with a text crawl across the bottom of the screen. "He's saying there has been a loss of power in the Çankaya district of Ankara. Two substations failed in quick succession, but the loss of power appears to be localized."

"There's our surgical strike. The Chinese have signed up," Talpa said.

"Or your general has. We don't know. If it's just him, they may not be able to supply all we need."

"I'm pretty sure that it is just him, as he insists on remaining the sole point of contact, but I'm not worried about capability. I have every reason to believe he can make good on whatever we need at this time. He currently heads the whole unit. Now we move fast. This blackout will signal to Bedia's compatriots that somebody is onto them. I give us twenty-four hours, max, before they either make their move or move their resources. We need to act quickly with the Chinese, exchange code samples, and make a go/no-go decision on a joint operation."

"What's the alternative?"

"We're not going there. Not yet. Right now it's flat out for the tech team, a busy night for the programmers, analysts, and software engineers. The rest of you probably can best serve by staying out of the way at this point."

Chapter 40

IN THE QUIET OF THE WEE HOURS, Dima rounded the corner of the hotel just as Bedia slipped from her window. "Any problems," he whispered. She shook her head, slipped on the backpack she had tossed out ahead of her, and motioned for him to lead on. When they were well clear of the building, Dima finally spoke again. "We have a hike ahead, about six miles. I didn't want to risk an early hiccup by borrowing or stealing a car. Our people may be preoccupied with wrapping up prep for the operation, but the tricky part will be getting out of the city at this hour without being spotted by somebody. Then it's mostly cross country on tracks and dirt roads." He pulled out a tourist road map of the area picked up at a kiosk in town. "We split up now and rendezvous northwest of the city, here, on highway 25, in one hour. Then we hike the rest of the way together. You're on your own picking your route between here and the rendezvous. I assume you can be resourceful."

"And from the highway? Then where?"

"Trust me. Or figure it out on your own."

"I'll figure it out. I trust that better than I trust you."

"Yet here you are."

"Limited choices at the moment: go with you or rot in a hotel room until they decide how to dispose of me. Let's get going. I'm turning left up here. I'll meet you at the highway."

"But that's toward the university."

"I pick my route, you pick yours. See you." She strode off at a fast clip leaving Dima wondering what she was doing and whether he would actually see her again.

≈ ≈ ≈

Dima prided himself in being in good shape for his age, but he was breathing hard and limping some when he reached the bend in the road and spotted Bedia already squatting on the ground. She stood as he approached.

"What took you so long?" she said. "Feeling the years? Maybe old war wounds? I've been waiting nearly twenty minutes."

"How'd you get here so fast?"

"I cut through the university campus and borrowed a bicycle. It'll get reported stolen in the morning but bikes get taken all the time around universities. And I dumped it well back from here, so there won't be breadcrumbs to track to our destination." She started to walk along the track running beside the highway. "North, right?"

"Yeah," he came alongside. "You know what's up?"

"I have a guess. There's a one-horse airstrip a couple miles up the road."

"Yeah, Teyman Field. Mostly general aviation and flight training."

"And you, who didn't want to steal a car, are now thinking of stealing a plane from an airport. Have you thought this one through? Are you crazy."

"Certifiable. Believe me, that helps. But it's all well thought through. Everything is set up."

"Like the rubber boat brigade out of Cyprus?"

"Exactly, except this is no IDF operation. It's just you and me. Fewer points of failure."

"All right. I'll believe it when we're in the air."

≈ ≈ ≈

The night desert air alongside the highway was cold, and Bedia set a brisk pace to keep warm. Whenever they heard the sound of approaching traffic or spotted the lights of the occasional truck, they moved away and ducked down. The worst thing to happen would be for someone to spot them and either think them a threat or, equally bad, to offer help or a ride.

The airport's only runway paralleled the highway on the west side. As they neared, a few safety floodlights outside the cluster of hangers and other buildings became visible, but the airport seemed deserted. "There's certain to be somebody around," he said. "Stay in the shadows and be quiet until I find our plane."

"What are we looking for?"

"A red-striped white Cessna 172. Do you know planes?"

"Not much. How many engines?"

"One. It looks something like that"—he pointed—"only that's the wrong tail number. And the wrong color. We're looking for 4X-Y . . . something. Oh, there it is. That's ours." He trotted toward the plane. "Quick, before we're spotted." He helped her in, then ran around to the other side and climbed into the pilot's seat. "Oh, shit!"

"What is it?"

"I picked the 172 because I flew these once, years ago, and because I assumed somebody here would have one. It's the world's best-selling plane, but this is not what I remember."

"How so?"

"This is all different, new cockpit instruments, electronics. It's got"—he leaned in and squinted to read the markings—"Garmin G1000 avionics. The one I flew in my relative youth had switches and real gauges, what we called 'steam gauges'.

Well, I see there are still some. Okay, airspeed, altimeter . . . and there's my compass, but the rest is now computer screens."

"Can you fly it?"

"I guess we're going to find out." He powered up the system. "Wow." He surveyed the two screens. "Just like one of those flight simulator programs. Too bad I'm not a gamer, but I think I can figure this out." He started speeding through an abbreviated mental preflight checklist.

"What about gas?"

"No problem, full tank. I called the airfield and pretended to be Mr. Ziv Macabbee, the registered owner of this baby—that information is all online if you know where to look—and told them to have it fueled and ready for an early morning takeoff. Course, I didn't tell them how early. See, they even positioned it to be ready. Now, what am I forgetting?" He cracked open the cabin door on his side and looked down, "Wheel chocks!" He hopped out and pulled the wooden chocks blocking the wheels. As soon as he was back in, he started the engine, which kicked over with a reassuring puff and roar.

Bedia was staring out the windscreen. "How are we going to be able to see. There's no lights. I can barely make out the runway."

"It's a straight shot. There's no wind. We point and go. Hang on. And don't touch anything." He gestured toward the yoke and peddles on her side. "We'll save the student pilot lessons for another time."

He throttled up, started to creep forward, and turned to head down the runway. For fear of running out of runway in the dark, he accelerated faster than necessary and rotated just short of the cluster of buildings midway down the field.

"Well done," she congratulated him above the din of the

engine. "And now that we're airborne, how soon before we show up on some radar and the Israeli air force scrambles an interceptor?"

"Not long, probably. Hatzerim Airbase is just over there, maybe five miles."

"Oh, great. And how long before they try to shoot us down?"

"We're going to avoid that if at all possible. Timing is everything. Once they spot us, they can scramble a jet in less than six minutes. By the time they're airborne, we'll be approaching our intersect with highway 31. We follow that, flying below treetop level, and—"

"Treetop? This is the desert."

"—and hope we start encountering nighttime traffic heading east. That way, even if we do get spotted, it would be damned hard for them to shoot us down while we're pacing a convoy of trucks." He banked right.

"We're heading toward the border, toward Jordan, right?"

"Yup. The border's about forty miles east of here, southern end of the Dead Sea. At this speed, we'll be there in less than twenty minutes, flat out, we can maybe cut it to under fifteen. We stay just above highway 31 most of the way, then cross at Neve Zohar."

"And then what?"

"We land just the other side, on the Jordan Valley Highway a little south of the Jordan Bromine Company. We're being met by a contact from the company, someone I . . . it's a long story. And then . . . well, we'll have to wing it. Ha ha. But we have friends. And you should be okay on your Turkish passport until we can get something else."

"What about you? You're Israeli."

"What's the problem? Have you seen the passport I'm using? I'm now an Arab-Israeli—don't I look the part?—and from here on, we speak nothing but Arabic."

"My Arabic is a bit rusty."

"No problem," he said, switching to Arabic. "We can brush up on the way. You'll be fluent by the time we land." He spotted highway 31 ahead and brought the plane down until the roadway was easy to follow in the faint light of the now-risen crescent moon. He concentrated on his flying as they skimmed along, barely clearing the wires paralleling the road.

Against the steady thrum of the engine, the radio chirped and spat out a rapid command in Hebrew.

"What was that?" she said.

"Air traffic control. They want us to identify ourselves."

"What do we say?"

"Nothing. It'll take a few minutes as they keep trying to make sense of our silence."

"And what now?" she said in response to more scratchy Hebrew over the radio.

"That's an F-15i now in a holding pattern somewhere above us. We're so close to the border now, that they're handing us over to Jordanian ATC, who are going crazy but will also take a few minutes to sort things out and take action. Hang on, we're almost there. All we need is a few extra minutes of indecision."

≈ ≈ ≈

It would have been impossible to miss their destination, with the towers and reactors of the chemical plant flooded in light. Dima banked the plane into a wide turn for his approach from the south. He gave himself plenty of space to allow for the possibility of having to let a truck pass before touching down, but the highway was clear.

It was a wobbly, two hop landing, but he managed to finally be rolling smoothly along on the tricycle landing gear until the plane finally stopped. "There's a spot ahead where we can pull off and wait for our welcoming party."

The lights behind them were the first warning, one they almost missed; the blast of an air horn was the second. A big tanker truck was barreling down the highway toward them.

Dima throttled up, maxed the engine power, and the plane accelerated as the headlights behind grew larger. "If I can reach takeoff speed . . ." He waited until the truck was almost on top of them before rotating and lifting off. By this point, they were going nearly as fast as the tanker truck. As it passed beneath, the plane bucked and pitched. "That could just have been turbulence from being so close, but I thought I heard something hit, maybe the landing gear." As they paced it, the truck continued to roll by under them, almost as if in slow motion.

"What do we do?"

"I guess we try landing as soon as we can, as soon as this tanker jockey gets out of the way." The truck, finally slowing, was beginning to slip behind them as it signaled to turn into the bromine plant ahead. "Okay, as long as we're up here, we might as well keep flying. I'll circle and try again. Unfortunately, everybody within miles now knows we're arriving. Our welcoming party might be a lot bigger than originally planned." He banked into a wide turn and circled to come in again from the south. "Any chance you could lean out far enough to see if we have any damage underneath?"

"I can try." She undid her harness, did a twist of the belt around her wrist, and tried to open the wide door against the pressure of the air rushing by. She finally managed to squeeze partway out nearly upside down, then struggled to pull herself back in and latch the door. "The front wheel is a mess. Must've caught on something on the truck."

"That's bad." He shook his head. "But maybe . . ."

"You have another crazy plan. I can see it."

"Yeah, I was thinking. The early Cessna's were tail drag-gers. Maybe with just enough flare, I can pull off a controlled tail strike and keep the nose up until the last second. It's hard-er to land that way, because you're pointed up but trying to look down and find the ground."

"I have no idea what you just said, but you're sounding like you think you're some kind of stunt pilot."

"More stunt than pilot, but I don't see other good options." He finished his turn and lined up again with the highway. "Okay, we come in low and slow and . . ."

It happened quickly. Just before touchdown, he brought the nose up enough so the tail struck at almost the same time as the two intact landing gear. He kept as much pressure on the tail as he dared as they screeched and slithered down the road. They were almost stopped when the nose-heavy plane pitched forward, collapsing the front gear and driving the nose and the prop into the pavement. The tail bucked up, but the plane didn't flip.

"Out, now!" They both scrambled out and ran to the side of the road. A second truck was now approaching from the south, and cars with flashing lights were making the turn out of the chemical plant and heading toward them from the north.

"Change of plans. Let's disappear." He took off at a run, trusting that Bedia was behind him. "Damn shame about the plane," he muttered. "I hope Mr. Ziv Maccabee has a good in-surance policy."

Chapter 41

YISHAI BARG STRODE ACROSS the helipad and climbed into the waiting car without a word. He was still rehearsing his lines when he reached Talpa's office and entered without knocking. "Do you think," he said, as he slammed the door behind him, "that there is any possible way you could fuck things up more than you already have?"

"Good to see you, too, Yishai. Second visit in a week. Actually, things are looking up around here. We think we found a way to break the cycle in one swift action."

"Have you, now? And what about losing assets and losing track of your own personnel?"

"Losing track?"

"Do you know where both of the Pohl brothers are? Do you know where that Turkish turncoat is?"

"I assume they are—"

"Never assume. Verify. And if you do, you'll find that neither Dmitry Pohl nor Bedia Tekın are where you think they are. We intercepted communications about an incident involving an Israel-registered private plane that crash landed on a highway in Jordan during the night, and Teyman Field here in Be'er Sheva reported a stolen Cessna 172S that so happens to bear the tail number of the crashed plane."

"Crashed? Was anyone hurt?"

"The Jordanians seemed to have lost track of the two spotted running from the wreckage. Current whereabouts and condition not known, according to the chatter we listen in on, but Mossad says they have reason to believe—I love that phrase, reason to believe—that the two are all right. So, it seems, our prodigal agent may have defected with our defector squared. But you know, that isn't even the biggest of my concerns about you and your team. No. I want to know"—his voice intensified and dropped into a hoarse growl—"what, in the name of Abraham, Isaac, and Jacob is this madness about collaborating with Chinese intelligence?"

"We're not collaborating. We are using some resources of Unit 61398 to carry out our mission."

"And sharing intelligence with them."

"Not really. We've merged databases and—"

"Jesus, Talpa, now you have finally gone too far. You can't do this, not on your own initiative."

"It's already done, or at least the artillery pieces are in place, ready to fire when they get the go-ahead."

"It ain't going to happen."

"At this point, it has to happen, since the Turks have already been tipped off that they've been found out. But you must know that already, since you must have tracked that power outage in Ankara."

"I just wanted to hear it from you. I'm pulling the plug on Operation Floodlight. Your team will stand down."

"I don't think so."

"If I have to, I'll have you arrested and throw you and anyone who doesn't cooperate in prison. You cannot, on your own initiative, decide to work with the Chinese. That sort of thing has to be approved at the Cabinet level. You have really overstepped this time."

"Out of bounds or not, the operation is going forward."

"The hell it is." Barg pivoted and reached for the door.

"Too late. It's out of my hands. General Zhang is calling the shots now. Once he fires the first round, if we don't join the fray, the fight is over, and you and your countrymen might as well put your hands in the air and walk into the sea. And if, somehow, you find a way to stop Zhang and the Chinese, the results will be the same, only maybe a little sooner from the Turks. No, Yishai, you are already committed, whether you like it or not."

"Well, I don't. And you better explain what you just claimed to be the case."

"Better yet, I'll show you. Let's go down to our so-called command center in the basement, because the show is about to begin, with or without us."

≈ ≈ ≈

The mood in The Pit was upbeat despite the fact that it had taken another all-nighter to put the last of the pieces in place. Every workstation was occupied and nearly every keyboard was clicking with last minute checks and double checks. Dan Shapiro was pacing up and down the row of workstations when Talpa entered the room with Yishai Barg. "Yishai, I didn't know you were coming down," Shapiro said.

"General Talpa here says I shouldn't miss it."

"Good morning everybody," Talpa said, looking around the room. "Arkady, by any chance do you know where your brother is?"

"I don't know. Should I go get him?"

"No, don't bother, unless you want to head for Jordan. You wouldn't know anything about that, would you?"

The look on Arkady's face as he shook his head made it clear this was the first he had heard.

"Okay, let's get started by bringing General Barg up to speed on what's going down today. Bini, the floor is yours."

Bini pushed back from his work station and stood to face the trio. "Well, our mission is to prevent the Russians and the Americans from escalating into full-scale cyberwar, including knocking out all or much of each other's electric grids. To prevent that, our operation has three phases. Before we can do anything about the Russians and the Americans, we have to keep the Turks from stepping in and triggering the shutdown themselves, plus trying to take us out."

"Do we know for certain it's Turkey rather than Russia or America? I mean, other than from the woman, the informant."

"We have confirmation. Unfortunately, we still don't know enough about the unit in Turkey, and we don't have enough time to put together a surgical cyber strike on their systems, so we are left with the nuclear option. We decided to launch a massive distributed denial-of-service attack on Turkish government sites at the same time that we do a repeat of the action yesterday and knock out the power in most of Ankara."

"Ankara is going to be super pissed at us. This could be a diplomatic nightmare."

"They will not know it's us. The DDoS attack will look like it's coming from everywhere, and if they ever work out a source for the grid attack, it won't point here. But I don't think they will work it out. Anyway, it wouldn't take long to start fending off the DDoS attack—the techniques for dealing with these are pretty well developed—and they would probably be able to get the power back on within hours, maybe faster. So, we have to complete the rest of the mission quickly before the Turks come back online."

"And the rest of the mission?"

"We essentially neutralize both the U.S. and Russia as far

as their offensive cyber capability goes, that is, with respect to attacks on the electric power infrastructure of both countries. The balance of power remains the same but they just can't turn off each other's lights."

"And we can do that?"

"Yes, thanks to Turkish intelligence already putting up signposts pointing to all the exploits already put in place by the Russians and the Americans."

"Signposts."

"Yes, the team that Bedia Tekın was part of, in effect, created malicious software that infected other malicious software, sort of like a virus that infects bacteria. The Turkish code enabled them to activate dormant attacks that had already been put in place by the Russians and the Americans. The Turks, like others, played all sorts of games to hide their code, to make it hard to spot, but there are some things that every one of their software levers had to have. It had to be able to call home, to pick up new code or instructions to trigger whatever piece of malware the Russians or Americans had planted. We figured out what that call-home bit was and used it to find copies wherever it had reached."

"Damn clever."

"That's what we do here. Anyway, we used the way pointers to infect the infected systems with our own code, sort of software disinfectant. The second phase of our mission removes the Turkish code along with whatever malware that it had infected and taken over. Bing, no more blackout battles."

"And that's it?"

"Almost. Then we erase our tracks and back out without leaving anything behind."

Barg put his hand to his face and stood thinking. "This is big. I tried to tell your fearless leader that we can't really go ahead without approval from the top. It will probably have to go all the way to the prime minister, and he'll probably have to take it to the cabinet."

Talpa shook his head. "You are under imminent threat. After the blackout in Ankara yesterday, the Turks know they've probably been exposed. They could literally pull the levers at any moment."

Barg took a slow breath through gritted teeth. "I don't know."

"Better to act now for the good of the country and ask later for forgiveness."

"Easy for you to say. It's not your country."

"But it is mine," Bini said, "and I'll point out what is not being said. Our hand is forced. The moment the Chinese launch their attack on Ankara—"

"The Chinese?" Shapiro said. "What the fuck do the Chinese have to do with this?"

Barg turned to Shapiro. "Dan, this is your unit. Are you telling me you don't even know what the hell is going on?"

"Don't look at me. You think your man Talpa keeps me in the loop? I don't know anything about the Chinese. Not in connection with this operation." He crossed over to Roni, who was closest. "Soldier, tell me what you know about the Chinese in connection with Operation Floodlight. That's an order."

Roni coughed and looked around. "I . . ."

"You've been given a direct order."

"Yes, General, sir. The Chinese army cyber unit in Shanghai is cooperating with us on this operation."

"What the fuck? Who authorized this?"

"I did," Talpa said, walking over to face the general. "And you know what my remit on this operation is."

Shapiro stared with his jaw clenched and his eyes locked

with Talpa's. "There is going to be fucking hell to pay for this. Heads will roll. Do I need to remind you"—he turned full circle—"any of you, that treason is the one thing that carries the death penalty in this country."

"You had your orders, Dan, and I had mine," Talpa said. "We needed outside help to carry out our mission, and we turned to the only place we could?"

"What about GCHQ in the UK? What about the Germans?"

"What about them? We needed an army."

"Well, you got your fucking army. Of all the armies, you have to team up with, you pick the fucking Chinese. Nobody trusts the Chinese."

"Exactly. We don't trust them either. That's why we took every precaution. They got none of our code, none of our data, and none of your fucking country's secrets." Talpa jabbed with his index finger on each point. "This is a one time, single purpose deal to keep the lights on. That's it. To the best of my knowledge, General Deming Zhang is the only one who actually knows the full story. Not even his troops know exactly what they are working on. It's a little like this op, Dan. Tell me, how many in Unit 8200 know about this operation, including ones that have been doing occasional programming or data acquisition for us? Who knows what it's for?"

"No one outside of this room."

"There you go, Dan. And I'd lay odds it's about the same in Shanghai, completely compartmentalized, need-to-know, off the books."

"I just can't."

"I'm with Dan on this," Barg said. "I'm putting the operation on hold as of this moment. I'm taking it up the chain-of-command. Until I get authorization from the top, we are standing down." He turned to the rest of the room. "Is that understood? Nobody touches a mouse or a key. We're standing down." He turned to leave.

"Excuse me," Marwa said. "I think you should see this." She nodded toward her screen.

"What is it? What am I looking at."

"It's a network traffic plot. Things are going crazy in Turkey. It seems the Chinese have just launched their denial-of-service attack. Something must have happened that set things off."

Adam Rabinowitz called out from the other corner. "We just lost the web cam feed from Ankara. Their power's out."

"Well, we're out of it," Barg said. "It's between the Turks and Chinese now."

"I'm afraid not," Talpa said. "If we don't act while Ankara is blocked, as soon as they're back online they'll trigger their Operation Lightning Bolt and wipe out most of the power grid in Russia and the U.S., and, as if that weren't bad enough, we're next on the list of targets. They intend to cripple us—permanently."

Shapiro looked like he was about to vomit. "He's right, Yishai. We have to act. They've forced our hand."

"All right, all right. But when this is over, I'm going to mop the floor with you, Talpa, and I'm going to see you court martialed, Dan, I swear. And why aren't they doing anything over there?" He made a grand gesture toward the crew at the line of workstations.

"They're waiting for me to give the go ahead," Talpa said. "Okay, people, let's wipe out some really evil code."

Bini got up and walked over to Roni. "Switch places with me." She gave him a quizzical frown but went and sat down at his machine. Each of them brought up login screens dominated by a cartoon nuclear radiation warning symbol. They quickly typed separate passwords and were taken to new screens titled "PHASE 2 – KILL TROJANS."

They positioned their mouse pointers over a button labeled "GO." "On my mark," Bini said. "Three, two, one, mark." They both clicked at the same time.

"That's it? It's done?"

"Hardly. Now we wait for our code to call home to our servers to pick up their instructions. It takes time."

"How long?"

"Our code is programmed to try every seventy-two seconds, but it depends on network traffic, how packets get routed, and so forth Those three progress bars show the percent of infections that have checked in, percent confirming the instruction to kill, and then percent confirming task completion."

The group watched in tense silence as the bars crept across the screen and the numbers displayed beside them ratcheted up. Progress slowed as the bars filled, then stubbornly refused to close to the end of the line. "I think that's all we're going to get."

"That's it, then," General Barg said, looking over Bini's shoulder.

"Not quite. We're still in mop-up. Our tailored-access team is working manually on the last handful of sites that we didn't get a call-back from confirming that the payloads have been wiped."

Roni turned from her station. "That's the last of them. I'm ready to confirm the self-destruct on the Operation Floodlight code."

"Okay," Talpa said. "Go to Phase 3."

Roni and Bini brought up fresh login screens, entered passwords, and were presented with screens headed "PHASE 3

–BACKDOOR CODE SELF-DESTRUCT."

"Wait a minute, what's this all about?" Shapiro said. "I thought we were going to erase our tracks."

"That's what this does. The attack payload, the planted code that kills the malware, provides a backdoor that allows repeated access to the same systems. We launch this phase and the payloads self-destruct, wipe themselves out. You ready, Roni?"

"Wait. You're talking about the Chinese code, right, wiping out the Chinese code?" Shapiro said.

"No, the team discussed it, and we agreed. It was unanimous. Leaving any of the malware in place, even our own, was too dangerous. Somebody in the future could use it to start this whole war game all over again."

"But this is a valuable capability, an asset of potential strategic value to Israel. No, we leave our access in place. It'll be like a software sleeper cell, always there in case we need it."

"Not a good idea," Bini said. "We're wiping out all copies. We're leveling the playing field."

"Absolutely not, we leave our code in place against future need. The backdoors planted by the Chinese are to be neutralized."

Bini frowned. "I was just assigned to write code to wipe all traces of Operation Floodlight code, whether from the Chinese or us. With this being such a massive op, leaving it in so many places is a threat in itself. Everybody will know, and everybody will start looking. Not only might pieces of the code itself be recycled, but our techniques could be reverse engineered and used in future cyber-weapons. No, we need to wipe the slate clean and leave a level playing field."

"We're good to go," Roni announced. "I'm ready to confirm self-destruct."

"You will do no such thing, Lieutenant. Lift your hands

from the keyboard. That's a direct order."

She held her hands just above the keyboard with her right little finger poised above the Enter key. She looked anxiously toward Bini who was mousing around at his station.

"Yishai," he said, "tell General Shapiro this is the right way. Roni and I wrote the code. It's all or nothing. It has to take out everything from the operation and leave no traces, no backdoors."

"You have your orders, Lieutenant Zimro," Shapiro said. He looked toward the door where a young soldier stood guard. "Corporal, unholster your sidearm. If the lieutenant so much as twitches, you will put a bullet through the back of her head."

The corporal stiffened but reluctantly unsnapped the holster and took out his sidearm.

"Now, Lieutenant Zimro, raise your hands and place them on top of your head, then stand and step back from your station."

She lifted her hands slightly but did not take her eyes from Bini. "Yishai," Bini said. "General Barg, General Shapiro, this is crazy."

"Maybe Dan's right," Barg said. "This is the fate of Israel. For once, we hold all the cards."

"So do the Chinese. They have the same deck. We just put a roadblock in the cyber arms race between the Americans and the Russians—or at least it's a detour—and now you want to put Israel and China in a perpetual stand-off."

"Unless I am countermanded," Shapiro said, "you have your orders. We will not destroy our own backdoor access. Stand down, Lieutenant Zimro."

"Everybody, chill," Bini said. "There's an interlock in the code anyway. It has to be confirmed from two stations simultaneously." He reached for his mouse.

"Stop! That's an order, Markham." Shapiro turned to the corporal. "If either of them so much as touch another key or reach for a mouse, you are to shoot."

Bini's hands hovered above the keys. He was looking toward Roni but thinking of Marwa. The technology side matters and the human side matters, she would say, but it's not about the code. It's about the people. It's always about the people. "I can fix this," he said.

Roni looked betrayed. Her mouth opened slightly and her eyes widened. "But there's no time."

General Barg said, "What's the issue?"

"If the implanted code doesn't get a confirmation from the C&C computers," she said, "the action times out and the code goes dormant."

"So?"

"So, that leaves the Chinese code time to call home and get new orders, whatever that may be. Standby, maybe. We hope."

"How long do we have?"

"Minutes, maybe. That's if the Chinese are not watching too closely or are still trying to suss out what's happening."

"Isn't there anything you can do?"

"Yes," Bini said. "I can write a fresh piece of code, a patch,"—he glanced toward Talpa—"a cut set to partition the graph into subgraphs." It was a coded message to play along. "We separate our implants from the Chinese. I've done this sort of thing before. Talpa can confirm."

Barg turned toward Talpa. "Professor?"

Talpa hesitated a moment, then caught Bini's eye. "Yes, he's done that before, on another op."

"Okay, but . . ."

"Look," Bini said. "I'll switch to another station. Dov, bring up our tailored-access dev studio and move over. I need to cut some code for a fresh hack."

Dov looked at him like he was crazy. "What are you going to patch? What are you going to hack? There's twenty-some variants on the self-destruct code out there."

"But it all checks in through our own C&C servers. That's the point of leverage that I'm patching." Bini sat down and began typing rapidly as Dov looked on in amazement. As fast as the dev studio software flagged errors, Bini backspaced and retyped. The first compile failed with a long string of errors and warnings. Bini erased a line and twisted to look over toward Roni, partially blocking Dov's view. He quickly typed two lines, submitted to compile, and watched. "There. Corrected, compiled. As soon as we execute the patch, we're good to go." He typed a run command, waited for DONE to appear, then typed a rapid string of characters, closing the dev studio window as he scootered his chair back to the other station. "Now, it's waiting for confirmation. Roni and I have to both confirm at the same time."

"This will work?" Barg said.

"You saw the code. It compiled correctly and executed. Should work. But it is a one-oh release, you know." Dov smiled and raised his eyebrows; Bini smiled back. "It's your call, General, but every second we waste leaves backdoors open for the Chinese."

General Barg looked again toward Talpa. "Rich?"

"I already told you. The kid's a magician with code."

Bini raised his hands above his keyboard. "Awaiting your orders."

"Okay, do it."

"Is that an order?"

"Yes, that's an order. I order you to send the command."

Bini looked to Roni. "On my mark: three, two, one. Mark."

They both tapped enter and a fresh screen with progress bars appeared, the bars already beginning to march across the screen. "That's it. And can you tell the guy with the gun to put it away? Makes me nervous." He stood up. "We're done here. From here on out it's all on autopilot."

Shapiro walked over to stare at the screen. "Wait a minute. There's two sets of progress bars, blue and red. What's that about?"

"Oh, that's just the display code. I didn't bother modifying that. No time."

"But it, uh . . . both sets are showing progress. Is one of those the Chinese malware?"

"Yeah, I guess, some of them got targeted anyway. I thought I had fixed that."

"Stop it. Quick, someone pull the plug on it—or something." Shapiro looked around helplessly.

"It's too late," Talpa said. "The code has already been sent to the command-and-control servers. That's it. It's over."

"Not for me, it isn't. And not for you, Binyamin Markham. I don't know how you did it, but you are under arrest."

"For what?" Talpa said. "He was following orders. He was given a direct command. Are you going to have General Barg arrested for giving the order? Apparently there was a bug in the patch. New programs tend to have bugs. What did you expect? If I were you, I'd forget about what's done and be thinking about what you are going to write in your top secret report on how Operation Floodlight saved Israel and civilization as we know it."

≈ ≈ ≈

General Barg, who had been consulting with Shapiro on what their report should and should not say, caught up with Talpa after lunch. "Exciting day. Looks like we pulled it off. That was some stunt you pulled in the situation room."

"Stunt?"

"You know, the code that failed. I figure it wasn't a bug, it was a feature. I'm thinking I should have a software forensics team maybe check it out. What do you think I would find?"

Talpa said nothing for a minute. "I would bet you would find correct code to do the job but with some small mistake, the sort that could easily be made under the circumstances, coding a patch to complicated software under extreme pressure."

"Perhaps. It doesn't matter, because I now believe you were right that we had to do it, regardless of the consequences. Officially, I'm going to take full responsibility for giving the go ahead."

"Smart move, Yishai. You'll be a national hero, even if nobody ever knows it. But, that's how the intelligence business works. Nobody ever knows about the good stuff, the wars we prevented, the attacks we staved off, the lives we saved. The only thing that ever comes out is about our screw-ups. Speaking of screw-ups, what's going to happen to Dan Shapiro?"

"Oh, I think he's probably going to retire. Stress is getting to him."

"Yeah, retirement is probably a good idea. He never did quite figure me out."

"Nobody does. Nobody ever has. You, Richard, are *echad*, unique."

Chapter 42

BINI AND MARWA WERE TAKING the air on the balcony, when Karl came out. "May I join you? Or is this a private conversation?"

"Both, Abba, we were talking about work."

"Well, I just wanted to tell you, the baby's asleep in Shira's arms. She finally got him away from Shoshi, and now she's relishing holding her grandson. I think he's tired after all the attention today. He was such a trooper through it all. I loved the way the Rabbi welcomed him into 'the community of souls'—Barak. Great name."

"Thanks," Marwa said. "We wanted something that worked in Arabic and Hebrew. He is blessed and he did sort of come out of the blue like lightening."

"I've never been to a *brit shalom* before. It was a beautiful ceremony. No, well, you know, no blood."

"It's not real common, as you can guess," Bini said, "especially not in Israel, but we wanted to leave some things up in the air. We found this rabbi through the Reform movement. At first she was a little hesitant, what with his mother not being Jewish, but we gradually won her over."

"Up in the air, huh? So I take it this is still an ongoing discussion, this whole affiliation-identity thing. Not that I'm poking my nose in, but . . ."

"Well, you are poking your nose in, but it's okay. You're a

first-time grandfather. Anyway, Marwa and I have even been looking into the Bahá'í movement. They take all comers and embrace all."

"Which also means that they are kind of a threat to just about everyone." Karl smiled up at the winter moon. "The Bahá'í gardens at the world headquarters here in Haifa are one of my favorite places to go just to go away and get in touch. You know what I mean."

"I do. We all need that break from the pressures."

"Yeah, and you two have had a busy year. How is that going, working together again, now that you have this big new appointment, my professor son?"

"No biggy."

Marwa elbowed him. "No biggy, just an endowed chair. The Ricardo Abram Talpa Chair in Complex Systems Modeling. You should see him strutting around the apartment, reciting his title."

"I do not strut. Besides, it was obviously an inside job. Who knew Talpa had that much influence with this Echad Foundation, or that they had so much money? You know, they also endowed a chair in Prosthetics Science at Worcester Polytechnic Institute and one in Social Systems Dynamics at the Massachusetts Institute of Technology."

"So, he's been busy. What have you been up to since that whole blackout thing?"

"Stuff." Bini shrugged. "Still saving the world. You know, stuff."

"Good for you. I guess I get the picture." He patted his son on the shoulder. "And thanks for today, for sharing all this with us. Our first grandchild. We are excited—and excited for you. How are you feeling, Marwa, a young mother and a media figure and . . .?"

"Relieved to be home, back at the university, relieved not to have a gun to my head." Karl gave her a shocked look. "Don't worry, I meant it metaphorically. I . . ."

Bini put his hand on his father's arm. "We're here, Abba, that's what counts. And you and Ima have your first grand-child."

"You really kept us in suspense until he was born, you know, wondering which was it going to be."

"Well, we didn't know either, but it just seemed fitting for us to wait and find out the old fashioned way."

"Good for you. Everything is all so high tech these days. For me, the only thing computers are good for is as fancy type-writers. And email. And online research. And . . . I guess I'm only a Luddite when it suits the argument. Changing the sub-ject, I see that the legion of tell-all, expose-all books coming out now are saying we may have narrowly avoided losing pow-er across much of the developed world. I know you still can't talk about it, but I'm guessing you two had something to do with the near miss."

"You know we can't say anything, Abba."

"No, of course not, but you know me. All those years paling around with spies and counterspies and writing about it—I can't help reading between the lines."

"Read all you want, but we still can't talk about it."

"Good, then. I'm going to go back in, get back to work on the book. My editor wants rewrites of the last few chapters by the end of the month."

"Your editor?" Marwa said. "You have a publisher? When were you going to tell us?"

"Well, I didn't want to take away from the baby naming and all. Besides, I just found out last week. Lev had passed on the manuscript to his publisher without even asking me. The rest is history, literally. The long-awaited novel is an alternative history of the founding of the State of Israel. I'm calling it *The Homeland Connection*."

"Well, congratulations, Abba." He and Marwa both hugged Karl at the same time.

"Yes, thanks, and I better get to it."

"This has been such a week of good family news and events," Bini said, grinning. "First Ima gets a commission to do a sculpture down by the harbor, and now you get a publisher for your novel."

"Yeah, she's going back to her roots. You know, your mother originally trained as a sculptor before turning to jewelry. Yeah, she showed me the sketches that earned her the commission from this new outfit, the Echad Endowment for Art and Technology. Talk about throwing money around. Anyway, her design is a series of watchtowers in architectural glass and stainless that she calls *Migdalim Gadolim*—Great Towers. Like I said, back to her roots. Amazing woman.

"Oh, by the way, I meant to mention we got a call from Arkady and Barbara. I'm getting forgetful. They said hello. They really wanted to fly back over for the *brit shalom*, but they're caught up in the midst of moving."

"Moving?"

"Yeah, they're leaving the city, moving into a mountain cabin in Spring Falls, Virginia. And DB has finally decided to retire from the malware scene. He and Suze Kirchoff are planning to expand the cabin and eventually move out to Spring Falls, too. Sounds idyllic."

"Or boring."

"You've always been a bit of an adrenalin junky, son."

"I was well trained, Abba."

"Speaking of your training, I wonder what you two would

make of these two pop-ups that showed up on my computer yesterday. Here"—he unfolded an A4 sheet from his pocket—"I printed out a screen shot."

Bina and Marwa looked over his shoulders from either side and then looked at each other. "Go ahead," she said. "He already knows about the SmokeSig conduit."

"The what?" Karl asked.

"The secret backdoor Richard Talpa left in the Scenaria antivirus software. It can serve as an end-to-end encrypted instant-messaging system. It got a lot of use during Operation . . . Well, the stuff we were working on."

"Okay, that makes sense of the second pop-up: 'MOLE HOLE DEACTIVATING. DELETE COMPLETE."

"So, Talpa finally closed the backdoor," Bini said.

"Looks like it. Or maybe that's to be taken literally. 'Looks like it' is a Richard Talpa guiding principle. My guess is that he has just pulled off another of his smoke-and-mirrors vanishing acts. Doesn't mean he won't someday appear onstage again. But this other message makes no sense at all. I had to get my reading glasses and study it even to be sure I was actually reading it right."

Marwa squinted at the screenshot and read aloud. "Antarctic anchorage landed red leaves tungsten BNF roots."

Bini shrugged. "Word salad. Must be in code, code words. Doesn't make any sense to me either."

"Well, if it came from Talpa or his cronies, it's yours to worry over. Anyway, I'm going to get back to editing while the baby's still asleep. And you two can get back to talking shop while you have a few minutes of peace."

≈≈≈

Marwa and Bini watched as Karl fumbled with the latch on the sliding door. She waited until Karl was gone and the door shut again. "Speaking of the SmokeSig app and Operation Flood-light, there is one thing I've always wondered about but was never sure it was okay to ask."

"It's always okay to ask, but that doesn't mean I'm always going to answer. So ask away."

"The code patch you wrote. What did it really do? What did you program it to do? I'm guessing you didn't tell it to separate out the Chinese and Israeli malware targets."

"You'd be wrong. That's exactly what I did, what it did."

"So you put some bug in it?"

"No, the patch was perfect, and it worked perfectly."

"Then how?"

"You want the magician to reveal his secrets?"

"Yes."

"But I think you can figure it out. Remember, it was a patch."

"So, let me guess. It patched the wrong thing or only part of the code."

"Yeah, something like that."

"Why then do that whole charade down in The Pit?"

"Because of what I've learned from you. It's about the peo-ple, you always say. I knew I had to deal with the people in the room. I figured everybody on the team was already with me, I just needed a way to get one of the generals to order me to send the command."

"You are something else." She hugged him. "You sneaky, brave, wonderful guy."

"I like the hug and the words, but I'll never admit to any-thing."

≈ ≈ ≈

They were back in their apartment, and Barak had just finished nursing. "I'll never keep up," Marwa said. "He's only eight days old and he keeps wanting more."

"It'll work out. Mother and baby synch up sooner or later."

"Says Mister Instant Pediatrician. What do you know?"

"Everything. I have internet access." He wrinkled his nose at her.

"Well, if you know everything, tell me what your father's pop-up message meant."

"Let me see it again. 'Antarctic anchorage landed red leaves tungsten BNF roots'," he read from the printout. "I don't even know who it's from. Talpa? No, not his style. Besides, it was sent via an encrypted messaging system. Why use code words? Maybe Dima. He always liked the word and mind games."

"Listen again," she said. "You have to listen to it with your other ear." She read it aloud.

Bini turned his head to one side, then the other. "Sounds the same to me either way."

"No, listen with your third ear, back here." She tapped him on the back of his head. "Just let me read it to you, and you listen to what echoes in your head. And remember who wrote it. Picture Dima having a conversation with you, free associate with what he's saying." She read it as if it were a bit of conversational. "What bubbles up?"

"Well, Antarctica, the South Pole, Dima's nickname was the Opposite Pohl. But anchorage? Where?"

"Alaska."

"Okay, you do that."

"What?"

"You said, 'ah'l ask her.' Right?"

"Oh, you and your godawful puns."

"That's the Pohl brothers influence."

"Wait. Ask *her*. Anchorage. Ankara. So it's maybe a reference to Dima and Bedia, maybe from them. Then what about landed red leaves?"

"I think I'm getting the hang of this," he said. "The Canadian flag, red leaves, landed Canadians."

"Okay, but then tungsten? And what's BNF?"

"The only BNF I can think of is Backus-Naur Form, an old notation for specifying the grammar of programming languages."

Her face lit up. "I think I know where they are."

"You do? From that?"

"Yes, and what they're doing. I'll bet you a dinner out I can prove it." She pulled out her smartphone and started thumb-typing. "See"—she turned the phone to him—"look at that, recent real estate sales in Nova Scotia, acreage near Wolfville, sold to a Benedicta and Dominic Cippolini. Look at the map. It's just down the road from that couple. Bedia and Dima are starting a new life growing red wine grapes in Nova Scotia. It looks like their exit plans may have worked."

"How in hell do you get that from tungsten and BNF and roots?"

"Don't you wish you were as smart as me?" She crumpled up the printout and tossed it toward the wastebasket but missed.

Bini scooped it up, turned his back, and sunk the paper ball over his shoulder. "And don't you wish you had my athletic talent? But really, how did you figure it out?"

"What's the chemical symbol for tungsten?" she snapped.

"W."

"Why that?"

"For *Wolfram*, the German name for tungsten, also the name of an American mathematical genius and the language he designed. And, yes, we used it in Operation Floodlight. Okay, so now I see how you get Wolfville, and maybe roots, like in planting, but where in hell did the red wine come from."

"Bacchus, Greek god of wine. And baco noir, a red wine grape. Backus-Naur, baco noir. See? Easy."

"You are one scary-smart lady."

"Had to be to get you. How about a game of Scrabble before Barak wakes up again?"

Epilogue

NPR Special Report: "Blackout Brinksmanship"

VOICE-OVER: "OPERATION FLOODLIGHT was not the end of the story. In fact, it was never a story at all, because nothing has yet been officially written or acknowledged by any of the parties about what really happened. Both Russia and the United States took credit for the cessation of 'cyber hostilities' and for the new multilateral cybersecurity agreements negotiated over the ensuing years. Neither have acknowledged that any of their offensive cyber capability had been lost or compromised. Security analysts, knowing that all détente is a temporary condition, assumed that both sides gradually reconstructed their penetration of the other's systems. In China, the only visible aftermath was the sentencing of General Deming Zhang to life in prison for unspecified 'traitorous actions.' Turkey, true to form, offered no comment on any of the events.

"The mysterious Richard Talpa vanished again shortly after wrapping up Operation Floodlight, although unsubstantiated stories of fresh antics by the Bionic Mole are reported to occasionally surface within the international intelligence community. Various of the world's clandestine services have hinted that they have proof that Talpa actually belongs to some other agency, but all have denied that he was one of theirs."

-30-

Fiction by Lior Samson

Distant Sons

The Homeland Connection novels:
Bashert | The Dome | Web Games
Chipset | Gasline | Flight Track | Exit Plans

The Immortality Quartet:
The Rosen Singularity | The Millicent Factor
The Intaglio Imprint | The Drucker Proxy

The Four-Color Puzzle

Death Rehearsals: Stories of Endings Dark and Bright
Requisite Variety: Collected Short Fiction

Appendix: Don't Look Down

INNERVASION WAS A SHORT-LIVED touring band formed by Israeli Chaim Hassan and Palestinian Abdullah Sirhan, former keyboardist and guitarist, respectively, from the legendary rap-metal fusion band, Blue-Green Algae Invasion. Performing a mix of new music and covers of the former group's pieces, they toured Israel, France, Germany, and the U.K. for several years, playing mostly in clubs and smaller venues.

Like Blue-Green Algae Invasion, their repertoire was eclectic in style and subject matter, but was often overtly political and thematically focused on conflict. Their layered lyrics intermixed rap, rock, and folk elements in spoken poetry laced with ambiguity and complex imagery. Hassan, who writes most of the lyrics, cops to the complaints of critics who claim he doesn't understand rap. "I'm not doing rap. It's a bit like with, say, Twenty One Pilots, you know. We're all just doing what we're doing. It's not stuffing words into some formulaic box. Maybe it's rap-like, but for me, I'm writing micro-narrative in poetic form set to music," he said, while on tour in France. "Get over it."

As a duo, they never cut an album but enjoyed some success on streaming music services. Their most popular song, just behind their remake of "Parallel Lines" from Blue-Green Algae Invasion, was "Don't Look Down." In an interview with the SustainedNotes podcast, Hassan and Sirhan said they had originally considered calling it "Narrows Abridged," a word-play reference to the famous dictum of Rabbi Nachman that "all the world is a narrow bridge." They dropped it because they thought it was too closely identified with Judaism and Israel, and they wanted listeners to hear the piece as a universal dive into relationship and distance in the broadest sense.

Long rumored to be romantically involved, the pair were married in a civil ceremony during a visit to the United States shortly before their final round of concerts in Germany. That last tour was cut short after several venues canceled out because of mounting concerns over threats of violence that seemed to come from both Jewish and Muslim quarters, as well as from anti-immigrant right-wing activists.

The couple now reside in Manhattan, where they operate an import-export business and occasionally play in local clubs.

Don't Look Down

words and music by Chaim Hassan and Abdullah Sirhan copyright, Planktonic Music Ltd (reprinted with permission)

> Like a river through the desert, mountains rising from
> the sea,
> Do you remember what you promised then, when you
> promised me?
> Like the snow on sunbaked sands or flowers flying up
> the sky,
> Do you remember what you asked of me when you
> asked me why?
> Like the earth above the treetops and the air beneath
> the plow,
> Do you remember how we wondered then, when we
> wondered how?

DON'T LOOK DOWN!
A dark ravine, a screen unseen, lying in between us.
—DON'T LOOK DOWN!—
But we don't know how to bridge it,
standing far apart so rigid,
angry echo from the frigid, hidden waters below.
And we neither of us know it,
how and why we would still fear it,
but the spirit arching bright across,
a line of life too quickly lost
in deepened gloom, without the room
for passing or returning
in a stomach-churning yearning
on a span that seems too narrow to be crossed.
—DON'T LOOK DOWN!—
Will we drown?
 Take a step!
No running and no crawling, and now no further
 stalling,
Or pretending to the ending,
and with neither of us bending and forever
 unprepared,
trying hard not to be scared to go
 far beyond the hurtin'
and of everything we dared to know
 always being certain.
Not by words but by our actions,
our committed retractions
of our still dividing factions.
 Take a step!
Your side, my side,
places where we hide

from behind our wary faces, the sole remaining traces
of our ancient shared beginnings.
We all started somewhere,
that where, over there.
—DON'T LOOK DOWN!—
A first step, another,
—DON'T LOOK DOWN!—
walking slowly like my brother or my father or my
    sister.
—DON'T LOOK DOWN!—
Stopping.
    Take a step!
Dropping.
    Take a step!
Falling, falling faster than a feather or a thistle,
an abyssal epistle.
—DON'T LOOK DOWN!—
    Take a step!
—DON'T LOOK DOWN!—
    Take a step!
    Take a step!
AND DON'T LOOK DOWN!

Appendix: Parallel Lines

INNERVASION UPDATED THE ORIGINAL version of Parallel Lines, branding it explicitly as "an anthem for our times." Their streaming video, backed by a full concert band orchestrated in a brass-heavy, almost martial, style, featured file tapes of protestors facing off at demonstrations around the world. After the cancellation of the last concerts on their final tour, a new section penned by Abdullah Sirhan was looped into the music video as a voice-under.

Parallel Lines: An Anthem for Our Times

words and music by Chaim Hassan and Samih Sayed
additional lyrics by Abdullah Sirhan
copyright, Planktonic Music Ltd (reprinted with permission)

> Parallel lines. Parallel lines.
> Parallel lines of opposing signs,
>   a shouting match of repeated attacks.
> And in the middle, between,
> Too subdued to be heard above the slogans and
>   screams,
> The voices of the many all murmur a dream.

A fanatical few invoking The Name:
    faithful fundamentalists and true reactionaries,
    orthodox extremists and revolutionaries,
True believers all distinctive
    but all sounding the same.
Controlling conversation,
Reciting revelation,
Shouting new invective,
Without nuance or perspective:
    Resolute truth and absolute right;
    black is still black and white is always white.

But the voices of the many all murmur a dream.
Too subdued to be heard above the slogans and
    screams,
The words and the whimpers of those in midstream
Are lost in the chaos of the stubborn extremes.

    Left-center, right-center, never centered, out.
    Always stay on message so you build your online clout.
      Bark your false distinctions,
      and mark your preconditions.
    Measure truth in decibels, reality in real estate;
    integrity is just a pose, another form of click-bait.

    Far-left, far-right, the meanings still stay out of sight.
    Each dystopic paradise sounds alike in sound bites,
    from irate Islamophobes and angry anti-Semites,
      marketing their racism,
      raising new antagonism,
    to the last evangelizing, selling scathing schism.
    From the social democrats to democratic socialists,
    communists and capitalists, keeping all their secret lists:

the enemies are everywhere,
everywhere, everywhere,
enemies are everywhere,
enemies are!

Parallel lines,
   parallel lines of opposing signs,
   a shouting match of repeated attacks.
And in the middle, between,
Too subdued to be heard above the slogans and
   screams,
The voices of the many all murmur a dream.
The voices of the many still murmur a dream.
The voices of the many . . .

Acknowledgements

WITH THIS BOOK, the series of novels known collectively as The Homeland Connection comes to, if not a close, then at least a point of confluence. I did not expect to be writing a seventh novel in what was intended as a double trilogy, but real-world threats started overtaking fictional nightmares. Sometimes stories choose us.

My thirteen-year writing rollercoaster ride has spanned a half-dozen countries and three generations. Babies have been born, children have grown up, and characters have matured and aged and died. I am deeply grateful to all the many readers and reviewers, among them fellow writers, who helped shape the steps along the way and who encouraged me to keep going.

For this volume, I am especially indebted to Ed Howe, who gave me the benefit of the rich experience of his life at sea and around the globe, including in Israel, where he actually once flew a Cessna 172 over the Dead Sea. His skepticism and un-varnished criticism were immensely helpful. My Haifa-based friend and colleague Yoram Chisik also helped me in getting many details right about life today in Israel and by spotting gaffs both great and small. It is a better book for their contributions.

Once again, I have turned for subject-matter help to people who know what they are talking about in areas outside my personal experience. I am grateful for helpful feedback and suggestions from Harrison Jones, an experienced airline pilot as well as a successful writer. Alan Hoffberg, another pilot, gave me supportive feedback on the manuscript. I also appreciate that Col. Dave Lewis, a retired Air Force pilot and lecturer on strategic studies, squeezed in time amidst a major job change to review and provide extremely valuable feedback on the manuscript.

The cover design was inspired in part by the photographic art of the brilliant Thierry Cohen, particularly his piece "Paris 48° 51' 46" N 2012-09-13 Lst 2:16". My ever creative and never-hesitant resident creative critic, Tovah Lockwood, helped tweak the cover art at the outset and then, as a poet in her own right, helped pound the lyrics of "Don't Look Down" into a more plausible instance of rap-metal fusion. Not for the first time, I am glad I listened to her pointed inputs.

Most of all, I am deeply grateful for the help of my best friend and perpetual muse, my wife, Lucy, whose influence and input resound throughout The Homeland Connection novels. For this last one, in the middle of finishing and defending her master's thesis, she made time to read and remark on the manuscript. Thank you. Thank you.

And usually last, but most definitely never least, I am once more indebted to my always patient and ever professional editor, Janet Lemnah. She is responsible for the editorial spit and polish that helps bring my work to its final shine.

About the Author

LIOR SAMSON is the pen name of a former university professor who has won awards for both fiction and non-fiction writing as well as for his innovative work in industrial design. He has more than two dozen published books, including thirteen novels and two collections of short fiction. As a consultant and teacher, he has traveled the world, lived in Australia and Portugal, and served on the faculties of two international universities.

He resides in Massachusetts with his family, where he cooks creative fusion cuisine and composes serious choral music. He is a freelance journalist and photographer and one-man technical support team for the three students in his life.

The readers who write with questions, kudos, and criticism are vital parts of the dialogue he seeks to spark through his writing. He enjoys hearing from readers and appreciates those who take the time to post reviews on Amazon and elsewhere. He can be reached by email at: lior@liorsamson.com

www.ingramcontent.com/pod-product-compliance
Lightning Source LLC
Chambersburg PA
CBHW021506240626
47154CB00002B/525